I0562957

Don't Want to Be Friends

Holly Kerr

Three Birds Press

Copyright © 2021 by Three Birds Press

All rights reserved.

No portion of this book may be reproduced in any form without written permission
from the publisher or author, except as permitted by U.S. copyright law.

cover figures by simplydylandesigns

www.threebirdspress.ca

www.hollykerr.ca

To all those who feel eclipsed by others—

You are awesome! Let your light shine

Don't Want to Be Friends

Chapter One

Neely

"THREE TIMES A BRIDESMAID, never a bride," April says with a rueful laugh as we hurry towards the church, the warm breeze moulding the skirt of the chiffon dress against her considerably pregnant belly.

"That doesn't mean anything," Ellie scoffs, her voluminous skirt caught in her hand as she brings up the rear with her father, Peter. "Who even says that?"

"*Anne of Green Gables*." I help the tiniest of the flower girls, a daughter of one of the many Scalzo cousins, up the stairs of Our Lady of Perpetual Peace. The sound of the organist midway through Ed Sheeran's "Perfect" floats out the door, meaning if everything goes to plan, the guests should all be in their seats. "I remember reading it in the book."

Like April, this is my third time as a bridesmaid. Two years ago I donned the burgundy sheath for the wedding of my brother Davis; twelve years ago, I had the unfortunate task of wearing teal taffeta with a big butt bow for my cousin Annalisa's wedding.

That dress had been especially traumatic for a fifteen-year-old who didn't have the chest measurements to pull off any dress, let alone one the colour that had haunted weddings and proms all through the 1980s.

The dress that Ellie picked is by far the best of the three, and for that, I should be grateful. Blush-coloured chiffon that is light and airy and perfect for the warm May afternoon, the twisted straps of the bodice are thick enough to hide a regular bra. Plus the way the chiffon drapes around my torso makes it seem like I have more curves than I really do.

It makes no sense why I remember the line from the book because I've always lacked the urge to get married, to my mother's dismay. Back then my focus had been on Anne's antics with her BF Diana rather than an old wives' tale that condemned unmarried women like they were a social failure, like today's version of having your Instagram account deactivated.

Anne was never on the hunt for a husband, preferring to live her life the way she chose, regardless of what Mrs. Rachel Lynde said about it. Anne was the star of her life.

I wanted to be Anne.

Instead, I've ended up being a Diana.

The supportive best friend, the sidekick. The Horatio to Hamlet, the Samwise to Frodo. The Ron Weasley of the story.

I've always understood Ron Weasley.

Loyal and courageous to a fault, Ron is always ready and willing to follow his best friend into danger, but he's got to wonder *Why Harry? Why does everything happen to Harry? Why not me?*

Why can't Ron be the hero of the adventure once in a while?

I understand those thoughts because Harry is Harry. And in my story, Shae is Shae.

As I position the frothy pink clutch of flower girls quivering with excitement, making sure they stay out of sight as I adjust dresses and hair, I peer around them into the church only to see Shae's pink hair, head and shoulders above the rest of the congregation. This means, because she's so short, she's once again standing on the pew. In a church. During a wedding.

Such a Shae thing to do.

Suddenly she disappears and I get a glimpse of Dawson's shock of black hair beside her. My stomach cramps and twists, like I'm constipated or have an ulcer.

I'm not, and I don't. My stomach issues are because of unrequited love. Being part of a wedding party when you're in love with a person who doesn't share your feelings isn't pleasant. I should know, because this is the third time I've done it.

I wonder if Dawson is wearing the blue suit. He looks good in blue.

The outside door to the church bursts open, flooding the vestibule with afternoon sunlight. Two figures appear in silhouette, obviously in a hurry because the guests are seated, the groom is already in position, and the wedding party is moments away from walking down the aisle.

It seems that none of the wedding party shares my annoyance towards the latecomers because the little group suddenly comes alive like a flutter of butterflies interrupted from an afternoon drowsing in a garden.

"Hey, Grayson!" Rufus, the young ring bearer, is the first to call out.

I hear the excited whispers of the other bridesmaids, so whoever this is, he's known to all.

His date tugs him by the hand, her shoulders hunched like she's trying to disappear. "It's his fault," she says.

"Isn't it always?" Ellie smiles and even I, who am only beginning to get to know her, can tell there's no anger in her tone. If this was *me*, and someone walked in two minutes before the ceremony was to begin, I'd march them right back outside and tell them they were out of luck. Punctuality is a virtue, and this couple doesn't have it.

"Sorry, sorry. At least we made it in time." His voice suggests he doesn't care about interrupting Ellie's wedding with his tardiness and I bristle with offence on behalf of my new sister-in-law.

The door closes behind the couple with an echoing *bang*.

Oh. Well.

This Grayson is model-pretty with caramel-coloured hair flopped over his forehead; tanned and toned, looking friendly and fun with a wide apologetic smile, like a surfer rushing in from the waves.

Whoever he is looks very good in that suit, which is definitely better quality than the one Shae and I found for Dawson at The Bay. The purple is so dark it looks black, with thin pinstripes of lilac, matched with a shirt and tie the same shade. I've never seen a man wear so much purple, but instead of looking like a Barney wannabe, he pulls it off.

I have no idea what his date looks like.

The organ music pauses before breaking into the opening chords of "A Thousand Years" and I tear my gaze away from him. I've met enough good-looking men not to appear impressed by a pretty face, but there's something about this one that catches and holds my attention.

It's because I'm irritated.

The song is the signal for the flower girls to start their slow procession into the church but the four of them stand stock-still in the doorway staring at the latecomers. "Girls," I snap. "Pay attention. It's time to go."

"Go sit down," Ellie tells him with a laugh. "I'm trying to get married here."

He—Grayson—first leans down to kiss her cheek, his dark blond hair flopping over his forehead. "You look absolutely radiant," he says, pushing his hair back with a graceful hand. "And it's Pepper's fault we're late, so you can't blame me."

"It is not. But I'm sorry we're so late." The woman pauses to hug Ellie before squeezing past the line of waiting bridesmaids. "C'mon, Gray. Good luck, Rufus," she says to the ring bearer with a wink.

Grayson follows, but unlike his date, he takes his time, his lazy gaze fixing on every woman in the wedding party with an appraising smile like he's the judge of a bridesmaids' pageant. "Y'all look gorgeous," he says. When his gaze falls on me, his smile widens, showing perfect white teeth.

I don't like feeling judged and I've never been one for high-gloss filters. I scowl in return. "We're waiting."

His eyes blink with surprise and he takes a step back. The eyes are blue. Very blue, and the smile is even better up close. "I don't want to *ever* keep someone that looks like you waiting," he says, clutching his chest for emphasis.

Another smile, but it only annoys me further with its perfection. Really, he's too pretty for his own good. "Well, don't. Please find your seat."

With a two-fingered salute and a wink of a very blue eye, he follows his date inside. I glance back to see Ellie shaking her head with a smile.

"At least they made it," Rufus says.

I push them from my mind and concentrate on the task at hand. One last check that everyone is in position and I loudly whisper. "Rufus. Take them in."

The young ring bearer looks back with a grin that's going to break some hearts in a few years. "Got it." With a gentleness that none of my brothers ever showed, Rufus nudges and gestures for the little girls to start down the aisle, before waiting an extra beat to bring up the rear with the oldest girl. I watch, soothed by his concentration, until he gets to the pew where Shae leans into the aisle with Dawson behind her.

"Hi, Shae," I hear Rufus greet her and a titter of laughter spreads through the crowd.

"You look so cool, and you're doing a great job," Shae says as if they're having a private conversation on the street and not in the middle of a wedding. I have no idea how Rufus even knows Shae since he's the nephew of the bride and I only met him last night at the wedding rehearsal. Even though she's marrying my brother, I've only met Ellie once. I like to think we've developed a friendship while I've been in Thailand with Shae and Dawson via her frequent DMs with the wedding updates, but we'll see how that plays out in the real world.

The vlog. Rufus must recognize Shae from her—our—travel vlog. It's become so popular that Shae has become a recognized social influencer, turning heads when she's in public and gaining thousands of likes for every posted picture, whether it's of one of our trips or her daily life.

When Rufus and the flower girls are halfway down the aisle, I nod at April, the very pregnant bridesmaid, to start. And then it's my turn.

The church, familiar from Christmas and Easter visits, as well as my confirmation, is packed as heads turn in my direction. The smiles of anticipation focus on me for a brief moment before looking past me for a glimpse of Ellie in her white dress. It's easy to notice Shae in the crowd; not only does her pink hair make her stand out, but she's still leaning into the aisle to watch me.

"You look amazing," Shae says in a whisper that is easily loud enough for the whole church to hear. Her smile, always so sincere and full of best friend love, warms my heart to see it directed at me.

To know Shae is to love her; to love her is to be jealous, at least for me. Not that her lot in life is anything to wish for, but she's still able to live every day like it's her best day.

Dawson stands behind Shae, a hand on her shoulder like he's holding her back from darting out into the aisle to hug me. Which, knowing Shae, is entirely possible.

Whenever I see Shae and Dawson together, I know exactly what Ron Weasley must feel, the tug of being left out of whatever bond ties them together.

I give myself the usual eight seconds to stare at Dawson, which is the perfect amount of time to focus on some part of him without seeming too obvious. His face is a study of contrasts, with the soft, smiling muddy-green eyes and full lips to the envious high cheekbones and slash of a narrow nose.

I take in his smile, or rather lack of it.

His mouth hangs open in sort of an awestruck expression, like when he first saw the expanse of the Wall of China and realized we were supposed to walk along it.

For a moment, I'm tempted to look behind me in case Ellie jumped the gun and is hurrying me along, but when my gaze flicks to Natasha standing beside Dawson, and I notice the absolutely furious expression on her pretty face, I know it really *is* me that Dawson is smiling at.

Or not smiling.

He's looking at me with wonder and admiration, and everything inside of me gets warm; my cheeks flush with delight, my stomach feels like I've downed a litre of hot chocolate, and my heart—

My heart can't take much more of this.

I tear my gaze away. Moment over.

Grayson

I SLIDE INTO THE pew beside Pepper, nodding at the heads swiveling in our direction.

"Isn't that Grayson Grant? From *The Suitor*?" I hear a woman across the aisle whisper. When I turn to glance her way and flash a grin, her face explodes like she won the lottery.

"Stop it," Pepper hisses, her own face twisted into a frown.

"Stop what?" My sister has always been like one of those critters sitting on a shoulder—sometimes they tell you good things and sometimes they tell you bad things. She's gotten me into trouble more times than I can remember, and yet loves to play the innocent.

Sometimes it's best to ignore her and her little voices. I glance over at the woman across the aisle to see if she's with anyone.

Nope. Three of them sitting together; my guess is single and looking to mingle with a former contestant of Canada's top reality show. I smile again.

"You're such a peacock."

"Did you just call me a peacock?" I ask under my breath as the first of the little girls in their cotton candy dresses step through the door. Two by two, they begin their walk, pretty faces screwed up with determination, much like Pepper when she's trying to be annoyed with me. It's impossible, and a gift. No one can stay mad at me, especially not Pepper.

"We were late. It's embarrassing and you sit here, loving how everyone is staring at you. You're like a peacock, shaking his feathers."

I give her an innocent expression, meeting her blue eyes that are the mirror image of mine. "I do have nice feathers."

She pokes me in the stomach and I retaliate by slinging an arm around her shoulders, tousling her hair in the process. The hair that took her an extra forty-five minutes to straighten after the curls didn't work out, and was the reason we were late.

Pepper growls and I bite back a laugh.

But I forget about all of it as Rufus steps through the door with the last flower girl clinging to his arm; my heart does something funny at the sight of him. "Ah, look at the little dude."

Pepper tucks her hands under her chin, her frown replaced by something warm and gushy. Both of us had been at the hospital the day Rufus was born, and it's safe to say the kid has a soft spot in both of us. "Ooh! He's so grown up, and *so* handsome. He looks like Emmett at that age."

At the front of the church, Emmett Pike, Ellie's brother and my best friend, beams proudly as his nephew makes his way down the aisle. "You think my best friend is handsome, do you?"

The softness in Pepper's expression vanishes as my sister gives me another sharp elbow. "Stop talking, Grayson. We're in church."

"You started it." I watch as Rufus takes his spot at the front of the church with the rest of the groomsmen. I don't have children yet, but I think it might feel like this, the pride and swell of love seeing Rufus deposit the flower girls in their spots at the front of the church before making his way across to where Emmett and the rest of the groomsmen stand at attention.

I've never felt prouder. Maybe when Rufus got his first strikeout using the two-fingered slider that I taught him, but it's a toss-up.

I turn back to wait for Ellie to make her appearance, just as the sharp-tongued bridesmaid begins to make her way down the aisle with measured steps, like she's counting every one of them. Masses of blonde curls trail down her slim back, which surprise me. The bad-tempered glance she gave me looked like it was from some miserable hair-pulled-back-in-a-tight-chignon type, not a girl who goes for wavy beach hair.

But you know what they say about women when they take their hair down.

Actually, I have no idea what they say, but the image of this girl shaking out her hair is sticking with me.

"Who's that?" I whisper to Pepper.

"Must be the sister," Pepper says in a low voice, and I tear my gaze away from the blonde as she takes her spot at the front across from Emmett, totally missing the third bridesmaid as she passes by our pew. "April is the pregnant one and I met Bettany at the shower, and that's Priya..." Pepper trails off as the maid of honour steps through the door, the congregation reacting with anticipation at what's to come next.

Part of me wonders if I should ask my sister if she's okay not being part of Ellie's wedding party but before I can say anything, Ellie appears on the arm of her father. A collective *aah* sweeps through the church as the congregation stands.

My heart gives another, different kind of tug as I watch Emmett's sister, the girl who blew my mind during one hot, life-changing, summer in my seventeenth year, glides down the aisle with her father, a radiant smile on her face.

"She looks beautiful," I say with awe.

"You missed your chance there," Pepper scoffs. "The only one you couldn't have."

I wisely keep my mouth shut and watch Ellie. When I finally glance back at Pepper, her eyes are filled with tears as we watch Ellie's father say the right words and step back to his seat as Ellie joins hands with her groom-to-be.

"That's going to be you next," Pepper whispers with a quick wipe under her eye.

"What?"

"You, getting married. That's what you want, isn't it? Your endgame in all this?"

Suddenly my stomach is free-falling like I'm on a roller coaster. Pepper is right, but her words are too final. The idea shouldn't sound that scary, but it does.

I can't look at my sister because she'll recognize the uncertainty in my eyes. "Sure," I say and gesture to the front of the church. "Look how awesome Rufus is. So proud of him."

I focus on the wedding at hand and do my best to forget that in six weeks, I'll be starting the search for my own true love.

Chapter Two

Neely

"WHERE'S SHAE?" APRIL ASKS me eagerly as the brides-maids pose in a tangle of shades of pink around Ellie under the welcome shade of a tree at the side of the Yacht Club. No one in our family but me has ever sailed, but we all share a love of the water. We've lived within walking distance of the shore of Lake Ontario my whole life and when I'm home, rarely a day goes by that I don't find myself down by the water.

James is the same way. Because Ellie's mother isn't in the pic-ture—I haven't heard the full story there—Mama got her way for the ceremony to be at our church rather than in the small town where Ellie lives, as well as the Yacht Club for the reception.

"I saw her in the church," April continues, posed with her hand on my hip, the push of her belly in the small of my back. "Love her hair! It's even pinker up close."

"She's not in the wedding party," I explain as I try to smile. "I imagine she's already inside at the bar."

With Dawson.

With Dawson and *Natasha*, I correct as the thought of seeing Dawson creates the usual twist of excitement and bitterness.

"Who is this Shae?" Ellie asks, her happy expression spoiled by the obviously fake smile pasted on her face. "She's all I've heard about from Rufus."

"Everyone say *James and Ellie!*" the photographer cries and the chorus of female voices answer him. I don't, because talking during pictures are a sure way of catching you with eyes closed, mouth open and looking like a gargoyle.

"I follow her on Instagram," April says as the photographer shuffles us into another "fun" pose. "She goes all over the world and posts videos doing all this fabulous stuff, like swimming with sharks and dolphins and surfing with the hottest Australian guys." She rubs her burgeoning belly with a role of her eyes. "If I'd only figured out I wanted to see the world before I got myself knocked up."

Ellie turns to me. "Didn't James say you travel with Shae? You were with her in Thailand, weren't you?"

"I was," I say, with just a *little* side-eye at April. "Sorry again I wasn't around more to help out."

"Is that why you missed the shower?" Priya, the maid of honour, asks.

"I'd miss the shower if I was in Thailand! Don't apologize." Ellie waves her bouquet at me. "If I had the chance to see the world like you do, I'd jump at it. I'm only glad you got back in time for the wedding."

"I wouldn't have missed it." I smile warmly at her. James didn't waste any time proposing to Ellie and because I'd been in Asia with Shae and Dawson for the last ten weeks, and Costa Rica before that, and Australia before that, I've only met my latest sister-in-law a handful of times. We've managed to cobble together a friendship from the email and texts, but I know nothing about the rest of the bridesmaids.

Nor do I really want to now.

"Besides, my brother would never have forgiven me if I didn't come back," I add.

"Neither would Mama S.," Ellie whispers a little fearfully. My mother is only slightly terrifying with her sharp tongue and strong opinions.

My family says I take after her.

"So, *you* were in the videos too?" April widens her eyes and gives an embarrassed laugh. "Totally missed seeing you there."

"I'm not surprised," I say with mock sweetness. It wouldn't be good to ask if her pregnancy has affected her sight. I may not be front and centre in the vlog, but I'm there. I'm always there, right beside Shae.

Even though I feel invisible at times.

The breeze blowing off the lake ruffles my curls and I wish it could blow away April, but she's solidly pregnant and unbudging at my side, asking me inane questions about the vlog, and obviously trying to make up for missing me in the videos.

The heaviness from the trip still hangs over me, a mix of exhaustion and general fog in my head that makes me feel like I'm coming down with a cold.

Maybe that's why I snapped at the guy in the purple suit.

I hate to admit I looked for him after the ceremony. Not to apologize, but to find out who he is. I heard the whispers at the church and it's driving me crazy not knowing what the big deal is.

Maybe if I knew Ellie and the others better, I'd ask them who he is. The easiest way would be to Google him but Mama confiscated my phone early this morning. She hates the thing; she tolerates me travelling with Shae because it's Shae, but my mother despises that my life is open to all via the vlog.

"You need privacy, for goodness' sake," she would say in her Italian accent, still thick even after living in Toronto for forty-seven years. "How can you find a man if he knows what you look like first thing in the morning? Those pictures you post. Horrible."

To clarify, I don't look horrible first thing in the morning, nor does my mother actually think that. At least I hope she doesn't.

"Where's Shae?" Adam asks when I join him under the welcome shade of a tree as Ellie and James finish with their pictures, posed to look like they're madly in love. It's nice that they don't have to pretend.

"Not you, too," I mutter as the heels of my shoes sink into the grass, forcing me to grab my brother's arm. "I am not her keeper."

"But you are." Adam smiles knowingly. "Someone needs to be."

"I'm sure she's inside, entertaining the guests. You know Shae. And I have no idea about Dawson," I add.

Adams gives me a side-eye. "I didn't ask about Dawson, but now that you mention him, I see he brought Natasha."

"He needed a date." *Please don't get into it*, I silently beg my brother. I let it slip *once* about Dawson, and now Adam always brings it up, like he expects an update to be part of the crawler on the day's news.

There is no update. There will never be an update. Maybe someday I'll stop feeling like this, but until then, there's nothing I can do but hide my feelings and let Dawson live his own love life.

Fortunately, I haven't had a problem with that since, according to Shae, Dawson is just too oblivious to realize what's right in front of his face. "For a brilliant guy, he's very stupid."

Unrequited love puts me in a bad mood, I decide.

"He's hot, isn't he?" I whirl around at Adam's words, thinking Dawson has suddenly appeared, or maybe the guy in the purple suit.

But no. Adam is staring at Emmett with an admiring smile. "Ellie's brother. Very hot in a farmboy-ish way."

"I thought he was a ballplayer." I'd rather comment on Emmett's profession than his hotness; which, in fact, I have noticed. Just like I also noticed Emmett staring at Shae throughout the ceremony. Not surprising, but I am surprised at the stab of disappointment I felt the third time I looked across the chancel to see Emmett smiling in Shae's direction.

"Former. I don't know the whole story, but word is that he got hurt and stopped playing. Kind of wild that Shae met him yesterday, isn't it?"

"Yesterday?" I parrot. "Where?" Shae meets people in the strangest places, but I haven't heard about this yet.

"Emmett was in Pain au Chocolate when we stopped there on the way back from the airport," Adam says with disbelief. "To think no one else wanted to go in. We could have met the hottie right then and there."

"We met him today, so that's fine."

"Yes, but is it? Now that Shae has him wrapped around her little finger, none of us have a chance. Not that I had one—or wanted one." He gives me the goofy smile he gets when he's thinking of his boyfriend.

"Yes, you're in love with Patrick," I say wryly. "Plus, I would say Emmett is heterosexual, which might make it an issue for you."

Adam gives his usual dismissive wave "Hetero, homo, what difference does it make when there's so much love to go around? Anyway, apparently young Rufus is positively *enchanted* with our Shae. So cute. He's a fun little dude."

"Fun," I echo.

I have an urge to ask Adam if he saw the guy in the purple suit and if he knows who he is, because next to Shae, my brother knows everything about everyone. And then I remember Purple Suit came with a date and I'm not interested in anyone.

I'm not.

"But the big news is that our Emmett was *married*." Adam drops his voice dramatically as he continues his gossip. "And she *died*. So sad."

"That is sad," I agree. "Let's not tell Shae that." I can only imagine what that would do to any interest Shae might have for Emmett.

"I concur." Adam turns wide eyes to the group posing, tracking Emmett as he laughs at something Rufus says. "We'll keep that quiet because he might be a good fit for her."

Adam and I are barely two years apart and have a closer relationship than I do with either James or Davis, and therefore he knows Shae and Dawson quite well. In fact, we've taken my younger brother on one of the trips, and Shae keeps pestering him to come with us again. But I know my brother, and I know he prefers to be at home, especially with his boyfriend Patrick in attendance.

Adam also knows all about Shae's illness—when she was fourteen, she was diagnosed with neuronal ceroid lipofuscinosis. Doctors gave her seven to ten years to live; she's made it to thirteen because except for the prospect of her dying, Shae is the luckiest person I know.

Knowing my best friend is dying, or will die, changes a few things in our friendship.

Like how I dropped out of university after only one semester to travel through Eastern Europe with her. Like how I put aside my plans in business management to manage the vlog, *ExpiryDate*, as well as any and all travel arrangements. I lecture Shae about vitamins and green tea and keeping her energy up, fixing her problems before they become issues, and acting as wingwoman, chaperone or shield, whatever she needs.

My best friend is dying and I do whatever I can to let her live her best life in the time she has left.

"You know Shae," I say with a shrug, like it explains everything.

Adam sighs again, a deep, dark sigh that has more to do with Shae's dating history than her expiry date. "Well, we'll see what we can do to help things along with Emmett, won't we?" When I don't answer, he nudges me with his elbow. "Won't we, Neely?"

It takes me a moment to find the words, and by the time I do, the photographer is taking the last shots. "Ellie thought we'd hit it off," I say in a quiet voice.

"You and...Emmett?" The surprise is evident in Adam's voice.

"She kept talking him up to me in her DMs," I admit. "But if Shae—"

"Shae would step aside in a heartbeat," Adam assures me.

"She doesn't have to. I don't even know him. I just thought..." I trail off, choosing my words as I watch Ellie and James.

"It's time for you to meet someone?" Adam finishes for me.

"Maybe." There's not a lot in this world that makes me self-conscious, but my sorely lacking love life is one of them. Romance comes effortlessly to both Dawson and Shae, even though Shae insists on keeping her love life as casual as a third-grade date. Neither one of them ever has problems attracting the opposite sex, and the string of broken hearts trails us across the world.

Unlike me, who has to force myself to give any man a second glance. If he's not tall and lanky, with greenish eyes, thick black hair and glasses that continually fall down his nose, I'm not interested.

But I did look at Purple Suit more than twice today.

"I think it's long past about time you met someone whose name doesn't rhyme with *Lawson Lacinto*." The eagerness is clear in Adam's voice and it makes me smile. There's nothing my brother likes better than watching a love story develop, whether it's two customers in the patisserie where he works, or on one of those crime procedural shows he devours on TV.

"Don't get excited," I caution. "It's been a while."

Adam coughs into his hand. "Never."

"It's not that bad," I say, even though I can't come up with the last time I was excited by a man who isn't Dawson. "It never makes sense when we're away, but if we're going to be home for a while...maybe when I start classes next month."

I've put off finishing my degree for two years now, prioritizing being with Shae over my education. I'm not the only one; Dawson has turned down countless requests from headhunters trying to recruit him. He's turned his years of playing video games into a real talent for game design. It must be every geek's dream—just not mine.

"So it's finally time for you to get over Dawson?" Adam has a knowing smile on his face when I turn to him. "Oh, come on, sister dear. You're going to have to stop being close-mouthed sooner or later."

"I really don't think I do."

"Adam and Neely, your turn to pose with James," Ellie calls to us.

"Dammit, I thought we were through," Adam says through gritted teeth. "Coming, new sister-in-law," he sings loudly, causing Ellie to squeal with delight. "You know, you could finally make your move on the boy. He'd kick nasty Natasha to the curb if he thought you were coming for him."

"I doubt that." There's no way Dawson would pick me over anyone. He had his chance years ago, and I don't give anyone a second one.

Even him.

Grayson

"**G**RAYSON! HAVE YOU TALKED to Chrissa?"

"Are you going to be the next Suitor?"

"I know I can heal your broken heart—DM me!"

The questions and comments blur as I maneuver around small groups of wedding guests on my way to the bar.

"Grayson! Selfie!" A woman pushes into me and I blink as the flash goes off.

"Let's do another one," I suggest. There's no sense having a pic of me looking like a deer caught in the headlights going viral right after my meeting with the *Suitor* producers.

I'm still not sure what I've agreed to. If things are this bad after I was one of twenty-five contestants, what's it going to be like when I'm the one and only?

A week ago, I agreed to be the next Suitor.

It's not official yet because I haven't signed the papers, but the rumours have been fast and furious across social media. *The Suitor* has a huge presence across Instagram, Twitter, even Facebook, and it was surreal to log on and find discussion threads about my suitability for the show, even before anyone even talked to me about it.

A year and a half ago, I had been one of the twenty-five contestants vying for the hand of the Suitorette—the second season of the female version of the show. I made it to the top five, but my journey was cut short when I was eventually sent home by Chrissa. I thought my reality show career was over, like my baseball career, but it turns out I'd made a big enough impression on the viewers for the producers of the show to come calling when they were casting the sixth season of *The Suitor*.

I know it's happening, but sometimes, like today, it seems really hard to believe that not only am I going to be the star of a reality show, but the purpose of the show is to find love. True love, the kind that after six weeks, will end up with me on one knee and offering a big rock of a ring to a woman I haven't even met yet.

It's the twenty-first-century version of arranged marriages.

"Have fun tonight," I say to the woman, as I detangle myself from her grip.

"Thank you!" she squeals, her voice high enough to shatter crystal. "If you have time, we should—"

I lift a hand in farewell without letting her finish and continue along to the bar.

"You don't have to enjoy it so much," Pepper says wryly as she tags behind me.

"What can I say?" I say, feigning confidence. "They love me."

I've always been fortunate to have more than my fair share of female interest. The worst—or best, considering how you look at it—was after my handful of starts with the St. Louis Cardinals. That had been the heyday of my baseball career and I thought I was going somewhere.

Unfortunately, the only place I went was back to the minor leagues for another half season before my arm burned out, leaving me on the list of the lucky Canadians who got to play in the Major Leagues.

I miss playing every single day.

Where did that come from?

Resting my elbow on the bar, I hold up two fingers to the bartender. Now that we're out of the church, the wedding seems to be growing with guests milling around the tables, waiting for Ellie and James to arrive. When I first got the invite, with Ellie's name embossed in white, I thought maybe it was a small affair, and Ellie was looking for guests to fill her side. Why else would she invite her brother's best friend and his sister? True, we've known Ellie forever, and she and Pepper used to be best friends, but things haven't been the same with our families since my father ran off with Ellie's mother.

Abandonment and wife-stealing tend to put a damper on relationships, even long-term ones.

"Grayson!"

I turn at the voice, this time a male one. "Peter," I say with a warm smile. "Great wedding."

"Wasn't it? Ellie looks so happy. How are you, Pepper?" Emmett's father leans in to kiss Pepper on the cheek.

"Great, Mr. Pike." She sounds like a nervous fifteen-year-old, which has never been my sister.

"Peter, please. I've known you since you were three."

Pepper smiles as some of the tension drops from her shoulders. I know she shares my guilt that somehow we're at fault for our father running off with his wife. Of course, there's no way either of us are at all responsible, but when a town puts the fault solely on your father for breaking up a much-loved couple, the kids get hit with the blame brush. That's just how it is.

"Ellie looks so beautiful," Pepper tells Peter. "And James seems nice."

"Great guy. And the family have really welcomed her. She's going to be very happy with him. And you, Pepper? I haven't seen you around much. My ever-expanding waistband keeps me from stopping into the bakery as much as I want to."

"You haven't changed a bit. You look the same as you did when we were kids," I cut in.

"I've had good feedback from the bread in your boxes," Pepper says. "It's helped business more than I imagined it would. Thanks for pulling me in."

Pike's Place is one of the new, community-supported agriculture farms that supply customers with fresh produce in return for them subscribing to the farm. Emmett convinced his father to move in that direction years ago and now helps Peter run things. "Good to hear." Peter squeezes Pepper's arm with a fatherly smile. "I'm sorry your mother couldn't make it, but I'm glad both of you are here. I'll talk with you soon."

"Whose idea do you think it was it to invite Mom?" Pepper asks in a low voice as we watch Peter make his way through a group, smiling his good-ole-boy smile as he accepts their congratulations.

"Emmett," I decide. "Peter's great, but he hasn't seen Mom in years. And Ellie..." I trail off as I contemplate Emmett's younger sister. "What do they say about a woman scorned? I think she holds a grudge."

Pepper raises her eyebrows. "You think?" With a rueful shake of her head, she turns to collect the beer glasses on the bar behind us.

"Grayson! Can I get a picture with you?"

There are some serious *Suitor* fans here and as I try to mingle with the other guests, a crowd begins with a lineup for selfies. Pepper starts taking pictures to move things along, but she's soon annoyed by being pushed aside and scoots away to find a few old school friends, leaving me alone to handle the constant questions.

"Are you still upset about Chrissa?"

"Have you spoken to her?"

"What really happens in the fantasy suites?"

I finally get through them all, my face cramping from smiling, wishing I had more time to talk with the couple who pushed in to ask me about baseball. "That's it for now, folks," I call over the excited chatter surrounding me. "Be sure to watch the next season of *The Suitor* when it starts."

"Are you going to be the next Suitor?" a woman cries.

With a smile, I wave the question away and make a beeline to the bar, where Emmett is standing with Rufus. It's not the first time I've been mobbed like that; I get recognized more and more recently as fans keep up the social chatter about who will be the next Suitor and my face is in most of the posts. And if things go as planned, it won't be the last.

I need a little breather though.

"Well, now," I muse approaching Emmett from the side in time to see him wave to a pink-haired girl. "Why is she trying to get you to dance? Doesn't she know what you look like on the dance floor?"

Emmett turns to me with a rueful grin. "I'm not about to dance."

"Don't. You'll scare her off, at least until you've had something to loosen you up. That the vlogger girl? Rufus already told me she was here." With a last look at the dance floor, I turn to the bartender. "Two cold ones, please, my friend. This dude here is getting desperate." I jerk my chin towards Emmett with a grin. "You can only be stuffed into a tux for so long without alcohol to ease the pain."

I smile my thanks as two glasses are pushed across the bar, both with a heavy foam heads and dripping with condensation, and hand one to Emmett.

"Shae. She's James's sister's friend." Emmett takes a long swallow.

"The sister is the tall blonde, isn't she?" I ask, glancing around for a look at her. "The one in the wedding party?"

"Neely." Emmett points out where she's standing by the entrance and I smile.

"Ah." Even the name is intriguing. She's smiling now, a big improvement from the earlier scowl.

Emmett nudges me. "I know that voice."

"I should hope so. I've only known you my entire life."

"She's Ellie's new sister-in-law. Shouldn't that make her off-limits?"

"Nobody said anything about sisters-in-law, and she's not mine. Besides," I say with a smirk, walking backwards away from the bar. "It's a wedding. You've been out of the game for too long, bro. Best time *ever* to pick up the ladies. You'd do good to remember that."

And then I make a beeline through the crowds to where the object of my new obsession talks with the pink-haired vlogger on the edge of the dance floor. I slide up to them with an admiring smile and overhear Shae speaking.

It's like she opens the door for me. "I agree with that assessment, but also that she looks hot." Both women turn to stare at me and I smile, trying to look innocent by showing lots of teeth. "If I'm allowed to say something like that without offending?"

"Why do you look familiar?" Shae demands. Her words are rude but her expression is one of interest—but not that kind of interest.

"Why do men insist on calling women *hot* when it only objectifies their sexuality?" Neely snaps at the same time.

I give a jerk of surprise. I expected a shy smile and a *thank you*, not a verbal tongue-lashing.

Maybe I secretly hoped for it, because Neely is seriously beautiful when she's annoyed. She looks like an Oscar award, tall and slim and golden with perfectly delicate features and natural blonde hair—my favourite kind—and sun-kissed skin like she's come in from the beach. Even her eyes are a hypnotic golden hazel that I can't turn away from.

Thank goodness she's not my sister-in-law.

"Whoa. I see I've interrupted something here, so I'll take my leave." The smile tickles the corners of my mouth and it wouldn't be fair not to let it free. *Smile, don't fail me now.* "But to answer your question—I hope you recognize me, if you're on social media as much as you are, Ms. Social Influencer extraordinaire."

Neely turns to Shae with a roll of her eyes. "Guess he recognizes you."

"Do you want a picture?" Shae asks.

This isn't going as expected. *How can they not...?* I need to step it up or I'm going to walk away without a dance partner tonight.

A dance partner would only be the beginning.

"And you"—I drop into a sweeping bow before Neely—"are the loveliest bridesmaid I've ever had the pleasure of watching. You are not hot, but your loveliness makes me warm under the collar. You're like a modern-day Cinderella, and I hope I get to take off your glass slippers because I give a mean foot rub." I let the smile run free, pleased when at least Shae smiles in return.

Neely, on the other hand, is expressionless in the face of my many years of orthodontics and teeth whitening. "You're a bit much, aren't you?"

How can there be no interest? Pictures of me have been posted on social media for weeks, and these two have one of the most popular vlogs around, so how do they not know who I am?

The realization is surprising, and not a little disappointing.

"They do call me Superman." I widen my grin, hoping I don't look as off-balanced as I feel. "I guess that makes me something."

"That's because his name sounds like a superhero," Emmett says from behind me.

Is this an interruption or an intervention? Either way, I'm glad for the help.

"Emmett!" Shae cries. I've never seen a bigger, goofier smile on a woman and it throws me off even more, because it's not me she's smiling at.

"Nice wedding," Shae adds, visibly trying to rein herself in.

"You seem to be enjoying yourself." Emmett's eyes skirt down to her feet. "Your toes match the flowers on your dress."

Of course, now I have to check them out too. Beside Shae's childlike toes, are Neely's feet, pushed into pink, strappy sandals with sky-high heels. I let my gaze drift up, past delicate ankles, her legs hidden in the gauzy fabric of her dress, to find Neely watching Shae with an almost imperceptible pucker between her eyes.

Why the frown?

I watch Neely watch Shae as she banters with Emmett, not wanting to say anything that would take her attention away from him. It's good to see him back in action, so good I don't even feel a hint of resentment that he is getting all the smiles.

"Did you eat the cupcake?" Shae continues, her hands clasped at her chest. "My cupcake."

"I haven't yet," he admits. "It's still waiting. Maybe we can share."

"You'd share your Reuben-made cupcake with *me*?"

"Yes," Emmett says simply.

If that's not a moment, I don't know what is. Emmett and Shae stare at each other, and the moment threatens to become awkward for Neely and me.

"So, Superman." Neely must feel it too. "What's your real name? Clark Parker?"

Could she...might it be possible for a girl who looks like her...combining two of my favourite superheroes? Is she a comic book geek too? "No, but you get points for a good guess. Grayson Grant, at your service. Happy that I have no power, nor responsibility."

Shae physically drags her gaze away from Emmett. "That would be a *super* superhero name."

"You were on *The Suitor*." Neely's voice is as cool as her eyes and for the first time I have a twinge of unease that this *really* isn't going as I hoped. "I remember that line. I'm afraid you lose points for originality."

"Ouch." But then Neely smiles and there are no words. I've met a lot of women with beautiful smiles, but there's something about Neely. With all of her apparent poise and confidence, her smile is just a little bit shy, almost self-conscious, like she's not used to flashing it.

Of course that realization is like waving a six-pack in front of me after pre-season training, and I vow to make it my goal to make Neely smile as much as possible tonight.

Which means spending as much time with her as possible tonight.

The voice of the DJ crackles over the speaker. "Our new bride and groom would like their dinner. Put your hands together and give a warm welcome for the stars of this evening, Ellie Pike and James Scalzo!"

The happy couple appears at the door, with the rest of the wedding party, including Rufus, clustered behind them.

Neely and Emmett share a horrified expression. "We're supposed to be with them," Neely says in a choked voice before she turns tail and races across the room in an odd run-walk that makes me laugh to see it. Emmett is right behind her, leaving his half-empty glass on the bar behind us.

"I guess they need to be somewhere," Shae muses.

We watch Ellie and James take their seats at the head table, followed by the rest of the wedding party. I notice Emmett's head bent towards Neely. Of course they're sitting together.

After the enthusiastic round of applause begins to taper off, guests are quick to start the convoy to the tables.

I yank my attention away from a now-laughing Neely and glance down at Shae beside me. "This looks like our cue to take our seats," I say. "And seeing as we've been left on our own, I'll escort you to your table, which will hopefully be the same one I'm at." I place my hand onto the perfect spot on the small of her back—too high and she'll feel like I'm pushing her, too low, she'll think I'm copping a feel.

I don't want anyone to think that, because I can already sense jealousy isn't the way to win over Neely.

I wonder what is.

Chapter Three

Neely

A S I TAKE MY seat at the head table, I silently fume like a carbon dioxide leak. I can't believe I missed the signal for the wedding party to assemble since *I* was the one who came up with the idea for us all to group and walk in together, and then I go and miss the song that was to tell us to gather by the door.

"I don't think anyone caught us drinking by the bar," Emmett says in a low voice as he holds my chair out for me.

"They all wish they were with us," I say, surprised when Emmett chuckles. "Especially Adam. He'll be propping it up all night."

"Sounds like a good deal to me. Brothers—and sisters—unite at the bar."

I laugh at the thought of my three brothers, along with Emmett and his brother Ethan, leaning against the bar in their tuxedos, like cowboys in an old-time saloon. I'm not sure how good the relationship is with Emmett and Ethan but there'd be an argument between the Scalzo brothers before the first beer was finished. "I'm not joining you for that," I say with another laugh. "Davis and Adam won't last the night."

"Grayson can keep the peace with anyone."

At Emmett's casual mention, my gaze slides across the room to where Grayson and Shae make their way to Table Eight, smiling and talking to everyone within eyesight. He even stops to take a selfie with my sixteen-year-old cousin, leaving Shae as the odd one out.

I watch covertly until they take their seats.

The room is full of chatter and the scrape of chairs as the guests take their seats. I noticed last night that the seating chart had been done with schoolteacher precision, which means Ellie must have done it. I had offered to help, sending her emails about which cousins needed to be kept separate from which uncles, and which of my mother's sisters would insist on being at Table One with my parents.

I'm not sure how Ellie did it, but Table One has only my parents, Emmett's father and brother seated together. When I glance over, Mama is happily talking to Peter Pike, with Daddy nodding in his quiet way at something Ethan is telling him.

None of my brothers are anything like our father, who is serene and passive in the face of the hurricane that is Mama. Strong-willed, strongly opinionated and not afraid to share their thoughts, all the Scalzo children take after our mother so much that I often wonder how Daddy played into it.

Emmett takes the seat beside me. After Ellie's feeble attempts at playing matchmaker, I might have been nervous about keeping up conversation with him all night if Emmett hadn't made his interest in Shae so obvious. Now he's nothing more than my brother's brother-in-law.

"So pretty." I look over on hearing Emmett's tone, assuming he's referring to the room. Done in shades of pink, centrepieces sit amid a sea of tealights, giving the room a rosy hue, like cheeks pink from the cold. But Emmett is staring at his sister with a rueful smile as she hugs her maid of honour.

"You okay?" I ask with concern.

"Yup." Emmett gives himself a visible shake. "It just hit me that my little sister is married. It's like she was playing with dolls last week."

"You sound like James. Every time we leave on a trip, he takes an afternoon to give me a self-defence refresher and I've had to stop him twice from buying me a Taser. He doesn't understand that his little sister is perfectly capable of looking after herself. But that does bode well for him looking after Ellie, if that helps."

"It does." Emmett reaches for the wine bottle between our plates and pours me a glass. "A Taser, huh?"

"I am currently unarmed, if you're worried."

"I'm trying to picture you holding one in that dress. So this is your second brother getting married? How do you get through it?"

I laugh loud enough for heads to turn my way. "Because they're my brothers. I love them both, but neither one of them were ever much fun to live with, what with the toilet seats left up and the laundry issues." I shake my head ruefully. "I should have warned Ellie because James hasn't done a load in his life. Mama takes care of that, and when she can't, he hides his dirty socks in my laundry basket so I'll do it. I'm embarrassed to admit how very old-fashioned things are in our house," I finish with a grimace.

"They'll have to learn pretty quick, because Ellie's no good at it either. Dad taught himself to iron when my—" Emmett's grin fades suddenly before he gives himself a shake—"years ago, and Ellie's only job was to put her clothes away and to take care of any unmentionables. I never ask if she has any of those."

"Probably better not to know." I raise my glass and clink with Emmett's. wondering what he stopped himself from saying. "Here's to more room in the house. I always wondered why James never moved out until I realized how much Mama was still doing for him."

Emmett and I chat as a few speeches begin and dinner is served. I make it halfway through Ellie's father's welcome to James and our family before sneaking a glance at the table where Shae is sitting.

I tell myself I'm checking out Grayson, but my gaze keeps sliding to where Dawson leans over to tell Shae something.

My stomach clenches from want or desire or whatever it is—I want to be the one sitting beside him. I want him to whisper into my ear, trying to make me laugh with one of his dry asides.

He does that, but it's not the same because I don't let myself enjoy it.

Beside Dawson, Natasha puts a hand on his shoulder to pull his attention back to her, but Dawson only raises his hand as a signal to wait while he continues to talk to Shae.

I wonder how long Natasha will be around for.

They had only started dating a few weeks before we left for Asia, so I've been a first-hand witness as the romance progresses. She's no different than the long line of Dawson girlfriends—women who have perfected the skill of makeup application and duck-lip smiles, looking for his influence to increase their social media followers.

He doesn't see it that way, and it's hard for me to argue that most of the women he gets involved with are using him because Dawson is truly a great guy. He's brilliant, funny and kind, with more than a passing resemblance to a Canadian actor who stars on *The Good Place*—because of that, I've binged on the entire series. There's so much going for him that women don't need some superficial reason to be with him.

I wouldn't need such a reason.

I came right out once and told him that a past girlfriend was only with him for the likes she got on Facebook but the hurt in his eyes made me wish I hadn't even thought it.

Now that I've let myself look over, I can't turn away from Dawson's table. Shae may be the light that brightens a room, but Dawson is my nightlight, warming the darkness and keeping my heart safe. He also keeps it out of the way of others.

With all the lecturing I do trying to get Shae to take a chance on love, I'm no better than she is. At least she has a good excuse—according to her, dying is a guaranteed get-out-of-falling-in-love card. Shae doesn't want to hurt anyone, doesn't want to leave them, like her father's death left her mother broken like a dropped wineglass. So she refuses to take a chance.

I wonder how Emmett will react to that little trait of Shae's, because it's obvious I'm not the only one watching the antics at Table Eight.

I've told Shae time and time again that falling in love would be worth it, but how do I really know? The only man I've ever loved is my best friend.

Maybe she's got a point.

Halfway through dinner, I hear the unmistakable sound of Dawson's laughter, big and braying and carrying through the room. He only laughs like that when he's having fun, his hanging-with-Shae laugh, but when I glance over again, I see that it's not Shae he's talking to but the woman who came late to the wedding with Grayson.

She flips her shoulder-length, dark blonde hair behind her shoulder, her smile wide and bright. Attractive in a serious kind of way. She and Grayson are like a couple of cardinals; his feathers—or purple suit—are showy, vivid and bright, and her more muted colouring and simple navy dress is definitely eclipsed by him.

Women should never be eclipsed by their dates.

Then I notice Grayson has his arm on the back of Shae's chair as he leans closer. Not the best date at all.

"Did you meet Pepper?" Emmett interrupts like he can tell what I'm musing about. "Grayson's sister?"

Sister... "No," I say, unsettled at the thought. "I mean, I saw them come into the church, but I thought they were together."

"Definitely not." Emmett chuckles. "Grayson'd never be able to handle Pepper."

There's a constant commotion at Shae's table as all eight guests serenade James and Ellie with another song. I thought taking away the clinking of the glasses would let the head table finish their dinner without it getting cold, but the restriction only encouraged the guests to be more creative. But I have to laugh as I watch Shae take centre stage. It's so natural for her. She should have been a performer, or a politician, or a cult leader because people naturally follow her, like a little pink-haired Pied Piper.

It's tough to watch at times. Knowing your best friend, the one person you love more than anyone, can wipe you off the map just by standing beside you, is hard. When Shae smiles, the world smiles with her and forgets all about me. April the bridesmaid wasn't the first—I've had people look at a picture of the three of us in some faraway country and ask where I am, when I'm standing just to the right of Shae.

But I love her dearly. It's impossible not to.

And it's not like Shae is grabbing the attention like a faux celebrity looking to hawk their next memoir—she does whatever she can to push me and Dawson to the forefront.

The candlelight glints off Dawson's glasses and I look away after only five seconds of staring. Maybe I'm getting better. And then I hear his laugh again and my stomach flips.

I really have to get over him. It's been too long—way too long.

Beside Dawson, Shae smiles as Grayson refills her wineglass. Grayson is exactly the type of man she goes for—fun and flirtatious who isn't looking for anything serious.

I see that Emmett keeps looking over at the table as well, and then I remember what Adam said earlier. Emmett seems solid; a decent, nice man. He would be good for Shae, I decide, much better than someone like Grayson. Emmett might actually make her pause before she tells him goodbye. "They seem like they're getting along," I muse.

"That's fine." Emmett sounds like it's anything but, and tries again. "It's good. They'd be good together."

"Really? You're just going to watch your friend take your girl?" My glass is empty again and I reach for the bottle of wine.

"She's not my girl."

"But you'd like her to be." I drain the bottle into my glass and wonder where the rest of it went. I've already drunk more than I usually do, and there's still hours of reception to go. Maybe I should switch to water as I take a sip, and decide water is overrated. "I talked to Adam who told me his plan."

"There's a plan?"

"There should always be a plan." Like my life, laid out with colour-coded squares. It's how I function best.

"So what's your story?" I ask, leaning on the table with my chin resting on my fist. "Since we're technically family."

Emmett doesn't seem like the type to open up so I'm surprised he tells me about his wife dying, how he destroyed his baseball career over grief. It's a sad story, one I hope he's not eager to tell Shae, because it would be all she needs to make an about face.

And the more we talk, the more I like Emmett.

I like him for Shae, not myself.

There's only one person for me.

But even as I take another glance at Dawson, the eight-second stare becoming longer because wine slows everything down, I find my gaze slipping once again to Grayson.

Grayson

M Y PHONE BUZZES AFTER my salad plate is removed and
I pull it surreptitiously out of my jacket pocket. Rude,
maybe, but when I see that it's my mother texting me, I decide it's
allowable to be rude.

MOM: How's the wedding?

I would have liked Mom to be here, and I think she would
have enjoyed it. But even after all these years, conversations are still
awkward with her and Peter, and nothing will ever change that,
regardless how much Mom might care about his children. Despite
the embossed invitation, she had decided not to come.

I send her a picture of Ellie that I snapped earlier.

MOM: So beautiful. Take notes because you'll be
next.

I hide my grimace. Mom's on the same wavelength as Pepper
when it comes to me being on *The Suitor*—they're all for it. I have
to wonder though, if it's because of the excitement of the show, the

chance I'll get to travel, or if they really think this show is going to be the only way I'll ever fall in love with a woman.

If my family thinks a reality show is going to give me a happily ever after, then I've done something seriously wrong with my love life.

Meeting women comes easy for me, like most things. But none of them last, which might be my fault. I'm sure it is my fault, but I'm embarrassed to admit that I've never given my exes much thought after it's over. Until my first stint on *The Suitor* showed the world what I looked like with a broken heart, I've never let a woman hurt me.

"You didn't let me get close," Chrissa had said after failing to give me a rose. "You're a great guy, Grayson, but I need more."

What more could I have given her? I started as one of twenty-five men, and quickly moved through the pack to become one of the frontrunners. Chrissa had been tall, dark and mysterious, but I had broken through her barriers without too much trouble, to find a smart, fun-loving woman with a vulnerable side. We bonded over absent fathers without me telling her how it hurt to be abandoned. I told her how I had given up baseball without getting into how it gutted me. We shared stories about growing up in a small town and I told her more about Emmett and Pepper than myself.

Apparently it wasn't enough for me to be funny and charming, sweet and considerate. Chrissa wanted me to *open up*. For me to be *vulnerable*. Show more *emotion*.

I need to talk more, and about myself. I can do that.

But with time ticking away before the next season, I'm beginning to think there's more to it. And since I don't want a replay of how I felt when Chrissa not only sent me home, but chose Aaron, one of my closest friends on the show to be her final Suitor, I'd better figure it out.

> MOM:The producers called and want to talk to you Monday.

I flip from Mom's text to check; I've gotten six texts from the show since last night. Maybe they think talking to my mother will ensure I'll get back to them.

I'm a grown man. I'll get back to them when I'm ready.

I send a quick text back to Mom that I'll get in touch with them, never admitting that my reluctance might have something to say about my readiness. There's no reason why I should have cold feet about doing the show, but they are definitely dragging when it comes to signing the final paperwork that will officially turn me from Grayson Grant, former pitcher for the St. Louis Cardinals, to Grayson Grant, the Suitor.

Suddenly, it seems like a lot to take in.

"Setting up a date for later?"

I turn to see Shae with a teasing smile. "Nope," I say, shoving my phone back into my pocket without responding to the producers. "That was my mom. I'm a one-woman man tonight."

"Oh, really? Have you told your admirers that? I see how Aunt Maeve has been watching you." She jerks her head at the table beside us, where a woman who must be pushing seventy is reapplying her lipstick. When she sees me looking over, she blows me a fuchsia-coloured kiss and nudges the woman beside her, who waves.

"Do you get that all the time?" Shae asks, more curious than irritated, like most of my female friends are. It's a nice change, possible only because Shae has absolutely no interest in me. At least I hope she doesn't. I'd rather she saved it for Emmett.

Maybe a little interest would be all right.

I shrug in answer to her question. "You must get the same thing. You're pretty big on Insta."

"Yes, but I don't have women constantly proposing marriage to me. Actually, there was one girl from Oregon." She laughs and I instinctively smile back. Her laugh—at least her smile—is contagious. "I let her down gently."

"No big boyfriend to scare her off?"

She gives me a tight smile. "I don't do boyfriends."

"Why's that? A cute little thing like you?"

"Were you really texting your mother?" she asks, completely ignoring my question. I don't blame her, since diving into personal territory with a strange guy you met at a wedding is never a good idea. Case in point: I went to a wedding five years ago and got drinking with a friend of a teammate; I remember somehow waking up in Montreal the next day, and having shared way too many secrets that ended up in his memoir.

"I was."

"That's surprisingly sweet."

"You mean surprising? Or sweet."

"Both. You don't seem like the mama's-boy type. Not that a mama's boy is ever a bad thing." She jerks her head to her friend Dawson who is talking to Pepper, leaving his date with a foul expression on her face. "I've never met any guy closer to his mother than Dawson."

"You haven't met my mom. It's only me and her and Pepper, so we're all pretty tight."

"That's nice." Her tone is wistful and just a little sad. "I lost my dad too, but it never did much for my relationship with my mother."

I don't tell her that my father might be very much alive, but I have no idea since I haven't spoken to him since my sixteenth birthday. And even that was a too-short conversation before Pepper grabbed the phone and things got messy with Emmett, who was there at the time.

Kids should make their parents' lives complicated, not the other way around.

A stab of clarity has me sitting up straight. When I was on the show the first time, I was escorted out before the last of the big dates, when all the scary stuff comes out. That's when they expect you to pull out the big guns that will make Chrissa—and the viewers—fall in love with you.

If I'm the Suitor, the women are going to expect to know all the dirty details about my life. And not only them, but the millions of viewers. And my dirtiest secret is about my father. How can I keep the fact my father left us for another woman, who happened to be my best friend's mother, a secret from the world?

I can't. It's impossible.

A waiter startles me out of my reverie by setting a plate of lasagna before me. "Thanks, but I thought I was getting chicken."

"This is a Scalzo wedding," Shae informs me. "Super Italian, in case you haven't noticed. They have pasta with every meal, except maybe breakfast. Although I've had cold spaghetti in the morning with Neely more than a few times." She forks up a mouthful of pasta. "It's not as good as Mama S's. Or Neely's. She's a really good cook too."

I'd much rather talk about Neely than try and figure out how to get through six weeks of being vulnerable. "Neely cooks, does she?" I muse, thinking of that slim figure swathed in an apron and little else.

"Neely does everything, and everything well," Shae says, the loyalty in her voice broken only by another mouthful of lasagna.

"She wasn't very nice to me at the church." I cut into my pasta, reflecting on those few moments. I'm not used to people disliking me, probably because it rarely happens.

"That's because you were late, and she hates it when people aren't punctual."

"You interrupted the wedding by talking. Was she mad at you?"

"I annoy Neely, but she loves me too much to stay mad. Plus, her bark is worse—actually her bite is pretty bad too." Shae laughs. "I'm glad she can't stay mad at me. I'd be scared of her if she wasn't my best friend."

"Do you think she'll be nice to me too?"

For the first time tonight Shae looks at me without a smile. "Do you want her to? Because Neely isn't one of your *Suitor* girls. She's serious about everything, and you need to take her seriously."

"Maybe all she needs is a little fun." I watch her at the head table talking to Emmett. He looks comfortable with her and has smiled more times than I've seen him smile at anyone in a while.

It's nice to see, but I'd much rather have Neely smile at me.

The girl did her best to bite my head off and I can't stop staring at her.

"She does need some fun." Shae's words surprise me. "She worries about me too much. And everything else."

"Why would she worry about you?"

Shae leans closer until her shoulder brushes mine. "I don't know if you've realized, but I'm a bit of a handful."

"I never noticed," I say with a grin.

The tiny gap between her front teeth is more noticeable when she smiles but does nothing to lessen her adorableness. For the first time I want to see Emmett with a girl that I like. Other than Pepper, I've never had a female friend.

Shae would be fun to have in my life. Plus, she'd be hilarious if I could get her to drop by the *Suitor* house.

My smile fades as I look across the room at Neely. How can I think of meeting the *Suitor* contestants when there's a woman I want to meet right in front of me?

"Hey, it's time for another song so they'll kiss again," Shae announces to the table, and I do my best to join in the fun.

Chapter Four

♥

Neely

As the dinner goes on, Emmett and I talk about our brothers and sisters. Fun stories about growing up, favourite things about them. I like learning more about Ellie, and the more Emmett tells me, the more I think we could be friends.

One more thing about the constant travelling with Shae and Dawson is that it cuts down on my friendships. I have lots of acquaintances, but other than Shae and Dawson, there aren't many I call friends.

It's easy to talk to Emmett. I even tell him about the dance routine Adam and I are going to surprise James and Ellie with, and how my dance background prompted it.

"You were a ballerina?" Emmett asks.

The question is like a hand clutching my throat. "I danced," I correct, trying to smile. It still hurts to admit it, to even talk about it. "I wanted to be a ballerina, but wanting and being are two different things."

"Oh, I know." A flash of understanding passes between us, one that warms my insides and soothes the tightness in my throat. "All too well. And so does Grayson, actually."

"Oh, really?" I glance over to the table to see Grayson gesturing wildly with his arms and sending the entire table into laughter. From what I've seen tonight, I doubt Grayson would understand disappointment and giving up dreams, of having the thing you want most in the world taken away from you in an instant.

One moment of distraction led the driver of the other car to run the red light, barreling straight into Dawson's car. Physically we were fine, just shaken up, but at my next dance class my arabesque had been shaky.

I chalked it up to being stiff from the accident.

The first time I did an assemblé, the gentle leap, my landing had been uneven. My brisé had been worse and I'd ended up a few feet off my finishing mark. Mme. Rue had accused me of being lazy, of not trying, but that wasn't the case. Doctors couldn't find anything wrong but I knew there was something.

Months later, I finally got my answer—the accident had left me with something wrong in my brain, or my muscles or my inner ear—somewhere, something broke. Something so slight that doctors couldn't detect it, but it threw off my balance enough that I lost the edge I had in dancing.

I could no longer spin. My leaps and jumps, always perfect, were off enough for my teachers to notice. And when I couldn't correct it, they gave my routines to someone else, relegating me to the corps de ballet, rather than the soloist roles I had worked so hard for.

I couldn't handle the disappointment of not succeeding, so I stopped dancing.

I drain my wineglass again. These aren't the thoughts that will make me switch to water tonight. "Well, back to our dance," I say stiffly.

And then it hits me like a lightbulb turning on: the perfect way to get Shae to notice Emmett.

The plan has always been for Adam and me to dance at James's wedding. It's long been a family joke that James's favourite movie is *Dirty Dancing*, and once he met Ellie and we found out it was Ellie's favourite as well, it was the sign for us to pull out the old routine.

About eight years ago, after watching *Dirty Dancing* with my brothers during Christmas holidays, Adam and I had retired to the basement, and perfected the iconic Patrick Swayze/Jennifer Grey dance routine. It had been the first time I'd danced in a while and I remember the heady feeling as muscle memory brought most of my ability back, even though I had been far less flexible than in my heyday.

Adam has always been a very good dancer, starting with ballet as a child but turning to ballroom in his late teens. We would push the ancient foosball table against the wall in the basement and he would meticulously go through his routines with me, sweeping across the floor in a foxtrot or counting off the steps in a tango. We performed a few times together at a school talent show as well as a church fundraiser, but most of our dancing was done in front of family or Shae and Dawson.

Adam had begun practicing the moves again as soon as James announced his engagement, and Shae would pull me onto the beach in Thailand at sunrise to go over the moves. She soon recruited Dawson to help instead.

I have no worries about the routine. Adam and I have performed it so many times over the years that I can do it in my sleep. Every time I hear "Time of Your Life," my body takes over and I find myself doing the steps, my hand clasped in my phantom partners.

I didn't need the practice in Thailand, but I took advantage of Dawson being willing to help.

It didn't matter that Dawson has never been much of a dancer; those hours spent dancing before the sun warmed the sand were some of my favourite times on the trip. Even Shae cheering us on didn't take away from the sensation of me being his arms, my hand in his, hip brushing against mine. Like the movie, we waded into the water to practice the lift and every time, Dawson would lift me over his head, water dripping off my clothes.

I got to share my joy of dancing with Dawson, and I'll never forget that.

However, yesterday when I finally had time to practice with Adam, it was quickly obvious that while my brother still has the moves, he's lost some of his upper body strength when it comes to lifting me.

That's where Emmett comes in.

"You just have to catch me," I tell him after I explain what I want him to do.

"It'll be easy."

Once I tell Adam, he jumps on board faster than Shae boards a plane, and the two of us drag Emmett to the hallway outside the kitchen to demonstrate. "Just stand there."

"I can't dance," Emmett says, standing at the end of the hall with fists clenched and shoulders hunched, like I'm about to attack.

"You don't need to dance," I promise.

"All you have to do is stand there and look strong and manly."
Adam winks. "Shouldn't be much trouble for you."

"I don't know about this..."

"Please, Emmett. I really don't want Adam to drop me again."

Adam throws up his hands. "It was one time!"

"He really dropped you?"

"Twice." I've never wished I had Shae's skill in convincing people more. She throws out an idea and the lineup begins. Granted,
I've asked Emmett to do a little more than skinny dipping at sunset,
but still. "It hurt," I say solemnly.

Adam snorts. "There was a mat under you."

"There's no mat here," Emmett says with a frown, looking between Adam and me. "Are you sure all I have to do is stand there?
No moving? You'll come to me?"

"Straight to you. Like I'm a fastball, and you just have to catch
it. Me."

My brother rolls his eyes. "Neely, you seriously need help."

"I thought it was a good analogy," I hiss as Adam puts Emmett
into position and I head down the hall to prepare myself.

I can still dance. It's like a mantra in my head as I shake out my
arms, give my shoulders a roll as I wait for the signal.

It's not Emmett stepping in at the last moment that has the
butterflies taking flight in my stomach. I have no doubt that he's
strong enough to hold me, lifting me high above his head in the
iconic Patrick Swayze move.

It's that dancing is no longer the second nature it used to be for
me.

There have been times I let myself go in a club dance floor, but
those times have become fewer over the years because it still hurts

too much. Even now, there's an ache deep inside to perform, to show I'm the best.

"You ready, Neely?" Adam calls.

It's been years since I've performed in public, but even longer since I've trusted someone enough to be there in the spotlight with me. I realize that as I stare at Emmett waiting uneasily for me at the end of the hall.

"And...go!"

A deep breath and I take off, seeing the smudges and scuffs on the white walls as I race by. A step, a leap, a *jump*, and Emmett's hands are on my waist lifting me.

Only a few feet up before Emmett takes a step back and drops me awkwardly. "Sorry," he gasps. "Are you okay? I didn't have a good hold."

"That was a good start," I assure him. "Again."

I lose count of how many times I run towards Emmett, but only stop when he's caught and lifted me perfectly three times. And each time the stabbing fear lessens a little bit, until the last time when I soar, smiling above his head, hearing the cheers of Adam like he's an audience of many.

♥

Grayson

I T'S THE EXPRESSION ON Neely's face that gets me, hits me right in the stomach like a well-planned punch.

During the dance with her brother, her face is set; stoic, like she's counting the steps in her head. But then Neely backs up and there's a gasp of anticipation from the more than half of the guests who have obviously watched *Dirty Dancing* and know what to expect. The expression on her face is part happiness and part fear, and I really want to know what she's thinking.

I've never been one for dancing, either myself or watching it, but it's something I could get used to if all the dancers look like Neely.

She's so slim and graceful, her body moving effortlessly. Every guest in the room has a matching expression of happiness and awe, including Ellie who has tears in her eyes even as her smile stretches wider.

And then Emmett—*Emmett*—is there. Emmett, who's never danced even when the entire Raptors Dance Squad dragged him onto the floor one night, stands there with his suspenders holding up his tuxedo pants, and *catches* Neely as she leaps through the air— her dress draped around him and hiding his face—holding her aloft for long moments. Seeing her practically float above him, his hands gripping her waist produces a strange sensation in me.

I want to be the one holding her.

Not only that, I want to be as happy as Neely is when Emmett makes the catch, like everything has gone right in her life. One perfect moment.

I've had a few of those in my baseball career: the first time I struck out a batter; the first time I struck out the side with the bases loaded; stepping onto the mound at Busch Stadium in St. Louis when I made my debut in the majors.

All pretty perfect moments, but as I watch Neely, I realize it's been a while since I've felt anything as good as it looks like she feels.

Ellie and James are on their feet as the song fades away, rushing to Neely's side as Emmett gently lowers her to the floor. Adam pounds his back and the expression on Emmett's face is one I haven't seen in a long time.

The last time had been when he hit a three-run homer to break a game wide open. Pride. Satisfaction. And like Neely, happiness.

It's about time my friend got a little happiness in his life again.

"That was amazing." Pepper's eyes are as damp and soft as they were in the church. "Ellie's always loved that movie. We used to watch it all the time."

"I know." I roll my eyes. "You used to make Emmett and me watch it over and over and over." But I throw my arm around her, giving her shoulder a squeeze.

The DJ says something but I watch Peter embrace Emmett, at how Neely's mother hugs her tightly. Suddenly there's a cluster of pink dresses and dark suits on the floor as the rest of the wedding party join in, wineglasses and bottles held aloft, big smiles and cheers as they tell Neely how amazing she is.

She is pretty amazing.

And then suddenly Shae is in the midst of the group, throwing her arms around Neely and Adam, and Emmett too. I had no idea she even got up from the table.

Just as suddenly, the scene on the dance floor shifts, so it's no longer Neely in the middle, but Shae.

Shae laughing with Adam, as the wedding party crowds around her, leaving Neely on the outskirts talking to a man I assume is her father.

The happiness still shines on her face, but it's dimmed a bit.

"Okay," James shouts. "Back to your seats. There's still more wedding to come."

I can't keep my eyes off Neely.

After everyone is back in their seats, the speeches begin, and then the lights dim as Ellie and James take the floor. Their dance routine doesn't come close to Neely's but it keeps me spellbound. The Ed Sheeran song is one I've never heard before but like all of his songs, the lyrics work for the occasion.

Even though I'm at his wedding, I've yet to meet James, and Ellie and I have a tenuous relationship at best, but I still feel wrapped in their love, like I'm part of their moment, one they'll remember forever. Does everyone here feel like that? Is that what a wedding should be like?

The last wedding I was at was three years ago in a hospital room. A growing steadily weaker Alex promised to love and cherish Emmett, through sickness and in health and my heart broke for my friend because there would be no time to create memories and share their love with others.

That had been a very bad day.

For me, watching Emmett pledge himself to a dying woman had been harder than Alex's death. At that time in my life, the possibility of marriage hadn't been real. The ruination of my parent's marriage had destroyed the part of me who believed in true love and trust and happily ever after. I didn't agree with Emmett's decision to marry a woman who was about to die, mainly because I didn't agree with getting married in general.

A lot has changed since then. Six months after Alex passed, I took the dare from a friend and tried out to be one of the contestants on *The Suitorette*. Did I want to find love? Sure. A forever love? Well...

I never believed in forever love, the kind where you love and cherish, sickness and in health, forgetting about selfish dreams and willing to sacrifice yourself.

My father didn't know anything about sacrificing himself. His actions taught me about being selfish, but that's it.

Now, as I watch Ellie dance in her husband's arms, I get it. What love should be. What it should look like—like Ellie and James together, smiling at each other.

The rest of the wedding party joins Ellie and James on the dance floor as I'm caught up in my revelation about love. But I do notice when Rufus arrives and whisks Shae away to dance, admiring his moves. I never had much confidence when I was his age.

Rufus won't have any problem finding love, or opening up to someone.

There's no way I'm learning from an eleven-year-old.

Neely is on the dance floor with Emmett, and then changes partners to dance with Rufus, leading him gracefully across the floor.

He could learn a lot by dancing with Neely.

I need to get out there.

The choice of partners at the table are limited—Dawson's girlfriend and Pepper. I don't give my sister a second glance as I lean across Shae's empty chair and offer Natasha my hand. "Could I have this dance or will Dawson be upset that I've borrowed you?"

Dawson, in the middle of a conversation with Pepper and another guest, gives a quick shrug of acceptance as Natasha pokes him.

"Dawson is never upset about anything I do," Natasha says bitterly as I lead her between the tables to the dance floor where couples sway to the deep voice of Lewis Capaldi.

"I'm sure that's not true," I say automatically, my gaze searching the floor for Neely. But then my attention is grabbed by Natasha pressing her body flush against mine, forgoing my offered hand to wind her arms around my neck.

All right, then. There's not an inch of space between us. Natasha's attractive and seems friendly and would be just my type if she weren't here with someone else. I go for fun, outgoing women, the louder the better; but it's not great when I end things in public. I've been attacked by sharp words, sharp nails, and a plate flying at my head. Everyone always tells me I'm a great boyfriend but the breakups need some work.

And I've never been one to steal another man's girl.

Natasha snakes her arms even tighter around my shoulders, stroking warm fingers against the back of my neck.

Okay. Maybe she's a little *too* friendly.

I needed someone to get me onto the dance floor so I can maneuver over to Neely and grab her for the next dance. I never imagined having to fight off the girlfriend of a guy I just met.

Should I tell Dawson his girlfriend is grinding herself against my leg?

I pull back as best I can, but Natasha has a grip like an anaconda. "So how long have you and Dawson been together?" I ask politely, hoping the mention of him might hose her off.

Instead it's like waving a red flag before a charging bull. "We're not really together," Natasha spits out, her breath warm against my ear. "It's impossible to really be with a guy who is so consumed with his friends."

"I like my friends," I say apologetically. "They're good friends."

"Do you do everything together? Dawson and Shae and *Neely*—" There's no hiding the vicious enunciation of her name. "It's impossible to be in the room with the three of them and not want to throw something. Preferably at one of them."

"Ah." I hope she doesn't know that I used to be a pitcher or she might try and recruit me.

"I'm convinced he's in love with one of them," Natasha continues, the vitriol in her voice making her less attractive by the moment. "Maybe both. He denies it but you can't spend that much time with a person and not hook up. You know all about that, don't you?"

I blink with surprise. "Actually, I don't."

"Come on. You were on *The Suitor*. You hooked up with everyone."

"Actually, I was only involved with Chrissa—"

"The Suitors go through the girls like they mean nothing. I'm so glad I never got on."

"You applied to be on *The Suitor*?

Natasha makes a face. "The second season. They said something about me not being a good fit, but they didn't understand how much I could have brought to that show." Her hand, which had been tangled in the ends of my hair, fists, giving it a yank. "I would have been the star."

I wince at the hair pull. "I'm sure you would have."

"I would have!" she insists. "Instead, I have to watch those idiots make fools of themselves. The girls are worse than the guys. At least the guys are just conceited jerks who only think of themselves."

Loyalty makes me defend my fellow Suitors. "Not all of them are jerks," I say. "When I go back on the show—if," I quickly correct. "I won't be like that."

"All guys are like that. Just look at him dancing with her!" Her voice rises high enough to worry about breaking glass, and somehow shifting her body so that she's looking to dancers to the right, still without relinquishing her grip on me. "She's practically humping him on the dance floor!"

"Who are we looking at?" Natasha gestures with her pointed chin and I see a smiling Dawson dancing with no other than Pepper. "That's my sister," I say coolly, firmly taking a step back in an effort to reclaim some space between our bodies. "And that's not humping."

"What do you call it then?" Despite the temper, Natasha still clings to me like I'm the last life preserver.

"Uh—maybe dancing?"

"Right," she scoffs. "It's disgusting."

What does she call what she's doing to me then?

For the rest of the song, which would have been a mere two minutes, although it seems more like twenty, Natasha mutters under her breath and glares across the dance floor, still while pressing herself against me. As the last of the lyrics trail off into an instrumental bit, I step away from Natasha with a tight smile. "Thanks for the dance."

Ever the gentleman, I politely escort her off the dance floor, cringing as she stomps in too-high heels like a toddler caught playing dress-up in his mother's closet.

Once we're back to the table, I'm ready to escape to the bar and wait for a turn with Neely. Maybe it's a gut feeling, or the need to give a word of warning, but I stay put as Dawson and Pepper, as well as Shae and Emmett, return with smiles on their faces.

Without a word of warning, Natasha throws a glass of wine straight at Dawson, who manages to step to the side in time, leaving Shae in the line of fire. "What the f—!" she cries as a wave of wine hits her mid-chest.

"What the hell, Nat?" Dawson exclaims. Instead of responding, Natasha turns and throws the wineglass at him. Dawson catches it before it smashes on the floor.

"Natasha!"

"Jesus!" Emmett grabs a napkin from the table and turns to Shae and her wine-soaked dress. "Are you okay?"

"Yeah, but Dawson..." Shae gestures at her friend, anger replacing the surprise.

"If you can't keep your hands off someone for *one night*, then we're through," Natasha shrieks, her voice cutting through the music.

"What did I do?" Dawson turns to Pepper with an incredulous expression, like he missed something important. "I was only dancing with her."

"With every inch of her touching you. My God, it was sexier than anything I used to do when I was on stage. You were practically humping her."

Did anyone else catch that little bit? About sexy dancing on a stage?

A jumble of voices erupts.

"Calm down a second."

"I was not!" Dawson cries.

"I'm a sexy dancer?" Pepper laughs, which doesn't help.

"Are you okay, Shae?" Emmett asks solicitously, ignoring the others. That's when I know he's got a thing for her, because the old Emmett couldn't walk past a bar fight without getting involved somehow. And a woman in the middle of it is just up his alley.

And then I forget about Emmett as Neely sweeps in from the dance floor. I was right—she looks even better when she's mad.

"Leave," Neely demands, jabbing her finger at Natasha. "You will not make a scene at this wedding. Out. Get out."

I stare in awe. The woman is magnificent in her anger. And Shae is right to be scared of her.

"You never liked me anyway," Natasha cries, her face contorted with rage. How could I have *ever* thought she was attractive?

"You're right," Neely snaps. "I don't. You treat Dawson like garbage, and it was a pain being nice to you on the trip. Get out of my sight. And far away from this wedding."

Natasha rounds on Dawson, eyes narrowed into slits. "Are you going to let her speak to me like that?"

Dawson holds up the glass that he somehow caught. "You threw a glass at me."

"And me." Shae steps beside him, slicking her hand down the front of her dress to send droplets spraying. ""This is a family wedding and Dawson was doing nothing wrong—not humping or groping or even touching the way he wasn't supposed to. I don't know what kind of dancing you're used to, but this wasn't it. Neely's right; this isn't the place. Get out."

"I should have known you'd pick his side," Natasha sneers.

The three of them stand like the Avengers facing off against Thanos. "Of course we're picking his side," Neely drawls in an icy voice. "It's Dawson."

Natasha throws her head back, long dark hair going everywhere. "See what your little followers think about this," she mutters under her breath.

"This is an awesome wedding." Behind Neely, Rufus's eyes are wide with delight. "Should I take a selfie for you, Shae?"

"Not this time," she says as Natasha storms away.

And then the Avengers break apart as Neely turns on Dawson. "She made a mess of everything—again!" she rages. Dawson steps back with surprise. "Just like in Kuala Lumpur, just like in Singapore. Why do you bother with women like that?"

"She's my girlfriend. Or was..." Dawson trails off with a confused expression. "Who was I supposed to bring?"

"No one," Neely spits. "For once, just no one. I'll go tell James everything is fine." Even stalking from the table in full furious mode, Neely is still the epitome of grace. I'm willing to follow her anywhere. I don't understand half of what happened here, but I'm on Team Neely all the way.

"Neely," Dawson calls after her, but turns to where Natasha stormed away.

"Go after her," Shae orders. She groans when he takes off after Natasha.

I turn to my sister. "What'd you do, Pepper?"

"Nothing! I did nothing. We were dancing, perfectly innocently." Pepper glances after Dawson and giggles.

"That doesn't sound innocent."

"It was." She throws up her hands. "I can't help it if I laugh at inappropriate moments. Emmett's dad is out there, along with all of Ellie's new family. I would never do anything to embarrass myself."

"Do you think Neely is okay?" Emmett asks into the awkward silence.

I couldn't have asked for a better opening. "I'll go talk to her."

Neely is trapped by a group of guests so it's easy to catch up to her. "Excuse me," I say to the wildly gesturing women, who stare at me with interest. "There's a situation Neely needs to deal with."

"What are you doing?" Neely snaps as, grasping her arm, I lead her away.

"Rescuing you."

"I never need rescuing."

I study her expression—tightly drawn lips, fury flashing in her eyes. Whatever is bothering Neely is more than an inappropriate Natasha. "Maybe I do," I say lightly. I let my fingers slide down her arm towards her hand. "She," I drawl, tangling my fingers with Neely, "is not a nice person."

Neely's face is frozen, but suddenly, to my amazement, it cracks into a smile. And then she laughs and something inside of me breaks wide open.

Chapter Five

♥

Neely

"**S**HE REALLY ISN'T," I agree as Grayson smiles widely, his blue eyes twinkling as I laugh. "I can't believe she threw wine at him."

"She threw the whole glass," Grayson reminds me.

"Poor Shae to get stuck in the crossfire." I glance back towards the table where Emmett sits with Shae.

"I think she can take care of herself. And if she can't, well, Emmett's there."

I glance down at where my fingers are still tangled with Grayson's. Why is he holding my hand? Why is he smiling at me?

And why did he come after me?

I pull my hand away, but Grayson holds firm. "I don't think so," he says, tugging me towards the dance floor. "I need to check out those moves for myself. You're an incredible dancer, you know."

"Thank you," I say stiffly, wondering why I'm following him.

"There's no need to be snippy with me," Grayson says over his shoulder. I pass Table One, and Mama stares at me with surprise. "You'll soon find out that it's impossible to stay mad at me." He stops where the shining parquet floor begins and slides a hand around my waist. "Although I can't seem to figure just *why* you seem to dislike me."

At this moment, I can't either. "You were late." It's a weak retort, since I'm caught off guard by the rush of warmth that floods me as Grayson pulls me close. Not too close—not as close as he held Natasha, but close enough for my entire body to be aware of him, like a sheet of plastic skimming the front of me.

Only he smells much better.

His shoulder muscles bunch under my hand as he shrugs. "It's not your wedding," Grayson says. "You shouldn't be the one who gets mad at me. Besides, we made it in time."

"Barely. It's my brother's wedding, so I have every right to be annoyed with whomever I like."

"It's good to hear that you're annoyed rather than angry. And Ellie is as close as a sister, so if anyone should be annoyed it's her. And she's not." To punctuate his point, Grayson waves at where Ellie is dancing with my brother Davis. "See?"

"Fine." My voice is cool, but nothing else is. Grayson dances like he's in grade six, swaying back and forth with little rhythm. He's not even moving in circles, just swaying with his hand resting gently on the small of my back, his other hand folded over my fingers like an envelope. "I'm over it."

"Over what?"

"Over your lack of punctuality..." I trail off as Grayson smiles again. "Nothing."

"Ah, now we're in agreement. Tell me how scared you were dancing with Emmett? That took a lot of guts to let Emmett catch you like that. Not sure I could have done it."

"It was easy." What isn't easy is getting used to Grayson's casual confidence, like he knows I can't take my eyes off him. It unnerves me. "I wasn't brave enough to let my brother catch me again."

Grayson narrows his eyes. "I have a feeling you don't lack bravery."

"You don't know me." Why would I say that? Why wouldn't I admit that he's right, since being seen as strong is so important to me?

"No, but I'd like to," he says simply. "You intrigue me." The moment lengthens between us, my gaze caught in his blue eyes. Grayson fascinates *me* because I'm not used to men like him. At least not used to them being interested in me.

Suddenly Grayson smiles, pulling away to spin me. The laughter bubbles out of my throat as my dress swishes around my legs. "Plus, I'm hoping you can show me some moves."

"My dancing days are over," I say when I'm once again back in his arms, one hand a little firmer against my back, the other holding mine a little bit tighter.

"From what I saw, I doubt that. Maybe not on stage, but you have *moves*." He wiggles his eyebrows and another burst of laughter bubbles out. "And I have to say I like them better than Natasha's."

"I would hope so," I say archly.

"Was she really a stripper?"

I blink with surprise. "I have no idea."

"It's just that she said the bit about being sexier than anything she did on stage...I assumed that's what she meant," Grayson says quickly.

"I have no idea," I repeat, my voice hollow. If Natasha is the type of woman Dawson is interested in—aggressive, assertive, *sexy*, with a sexual confidence that can land her onstage as a dancer, then it's no wonder he's never looked twice at me.

"What did I say?" Grayson asks with a frown.

"Nothing." I smooth my expression back to my usual cool disdain. I know that's what I look like. My resting bitch face, as Shae calls it.

I can hide my feelings better that way.

"I don't believe that, but I don't know you well enough to pry." Grayson studies me like he's observing an onion skin under a microscope, and it's unnerving. "Maybe I should apologize for whatever Pepper did to start that little brawl."

"Why do you assume it's something she did? Dawson has a habit of enjoying the company of pretty women." Do I hide the bitterness? Can he tell the Band-Aid I keep over the crack Dawson made in my heart has just been ripped off?

"Can't say I blame him." Grayson's smile widens. "I'm enjoying myself a great deal right now."

How can he keep getting better looking when he spouts lines like that? "I'm so happy for you," I say coolly.

Grayson studies me with eyes that are entirely too blue for my liking. "You're a tough one, aren't you?"

I murmur my acquiescence but he's not finished. "Or at least you pretend to be. What did Natasha do to you, or are you in the habit of defending all your friends from flying wineglasses?"

"It's rude to act like that at a wedding."

"Actually, it's fun for the other guests, especially if it's not family that's acting like that. Or is Dawson related?"

I practically choke at the thought. "No. Definitely not."

"Just a friend?"

"That's all." Grayson studies me for a long moment until unease pricks me like a needle. Can he tell that I'm lying? That my love for him flows as long and strong as the chocolate fountain on the dessert table?

How pathetic is that? I'm in the arms of a extremely good-looking man, who followed me to see if I was upset, and I can't stop thinking about Dawson.

But the thoughts about him seem to be a little fewer and farther in-between now that I've met Grayson.

He spins me again and my dress flows behind me. "Beautiful dress," he says. "You really are amazingly gorgeous, you know."

"Thank you," I murmur.

Grayson pauses so that we both face the floor. "So which one is your plus one? I haven't seen you with anyone."

I shake my head. "I brought Shae," I admit. "Or technically, Shae had her own invitation, so she brought Dawson...I guess that means..."

"Natasha! You just kicked out your date!"

Despite myself, I find myself joining his laughter. "If I realized she was my date, I would have done it sooner."

"Not a fan?"

"We spent nearly three months travelling with her. I had enough of Natasha after the first week but Dawson was fond of her."

"Some guys have no taste," he says easily. "Not me, though. I have great taste in women."

"Is that why you went on *The Suitor*?"

Grayson cocks his head. "From that tone, I'd think you weren't a fan. How can you not be? *The Suitor* is the most popular reality show in Canada!"

"There are no other reality shows in Canada."

"That's not true. You're forgetting *Canada's Best Chef*, and some baking shows, and hey, how about *Amazing Race Canada*, which I seem to recall seeing you on, so you must be a fan." He smiles smugly.

"So you're stalking me now?"

"Not at all. Rufus is Shae's biggest fan. I heard all about the three of you over breakfast this morning. I'm sure there'll be more to come."

I smile tightly, appeased by his explanation. "He's a good kid."

"The best. I have to admit, I was as nervous as anyone when Ethan got Darcy pregnant, but it turned out great for the kid."

"Have you known them long? The family?"

"My whole life. I'd tell you stories about Emmett and Ellie and Ethan, but I'd rather take this time to get to know you."

I study his face—the bluer than blue eyes that crinkle in the corners when he smiles, the straight teeth that must have needed help, the nose that's slightly crooked. Did he go to an orthodontist? Was his nose broken? Is there anyone he doesn't smile at?

These are things I know about Dawson, but I have an urge to find the answers from Grayson. "You're good, aren't you?" I finally ask.

"The very best." This time he doesn't smile, but holds my gaze long enough for a pitter-pat of goose bumps to run up my arms.

"I'd like to make that determination myself, thank you." I don't think I can pull off a flirtatious voice, but I do it as easily as flipping a switch. I smile smugly as Grayson's eyes widen with surprise.

"That could be arranged," he murmurs.

Grayson

"**G**RAYSON!" THE EXCITED FEMALE voice travels over half the dance floor, right to where I enjoy holding Neely in my arms.

Neely stiffens at the sound of my name. "Friend of yours?" she asks in an icy voice as we watch the middle-aged woman, red-cheeked from embarrassment or too much wine, making her way through the couples.

I wince as the woman careens off Ellie's father. I'd say too much wine. "Not really."

"I knew it was you," the woman says in a voice loud enough to turn heads. "I saw you in the church, but I didn't want to make a scene."

"Like now?" Neely murmurs.

"I loved you on *The Suitor*!"

Inwardly I groan as Neely stiffens even more and takes a visible step back from me. "Thanks."

"I think Chrissa made a horrible mistake sending you home," the woman continues. "You were my favourite, my very favourite. I almost liked you as much as that Nick Viall from *The Bachelor*—he is a *cutie*. Do you know him?"

"I've never met Nick, no."

"What about Virgin Colton? Do you know him?"

This time I can't hide my grimace. I have met former Bachelor Colton Underwood, and he's a good guy. Much more interesting than just his sexuality. "He's great."

"I thought so too. I really like how *The Suitor* copies from *The Bachelor* but is still its own—"

"Would you like a picture?" I ask, to make her stop talking.

"*Omigod*, yes!"

Neely takes her phone and poses the woman beside me. She must do this with Shae because she's very good at it. Pictures are quickly taken, and I pull Neely back into my arms in an attempt to dismiss the woman, who thankfully goes back the way she came, clutching her phone with a silly smile on her face.

"You made her night." Neely stands awkwardly, barely moving to the music.

"I'm very good at making nights." She sniffs in response as she pulls out of my grasp. "So, do I get to finish the dance with you?"

"I'm sure there are other fans who will be happy to dance with you."

I'm not letting her get away yet, at least not while irritation stiffens her spine. "None as beautiful as you," I say quickly. "Or as good of a dancer. Really, that performance with your brother was incredible. And the fact you got Emmett out there...wow."

I really think it's the mention of Emmett's name that settles her back into my arms. I'll have to rethink that later, but for now, whatever works. She slides her hand into mine. "He was really good. I was a bit nervous, but a lot less than if Adam was there to catch me."

"Shae said you've done that before?"

"A few times. He hasn't dropped me in public, but private is another story. And it's been a while, so I thought I was safer with Emmett."

I can't help but chuckle at the thought. "Your brother actually dropped you. Pepper would kill me if I did that to her."

"You have no idea how I made him suffer." She gives her impression of a wicked smile and it's somewhat believable. For a girl this gorgeous, she's got a tough side to her. Shae is right to be a little afraid of her; part of me is too.

But the other part wants to get under that toughness to see what else is there.

"Adam's a smart guy to step aside," I say. "You're always safe with Emmett. He's the best guy."

"He seems like it. How long have you known him?"

"All my life. And Shae? How long have you known her?"

"Same."

It's easy conversation, mundane chitchat but I'm not finished, even though the song ends. There's more I need to know about her but Neely begins to slip away. "Another?" I ask with my most winning smile. "Since we were so rudely interrupted by Nick Viall's girlfriend."

I take that as agreement since Neely keeps moving. "Does that happen often?" she asks.

"Only two or three times—"

"Grayson! From *The Suitor*!" another excited voice cries out behind us.

I grin apologetically. "—a day. I'm really glad the show is so popular. It was fun to do."

"Even though you didn't find love? Or the kind that lasts."

Did I find love with Chrissa? I certainly thought I did, but the more time passes, the more I wonder if it was something else. I was head over heels in *like* while on the show, and who could blame me? Chrissa had everything going for her; small-town values mixed with enough sophistication and poise to make it in the city; smarts, funny and, of course, beauty . Every guy on the show thought they were in love with her.

It makes me wonder how much of the emotion was fabricated by the show. And then I wonder if I should be thinking that since I'm signing up for another go at it. "It was a great experience," I finish, my usual response.

"How did you get on the show anyway?"

Neely studies me and I realize it's been a while since a woman has listened to me so intently. "Funny story. Or, at least for me. One of my baseball buddies talked me into auditioning. There were three of us—I tried to get Emmett on board, but he wasn't ready yet." I glance over my shoulder to where he's sitting with Shae. "So it was the three of us, and Anton was the most excited. But it turns out he'd met Chrissa a couple years ago and forgot all about it. She remembered, and apparently, as soon as she saw his picture, put the kibosh on him, and he never made it on. Roman and I did. I don't think Anton ever forgave us. Worked out best for him, because now he's happily engaged to a great girl."

"What happened to your other friend? I don't remember seeing him—" Her lips snap shut once she realizes what she's admitted.

"Ah! So you did watch it."

"Maybe a few episodes," she hedges. "Enough to notice there was a lot of kissing going on."

I'd have to be blind not to notice the way her gaze skips to my mouth. "That's what gets the people watching. See anything you liked?"

Another sniff. "Roman? Did he get to do as much kissing?"

"Alas, no. My friend never made it out of the first cocktail party. I don't think Chrissa even knew his name."

"And you made sure she knew yours with the Superman comment."

I shrug. "Whatever works."

"And that works for you? Cheesy comments that get women's attention?"

"That's harsh."

"But accurate?"

"What are you saying?"

"That you're as much of a playboy as you come across as."

"Is that what you think?"

"I think I don't know you. And really don't care to."

I study her face, looking deep into those eyes with such a mix of colours—flecks of green and different shades of brown. The combination is stunning. "You have amazing eyes," I blurt out.

Neely rolls her eyes. "I know. Compliments don't change anything."

"Really? Then why haven't you noticed that Lewis Capaldi is over and now we're dancing to the Backstreet Boys?"

With wild eyes, Neely looks around us. Before the confusion can lead to embarrassment and possibly anger, I spin my arm to twirl her, pulling her into a low dip. "Don't run away, because I'll chase you. I'm stalkerish that way."

When I pull her back to her feet, Neely just looks at me. And then she laughs again.

Chapter Six

Neely

I LIED WHEN I said I didn't want to get to know Grayson.

The last time I was attracted to a man was seven months ago, when I fell in lust with our guide as we explored the Costa Rican jungle. Unfortunately, my covert glances were a little too covert and by the end of the first day, Carlo was entwined with Shae, both emotionally and physically.

The last time I was interested in a man was a year ago during a short trip to Cuba where I was wooed for three heady days by Juan, a salsa instructor. That led to exploring Havana on the back of his motorbike and hot kisses in the moonlight, but we flew home two days early because Dawson's girlfriend at the time caught a nasty virus.

I didn't even say goodbye to Juan.

There are more stories like that, times when I didn't speak up and let someone get away, but I've never regretted them because I love Dawson and somehow, despite his relationships that trail after him like peacock's feathers, I still hope that someday we'll end up together.

I've been in love with Dawson since I was fifteen, and tonight, once Natasha leaves, there is no one standing in my way. Seeing her walk out—technically I kicked her out, which was *very* enjoyable—takes a weight off my shoulders that I didn't even realize was there.

I've spent so much time with Dawson and his girlfriend in the last three months. Natasha got irritating in Singapore with her insistence of touching Dawson and it only got worse as the trip went on. If they were together, she held his hand or put her arm around him—or my personal favourite—stroked his face with fingernails that could take out his eye if she made one wrong move.

But now she's gone, her walkout dramatic, but I kept it discreet to not upset Ellie and James. More importantly, Dawson didn't go after her. Sure, he ran after her, but he walked back to the table alone, and that's when I knew I had a chance tonight.

It's about time that I learned my lesson about grabbing the moment.

But instead of stepping up to console Dawson, I keep dancing with Grayson.

He makes me laugh.

He's very easy on the eyes.

He's a tolerable dancer.

But more importantly, Grayson stops me from thinking about Dawson.

It's like I've shaken off a thick wool sweater in the heat of summer. I had no idea how conscious I am of Dawson, until I'm not.

For the rest of the night, I don't obsess over Dawson. In fact, I don't know where he is most of the time, and I'm rewarded by a huge surge of energy that keeps me glued to the dance floor.

Or maybe doing the routine unlocked something in me. Suddenly, I don't just hear the music, I *feel* it, just like I used to. Fast songs, slow songs; songs from this century and classics from the past.

"This is the best wedding playlist," I announce to all who will listen.

I rule the dance floor with Shae. I take turns with the rest of the wedding party, including James, as well as every other family member who asks. I dance with Rufus. For most of it, Grayson is there with me, moving through the years with the Beach Boys, the Backstreet Boys and One Direction.

It's possible the amount of wine I've drunk helps my inhibitions, but I'll worry about that tomorrow. For the first time, I choose not to worry about something and let myself have fun.

With Grayson.

He smiles every time he looks at me, and despite the constant attention from *Suitor* fans and even a few baseball die-hards who followed his career, he keeps coming back to my side. It throws me at first. I'm not the magnet that draws people to me like Shae, but it makes sense for Grayson to couple with me, seeing as how Emmett and Shae are suddenly inseparable.

When I'm with Shae, I've learned to step back when men approach. The two brothers in Prague who ended up in a fistfight over her at the end of the night, rather one of the them deciding on me; the friend of one of her admirers who preferred to find someone else rather than talk to me for the night; countless men and women who push me aside to get close to Shae, or worse, ask me to take their picture.

Shae is the sun; shining brightly to provide light and warmth that keeps the world going. I'm the halo around the sun, caused when the sun's light is refracted as it passes through ice crystals. Rare and beautiful, but ultimately created by the sun.

But Grayson sticks with me despite feeling the heat of the sun, and that makes me warm all over.

Except for my feet. I fell in love as soon as I saw these shoes, but the heels are not meant to dance in all night. By the time the night draws to a close, it feels like chunks of concrete have been attached to my aching calves.

It's no worse than eight hours of practice for a ballet recital, so I keep dancing.

By the flurry of activity passing through the doors leading into the kitchen, I can tell the staff of the Yacht Club is getting ready to begin the cleanup. It's been a good wedding, one of the best I've been to. And even though the tiredness is making things a little fuzzy, I'll be sad to see tonight end.

I'm grouped in the middle of the dance floor when Dawson pushes in beside me so I'm sandwiched between him and Grayson, shouting the words to "We Are the Champions." He looks over at me with a smile and a flood of memories hits me—sitting on the floor with Shae as Dawson listing the merits of Queen as the best band in the world, him passing me his headphones to listen to a song, singing along to "Bohemian Rhapsody" every time it comes on in the car.

Why can't it be easy to love him?

It is easy to love him. What's not easy is that he doesn't love me.

There's so much history and memories and shared time with Dawson that there's no way to extract myself from his life without ruining everything. And both Dawson and Shae mean too much to me to destroy our friendship.

The acoustic sounds of an Ed Sheeran song follow after Queen, and as I'm about to turn to Grayson, Dawson grabs my hand.

"You haven't danced with me yet tonight," he says.

There's no hesitation as I step into his arms, not even a backwards look at Grayson. I've danced countless times with Dawson; his warm hand around my waist is as natural as crawling into bed.

"Nice wedding," Dawson murmurs into my hair. With my heels, Dawson is only a few inches taller than me. His jacket has long ago been thrown over the back of a chair, and his shirtsleeves are rolled up, but his tie knot is still as perfect as it was when he left his house for the church.

"I like Ellie a lot. They're good together."

Dawson stumbles as he moves us away from another couple, and I instinctively begin to lead him into a modified boxstep.

His shoulder would be the perfect height for me to rest my head on. I breathe in the faint scent of his cologne, which he only wears on special occasions. It strikes me as ironic that Shae and I picked it out for him two Christmases ago, spending hours sniffing perfume in The Bay before deciding on Jimmy Choo's Man eau de toilette for him, and now he only wears it when he's with other women.

His hand splays on my back, and I feel the gentle stroking of his thumb through the fabric of my dress.

His hand on my bare stomach, the soft stroking of his thumb lulling me to sleep...

"I'm sorry about Natasha," Dawson offers, pulling me out of the past. "Neely?" he adds.

I take a deep breath, and another, banishing the image and the emotions that come with it. "Mm-hmm."

"I'm sorry," he repeats.

"So you say. I'm waiting for you to tell me I'm right."

"Why do you need me to tell you when you already know it?"

"It's always nice to hear."

"You were right, okay?" He squeezes me around the waist with familiarity and fondness, and my heart sings along to the song. "Happy?"

"Happier," I correct with a smile.

"Like the song," he says, meeting my gaze. His eyes are a mixture of mossy green and muddy brown behind his glasses, as familiar as my own.

We sway to the music; Dawson mumbling an apology when he steps on my toe. I don't complain. It's better not to say anything and enjoy being close to him.

The first time I danced with Dawson was at our senior prom. The three of us had decided no dates, but at the last minute Shae ended up accepting the invite from the student council treasurer, which meant, technically, Dawson was my date.

It had been a night like this—full of fun and friends and dancing. I had let myself imagine that there *might* be the *hint* of a possibility of something happening with Dawson, but at the prom after-party, I spent most of the time with Shae, sick from too much tequila. We'd left early without even a hug from Dawson because I smelled of Shae throw-up.

Just another night that peppered my daydreams of what-might-have-been with Dawson.

"This is a really sad song," Dawson says, breaking the moment. "Have you ever listened to the words? It's about breaking up."

"He let her go because he loved her," I correct. "It was the best thing for her. But he still loves her."

My breath catches in my chest as I realize what I've just said. How I've described our relationship. I let Dawson go because it was best. For him, for me—for everyone.

I have to keep telling myself that because if I don't believe it, then it starts to hurt more than I can bear.

I have to find some way to get over Dawson.

Grayson

"Y OU'RE STARING AGAIN." PEPPER gives me a tap on the side of my head with the flat of her hand, which means it's more like a slap. "Stop before it becomes obvious."

"Do you blame me?" As I dance with my sister, my attention is wholly fixated on Neely swaying with Dawson to Ed Sheeran. Once she worked the room like a dutiful bridesmaid, dancing with the groomsmen, family members, and a drunken uncle whose attempt to jive to "Despacito" leaves the entire room applauding, I've managed to commandeer Neely as my partner.

It's not just because she's a fantastic dancer either.

"Look at her," I say to Pepper, unable to break my gaze. Neely is leading Dawson around the floor, her hand in his, the other curled around his shoulder. Even though her hips under the gauzy pink skirt sway in an intoxicating pattern, it's her expression that keeps me fixated. "She's absolutely gorgeous, but the best is that she looks so happy when she's dancing. Whoever she's dancing with."

"You don't think it's because she's dancing with Dawson?" Pepper asks skeptically.

"They're only friends."

Are they only friends? Pepper has me wondering, but not worried. I know when a woman is interested in me—they smile more, the increase in heartbeat when you hold their wrist, the faint pant of breath. I never understand how a man can't tell when a woman is attracted to him because, to me, it's always crystal clear. "Speaking of Dawson, you seem to be hanging on to his every word tonight," I point out. "Has he said anything about Neely?"

"Grayson," Pepper says sharply. "You're crushing on her."

"So?" I love feeling the first flush of infatuation for a woman. Attraction is instant; interest takes at least a conversation but infatuation can be slow and drawn out during the course of an evening together—or happen in a flash.

It's never happened as quick for me as it has with Neely tonight. From the moment she tried to bite my head off in the church, I was smitten.

"'So', he asks?" Pepper frowns, her eyes narrowed with disappointment. "Do I have to remind you that you've signed up to do *The Suitor* again? You're going to have a pile of girls you need to pick through, and Neely won't be one of them."

It was an easy decision to agree to be the next Suitor, just like it was easy to be convinced to sign up the first time. The thought of twenty-five women presented for me like an elaborate buffet for me to taste and sample to help me find the perfect one for me is great, and I'm looking forward to it.

But tonight, I'm not excited about the thought. The constant attention at the wedding has been exhausting, and I'm tired of the demands for pictures, questions about Chrissa, and contact info programmed into my phone, given with flirty smiles and orders to

Text me. I had no idea there would be quite so many single women here tonight.

"The show doesn't start for another six weeks," I say in a sullen voice.

"Don't pout, brother dear. You signed up for this."

"I'm not pouting."

"You want to fall in love and now you met a girl. But the problem is that Neely isn't your usual type. I don't know her at all, but she seems a little too serious for your usual kiss-and-fly, one-night type of girl."

Pepper's words are sobering. Is that what I want with Neely? I've already programmed her contact info into my phone and have the next few days plotted out—casual, fun texts and GIFs leading to questions and answers on DM. Deeper discussions via text, a few FaceTime calls until I can plan the perfect date for her.

But what comes after that is a blur.

"You need to think of that," Pepper continues. "Don't start something with her you can't finish."

I open my mouth to make a crass remark about always finishing before I remember that this is my sister and I'll no doubt get another slap on the side of the head. "I barely know her," I drawl instead.

"What's the longest you've gone without a date?" Pepper asks suddenly.

"How am I supposed to know?"

"If you don't, who else would? I know that I've once counted that you went three days without mentioning a girl's name, and you tell me a lot about your love life."

"You don't know everything," I protest.

"First kiss—Amy-Lyn Shuler, grade two. First time—Beth Robbins, in the back of Mom's car right after you got your license. First serious girlfriend—Dineen Crabbe, senior year. You told her you loved her and got her a promise ring, only to leave without saying goodbye when you and Emmett got drafted."

"It was a last-minute thing. I came back to say goodbye." The memory of Dineen is one I'm not proud of. Noisy sobs, the front of my shirt soaked with her tears, the expression on her face as I drove away.

"Three weeks later. How many other hearts have you broken? And how many times has it happened to you?"

"Are you forgetting about Chrissa?" I sneak another glance at Neely, looking pensive as she dances with Dawson. I don't like being reminded of my past mistakes, something Pepper is often prone to do, especially within hearing distance of Neely.

I'm not the only one with skeletons in his closet. There are things I'm not proud of, but nothing had a long-term consequence. Dineen got over me; a year later, she was engaged. Now she's happily married with three little girls. Broken hearts heal.

Except for my mother's. She's never gotten over my father leaving.

"Chrissa was once, and I still think you were more embarrassed than broken-hearted," Pepper says, oblivious to my discomfort. Or maybe she's aware of it and wants to rub it in, like good sisters do.

Not for the first time, I wish Pepper had more of a past that I can use against her. At twenty-eight, she's had three serious relationships—her high school boyfriend of three years who proposed but then dumped her two days after they graduated; a messy attachment to an investor in her bakery that I don't like to bring up because I paid for the lawyer to get her out of the contract, and Pepper gets weird when I tell her she doesn't have to pay me back; and last year when she suddenly fell in love with a woman.

Her past is pretty interesting, but nothing that I can tease her about. Maybe if she was in a happy, committed relationship, I could get in my little digs, but my sister has been adrift in the world of dating for years with no sign of anyone throwing her a lifeline.

"Why are we talking about this now?" I ask.

Pepper smirks. "So you'll stop watching Neely. Talking about yourself is a sure way you'll pay attention. Song's over, brother dear, and from the looks of it, this wedding is almost done too."

Chapter Seven

Neely

"Neely?" Dawson murmurs. "Shae's waving us over."

My head jerks up from where it was about to rest on Dawson's shoulder as the room suddenly floods with light. I blink to adjust my eyes as his hand flexes on my back as I pull away.

"It's over," I say stupidly. The music has ended, the lights are on, and I was so caught up with Dawson that I didn't even notice.

"I guess so." The light bounces off his glasses so I can't see his eyes. His smile of amusement seems directed at my obliviousness and I step away from him, the spots where my body touched his suddenly chilled. He points across the room to where Shae stands with Emmett, Grayson and Pepper. "Shae."

"Right. Shae." Without another glance, I stalk across the still-shiny floor, forcing my head back into the wedding, leaving the three minutes of being held by Dawson in my stock of memories.

Shae meets me halfway, swinging her hips so her dress dances around her bare legs. "I lost my shoes. Have you seen them?"

I can't imagine what the bottom of her feet look like after going barefoot all night. "Head table," I tell her.

"This was fun," she says with a grin, looking impossibly awake even though the shadows are beginning to pool under her eyes. "You look—" Her gaze is caught on something behind me, and even without it, I know Dawson is there. "I don't want to go home."

"You need sleep. We all do."

"We need fun. We have new friends so let's play." She skips away without waiting for a reply, and I inwardly groan, thinking the comfort of my bed is still far away.

"What do you think?" Dawson looks down at me. "Keep going?"

"She needs to sleep," I repeat, sounding like a broken record. Reining Shae in is one of the most exhausting things I do, and the least successful.

Because, in part, of Dawson. "She can sleep tomorrow. We all can," he says, giving me the half smile he uses when he disagrees with me. "Do you want tonight to end?"

What am I supposed to say to that?

Before I can say anything, Grayson leads Emmett and Pepper over to us. "Where'd she run off to?" he asks looking after Shae.

"Shoes." I'm befuddled because of the sudden brightness, the end of the evening, *Dawson* standing beside me smelling of Man, and Grayson smiling down at me.

"Is there someplace around here we can go to grab a drink?"

"I—" I honestly don't know why he would ask something like that, after spending the evening at a wedding reception with a free bar. Maybe he likes to drink. "Why?"

"So we can talk some more?"

"Oh." I blink with surprise, resisting the urge to glance over at Dawson. "Okay."

"Shae wants to do something," Dawson says, including himself in Grayson's invitation. "We can head up to Queen Street, find someplace. It's not far."

"Sounds good to me." Grayson grins at both of us, leaving me struggling to find my balance.

There are times that Shae drives me crazy with her ideas. She comes up with them, and I have to make sure they work, and then fix things when they don't.

Like her plan to "steal" the wedding car.

There's no way that the limo has time to drive us to Fred's diner, like Shae wants, and then make it back to pick up Ellie and James. I can't even believe she suggests it.

I can't believe I let her lead me along, like I'm some sort of protector that will make everything all right for her.

"This isn't a good idea." I announce as the car pulls away from the Yacht Club. I'm squeezed in beside Emmett, the disapproval rolling off both of us in waves. Everyone else is enjoying themselves, looking at Shae like she came up with a new ride for Disneyland. "James is going to be so mad at us."

"We're stealing the car." Emmett won't look at Shae, and Shae can't meet his eyes. She's done it again—taken a nice guy who was clearly interested in her and pulled out his heart and stomped on it. And to do it right when I'm heady with happiness at my dance with Dawson makes it worse. All I want to do is relive the touch of his hand on my back and the whisper of breath in my hair and—

Across the car in the far seat of the limo, Dawson is scrunched beside Grayson. I barely notice Pepper on Dawson's other side because I notice the expressions of concern on the faces of both men.

Directed at me.

Dawson knows that I'm annoyed with Shae, and Grayson isn't blindly going along with her plan like I expected. They're concerned about me...

Warmth blooms inside of me, washing over the annoyance with Shae.

"I asked if we could borrow it," Shae admits.

And just like that, it's back to her.

Fred's Diner hasn't changed since it had been our go-to place in high school. Still tired and dumpy looking, with a slick coat of grease that seems to cover everything, the diner was where Shae, Dawson, and I would hang out when everyone else was at parties, or on dates, or doing things that teenagers who weren't dying did.

There are experiences I know I missed out on in school, but I don't regret them. My brothers used to go out with their friends every weekend, spending Sundays in bed, and when they got older, recovering from hangovers. I don't mind that I missed out on that. I had friends, and they were good ones. Just because we never followed the masses doesn't mean we didn't have a great high school experience.

Who am I trying to kid? No one has a great high school experience.

Grayson holds open the door to the diner for me and I smile my thanks without meeting his eyes.

I feel awkward. Uncomfortable, like I'm doing something wrong if I look at Grayson.

Which makes no sense. I spent most of the evening with him—laughing, talking, dancing. He held me with a gentleman-like ease, doing absolutely nothing that should make me uncomfortable.

It's the way he looks at me, and smiling. I'm not used to it, and I don't know how to react. Does this mean he likes me? Is he interested? Dawson...

This has *nothing* to do with Dawson.

"What is this place?" Pepper asks, wrinkling her nose as we move, en masse, towards the tables in the middle of the room. Dee, who had been the night-shift waitress since we'd been coming here, raises an eyebrow in greeting but keeps her face otherwise expressionless.

"We used to come here a lot," Dawson tells her as he and Emmett pull the tables together. "Me and Neely and Shae."

It's been the three of us since we met Dawson in grade nine; there are often additions, like the Natashas that flock to Dawson, or Adam, but with this group, for the first time in a while, there's the potential to make a bigger group.

There's something between Emmett and Shae—that's obvious to anyone with a working eyeball. Chemistry flows between them in a jagged current, stopped only when Shae begins to doubt herself. *Stop*, I plead silently, her conflict apparent on her face. *You can do this. Go for it.*

I'm like a silent cheerleader urging her on. I won't be silent tomorrow, but right now I have to remember that Emmett and Grayson don't know about Shae dying. She hates telling strangers about the disease.

"It changes how they treat me," she said when I first asked her about it. I've seen it firsthand: how Mama indulges Shae more than me and my brothers put together. And how at high school, Shae was looked at, picked apart, and gossiped about more than regular kids, so much so we stopped going to parties and events.

Even I treat her differently, as does Dawson. She always gets her way when it comes to making plans, since who wants to tell the dying girl we can't do something? We make excuses for her, like she's a spoiled child, which thankfully, she's not. Sometimes I feel like I'm her babysitter more than a best friend. I look out for her, take care of her, give her whatever she needs.

I pull myself back into the conversation when Shae returns to the table and asks Dee to serve food to the homeless man by the window. I make a mental note to take the cost from our account—along with the vlog expenses, the three of us have started a charitable foundation with some of the sponsor monies, helping people like the homeless man who we come across, as well as making yearly donations to research for Batten disease.

There's a lot Shae wants to do before she goes. I just hope that she'll have time for all of it.

"I'll chip in as well, if Jacques will let me watch him cook." Dawson flips the hair out of his eyes and gives Dee a hopeful smile. "I forgot everything he taught me before." Years ago, during one of our late-night sessions at Fred's, Dawson decided he wanted to learn to cook and spent weeks looking over Jacques' shoulder until the cook handed him the spatula and told him to, "Have at it."

"Women will love it," had been Dawson's reasoning even though he doesn't have to lift a spatula in a kitchen for women to love him.

"It's pancakes, for God's sake. How hard can they be to make?" I mutter to no one.

Dawson can do what he wants, and I can— I glance across the table at Grayson, pleased not to find him looking at me. His hair has escaped whatever product held it in place for the wedding and flops onto his forehead in an unruly hunk as he looks around the diner with interest.

Is he uncomfortable here? Is he used to places like this? From his suit and the way he carries himself, Grayson gives the impression that he likes the finer things in life. He must be well-off from the years playing baseball, not that it matters.

I'm not sure what matters right now. Or who.

Dee gives a bark of what might be laughter and thumps the rest of the glasses on the table, and I look over with surprise that I missed the punch line in the conversation.

Grayson turns to Shae with a look of amazement. "Who are you? You wow the wedding, help the homeless, and make love connections. Is this a usual night for you?"

She bends her pink head to suck at her straw. "I guess."

Grayson shakes his head. "You're a strange girl. But I'm impressed with the love connection thing. You should come on *The Suitor* and be my Obi-Wan, whispering in my ear about who's there for the right reason."

"Obi-Wan would let you figure that out yourself," I say auto-matically, comfortable discussing everything *Star Wars* because of years of listening, and then arguing, with my brothers and then Dawson about the series. "I think you're better off with a Yoda than an Obi-Wan."

Grayson's jaw drops open. "Are you debating *Star Wars* with me?" he whispers in a hoarse voice.

"Obi-Wan is overrated. Yoda's better."

"Yoda's better..." Grayson echoes with disbelief.

"Shae kind of looks like Yoda," Rufus pipes up. "Especially Baby Yoda."

"I'm going to take that as a compliment," Shae says with a grin. "I thought you were already on *The Suitor*?" she asks Grayson.

"Gray." Pepper groans. "You have to keep quiet about it."

You'll have to come on The Suitor with me...

How did I miss that?

When he talked about the show, I thought it was in the past. I never imagined he would be doing it again, and that he is planning to be *the* Suitor—the bachelor who gets to pick from countless beautiful women, who ends up proposing to one of them at the end of the show.

Grayson is planning on being the next Suitor, so that means...

Nothing. Nothing for me. Literally nothing. He's just a man I met, and now I'll do my best to forget about him.

Grayson

"**A**RE YOU GOING TO be the next Suitor?" Shae's eyes are wide with surprise. She glances at Neely, whose face has shuttered to hide her emotion.

I did not mean to tell her like that.

I didn't want to tell her at all.

When I open my mouth to explain, to apologize, to...*something*, Pepper pushes in. "He's not supposed to say anything."

Some days she acts more like a big sister than one who is four years younger.

Maybe I can pretend this isn't a big deal. Maybe it isn't a big deal. "We're all friends here," I say with an easy wave of my arm.

"Maybe so, but Shae is on social media an awful lot." Pepper's voice is curt and crisp. Now she's acting like my lawyer.

"I wouldn't say anything," Shae assures Pepper with a stricken expression, which makes me feel guilty. Pepper overreacts to the smallest things and—

"Please don't. They'll sue him if he releases the news first. It's in the contract."

"It is?" I turn to my sister with surprise, and a little fear. No one has ever said anything about suing.

"Yes, brother. You should read the thing. I do, and I'm not even your lawyer."

"We won't say anything, but you have to agree to let us post something as soon as it's official." Neely won't look me in the eye, and her tone is as cool as Pepper's.

Despite the chill in the air, I can't help but wonder what would happen if the two of them went up against each other.

"Like an interview?" This might be the perfect way to explain if I can't at least get her to look at me tonight. This is not how I wanted this to go down.

"Sure. Anything, really." Neely brushes nonexistent crumbs off the table and I get the sense that she considers me just as insignificant.

Of course, that only drives my interest up.

"Sounds good. But I'll only talk to you." I glance at Shae with an apologetic smile. "No offence, of course. But this is a good way to make sure that you'll talk to me again." I turn to Neely, willing her to look at me with the force of my smile.

Dawson mutters under his breath.

"What's going on?" Rufus whispers.

It's a game of chicken between me and Neely. Will she look? Can she help herself? Just as my resolve begins to falter, the corners of her mouth begin to curve up.

"Oh, all right," she says begrudgingly.

"Such enthusiasm. I love it!" I beam at her, but when Neely finally meets my gaze, there's something missing from the way she looks at me.

Something that I enjoyed seeing tonight.

"I should have told you," I say softly, to my ultimate surprise. I rarely apologize, I never admit defeat, and I can justify any action. But I liked the way Neely looked at me tonight, and now it's gone. It's up to me to get it back.

Because, possibly, it's my fault.

Neely shrugs. "It's not my concern what you do or don't do." Her tone is cool and dismissive, meeting my eyes straight on like she means what she says. But after she drops her gaze, she looks at me quickly under her lashes, and I know I still have a chance.

I'm not sure what I have a chance at, but whatever it is, I'll take it.

The door to the diner bursts open, turning the heads of all. It takes a moment for me to recognize Neely's brother Adam and his boyfriend, Patrick, who sat across from me at dinner. Both have shed their suit jackets, Patrick wearing a different T-shirt from his wedding outfit, and Adam still with suspenders and a bow tie, along with his white dress shirt.

They hold hands, each with a smile on their face, bringing in a gust of cool night air. "I thought we'd find you here," Adam calls. "After you ran off with the limo—*what* was that stunt? *Shae*?"

"I asked first," Shae protests. She's perched on the counter videoing Rufus flipping pancakes, his little face tense with concentration. "Benjamin got back in time, didn't he?"

"Yes, but the look on Mama S.'s face when it rolled up." Adam laughs and Shae's shoulders slump with what might be relief.

Patrick seems like a good guy, but I'm quick to find out that Adam is a character—outgoing, loud, and effusive with his comments. He fits into the trio of Neely, Shae, and Dawson like he was meant to be there.

Soon, the tables in the diner are pushed back so Neely and Adam can give a repeat performance of their dance routine. It's my suggestion, mainly because I want to see the expression of happiness on her face.

They leave out the lift since Emmett isn't keen to try it again.

Even before the song is over, I have my Apple Music queued up for Lewis Capaldi and cut in on Adam.

Neely doesn't complain as I sweep her away by the front door, watched by a smiling couple near the washrooms and an older man sitting alone by the window.

"So this is where you hang out?" I say, eager to find out more about her.

"We used to."

"Not anymore?"

"We're not in the city much."

"Yes, the travelling for the vlog. Is that something you enjoy?"

"I wouldn't do it if I didn't."

I cock my head. "I don't believe that. I think you'd do anything for those two."

Neely stares over my shoulder where Dawson is at the stove being taught the art of making pancakes for a group. Good on him—I have no interest in learning to cook, or even worse, getting involved in the cleanup. Pepper's a great cook and keeps me fed, and when she doesn't, there's always takeout.

"I would," Neely murmurs.

"They're lucky to have you as a friend."

"Do you think so? Not that I'm lucky to have them?"

I shake my head, amused at the earnestness of her question. I think Shae is right—Neely needs some fun in her life, because she's as serious as they come. "Anyone can tell you are the cog that runs that wheel. I just met them tonight, so I obviously don't know the whole story. Shae is great, but I have a feeling she can be a handful. And Dawson." I turn enough so now I'm facing the counter. "It's almost like there's a Dawson world that he goes to, that no one is allowed in."

Neely's eyes bug out a little before she laughs. "You can tell that just from sitting with him at dinner?"

"From things he said, plus how could he not realize what kind of girl that Natasha is?" I make a face. "She shouldn't talk about the way Dawson was dancing after what she pulled with me. Not that I'd complain if she wasn't with anyone."

"How was she dancing with you?" Neely asks.

"Want a demonstration? But you have to promise not to be offended or smack me or anything."

"Now I'm really intrigued—"

Before Neely finishes speaking, I pull her close to me, close enough that there isn't room for a breath between our bodies. It's like she's molded to me. My hand is high on her back, stroking softly, the other clasped with hers and tucked against my chest.

"Oh," she murmurs. "It's..."

"Pretty close," I finish, looking down at her blonde head. Her hand droops between my shoulder blades. "But there was no grinding or any other move that she might have done on stage in her previous life. In fact—are you holding your breath?"

"No." But her quick exhale tells differently, and I fight to hide my smile.

I relax my hold, but only a little bit.

Chapter Eight

Neely

G EORGE BERNARD SHAW ONCE said that dancing is a per-
pendicular expression of a horizontal desire.

Tonight, I agree with that.

The way Dawson held me was like being in a bathtub full of
bubbles. Warm and relaxing, and where I'm meant to be.

The way Grayson holds me makes me wonder what it would be
like to be in the tub with the bubbles—and him.

He makes me breathless and unsure and wonder why I laugh so
much.

I still don't know what to think about Grayson, but the problem
is that I'm thinking about him.

Or at least that wasn't a problem until he let it slip about being
the next Suitor.

Before that, I liked letting myself be distracted by him. For the
first time, Dawson faded into the background. Even after our
dance, there was none of the giddiness that usually shadows him
making an effort.

When Dawson surprised me with opening-night tickets to the last *Star Wars* movie, I spent most of the two-and-a-half-hour movie replaying the moment when I opened the door to him ready to whisk me away and debating what it all meant and had to rewatch the movie two days later.

When he picked up a new hat for me in Thailand, I was beyond thrilled with his consideration, before I found out Natasha had borrowed mine and it had blown off into the ocean.

It's sad how little it takes to make me happy. Maybe that's why it never lasts; after the joy fades, I'm still left in love with my best friend who has no idea.

This leaves me with an ever-present, slow-simmering anger to-wards Dawson, even though, deep down, I know it's not his fault. I want Dawson to *see* me—see the love I have for him, see how good we'd be together. I want him to look at me and know that I'm the one he's meant to be with.

And I want him to see all this without saying a word to him.

I fell in love with Dawson without him doing anything—no grand gesture, no declarations of devotion. One day, he was my best friend Dawson, and the next, he was everything. I want him to do the same thing. I want him to look at, really look at me, and see the Neely that I would be for him.

It's impossible. I know this, but I still hope.

The confusing part of tonight is that the way Grayson looked at me, I thought there was a chance that *he* might see me like that.

After the empty plates smeared with maple syrup are cleared from the table, there's no reason to hang around Fred's. We sit and talk for a bit, until Shae starts to yawn, the shadows under her eyes growing darker.

"We should get home," I finally say. "You're tired."

It's always Shae I think about. I would never complain about how my eyes feel grainy, like I've rubbed them with sand-crusted hands, how my feet are so sore that I expect to collapse into bed when I get home still wearing the shoes because I won't be able to get them off my feet.

My shoes—my wonderful, beautiful shoes with the pink straps that laced around my ankles and the sky-high heels that make me feel like I'm back in toe shoes—are uncomfortable, to say the least. As we sit at the table, I want so much to slip them off, to sit barefoot under the table like Shae and Pepper, but I'm so afraid I won't be able to get them back on. That my feet have swollen so much that they won't fit.

Plus, my feet aren't meant to be barefoot. Years of dancing has made them bruised and battered; broken toes that have never healed properly because I don't let them, callouses that no pedicure will ever dissolve, and a mashed baby toe.

Despite my exhaustion and very sore feet, I will never be the one to call it a night, to call off an adventure, because I don't want to be the one who makes Shae miss out on something.

"Let's go for a walk along the beach," she suggests instead.

It's either a sign of how others are willing to follow her, or how fast Emmett has fallen, because the only ones who take a pass are brother Ethan, who has a sleeping Rufus to consider, and Patrick, who had spent the day hauling bags of compost for his cousin's landscaping business before coming to the wedding. The rest of us gather outside the diner, prepared to continue with the fun.

I don't know what time it is, but the busyness of Queen Street has hushed, a single car following the ever-present streetcar. There is still faint music drifting up the street from one of the bars, but for the most part, the area seems settled for the night.

"Dawson, you need to carry Neely," Shae instructs, knowing without me saying a word that my feet hurt.

"I'm fine," I say quickly. It may be some women's wish to be carried by the man they're in love with, but it's not mine.

"You know what they call a woman who says she's fine, right?" Grayson jokes, giving Adam a nudge with his elbow.

Adam shakes his head. "No, we don't." He steps away from Grayson.

I shoot a laser stare at Grayson. Using the word fine as an acronym has always been one of my pet peeves. "We call her able to walk on her own two feet." To punctuate my words, I step off the curb and wobble on my heels.

"Stop being stubborn." Dawson grabs the crook of my elbow to steady me and trails his finger down my arm. "I'll give you a piggyback, just like in Portugal when you got stung by the jellyfish."

"Don't remind me." Back then, having Dawson so close was overshadowed by the pain of being stung, as well as Shae's insistence of peeing on my foot. After a moment's debate, I hop onto Dawson's back and he tucks his arms around my legs.

Does every woman wonder if she's too heavy to carry, or is it just me? Dawson manages just fine, stepping carefully over the streetcar tracks in the middle of the road

"Is there anywhere you three haven't been?" Pepper grumbles as she follows us across the street.

"Antarctica," Shae pipes up as she brings up the rear with Emmett. "That's where I want to go next."

"No," Dawson and I say in unison.

"Come on," Shae wheedles. "I let you pick. We can see the penguins."

"I'm okay going to the zoo for that," I say.

"I'm fine watching *Little Feet*," Dawson adds.

Pepper laughs. "This seems like it's been discussed before."

"Many, many times."

From my perch on Dawson's back, I see the way Pepper looks at him. My heart gives the usual tug of unhappiness at the usual sight of Dawson with someone else. He's a great guy and it's not surprising that other women always find out. But still...

It's exhausting being in love. I wish I could turn it off, like my bedside lamp before I go to sleep. Or at least change who it is I'm in love with.

"How you doing up there?" Grayson calls from beside Pepper. "Let me know if you need a change of pace."

He does have a nice smile.

♥
Grayson

I watch Dawson carrying Neely piggyback down a quiet residential street leading to the beach, her brother Adam dancing along beside them. They lead the way, with Emmett trailing behind with Shae.

I want to be the one who is carrying Neely. And not because I want to show off that I'm still in fighting shape, much better suited to carry Neely rather than Dawson, but because I could tell her feet hurt from those silly shoes hours ago.

I'm sure she doesn't think they're silly. Girls have a thing for shoes. Pepper has taught me that.

I glance over at my sister walking beside me. "You good with hanging out with them longer tonight?"

"Do I have a choice?" Pepper laughs. "Seriously, though, they seem nice. And Emmett looks happy. I haven't seen him like that for a long time."

"Yeah." As I glance over my shoulder at Emmett, Shae laughs and grabs Emmett's arm in a hug. And then she tangles her hand with his. It's good to see my friend like that. "She seems cool."

"Cool?" Pepper scoffs. "Selena Gomez is cool. Shae is...I think I'm crushing on her."

"Do not mess this up for Emmett with your girl crush," I warn her, only half kidding.

"Oh, so you'll take his side over me?" Pepper smacks my arm. "I'm your sister."

"Why don't you pick up someone your own speed?" I jerk my chin towards Dawson, now visibly stumbling with Neely as we reach the edge of the sand. "I saw you two on the dance floor."

"Cute," she agrees. "But I think he's otherwise occupied."

"We'll see about that. Hey, Dawson," I raise my voice. "Want me to take a turn with the princess?"

Dawson stops at once. "That'd be great." He lets a protesting Neely slide to the ground. I shoot a gleeful grin at Pepper before positioning myself before Neely.

"Jump," I order her.

"I can walk," she protests.

"Why, when you can ride? Jump."

With a huff of displeasure, she climbs aboard and I give her a boost. "Hang on." I start across the beach on a run, leaving Dawson behind to keep Pepper and Adam company.

"Stop!" But there's laughter in her voice, so I keep running, her skirt flowing behind us.

The deeper sand makes my calves burn, and it's been a while since I've run, so I eventually slow, but not before I've put some distance between us and the others. "So are we swimming?" I ask.

"And ruin my dress? No way!"

"Clothing could be optional."

"No, thank you."

"Really? Are you telling me you've never once skinny dipped with Shae and Dawson?" It's Dawson that I want to find out more about. My gut tells me this girl isn't available, but the only thing I see standing in my way is her friendship with Dawson. Or maybe it's more than friendship.

Inquiring minds want to find out.

I slow my steps more to make the trip down to the water last longer. I like the feel of Neely's slim legs in my hand, her arms around my neck. I like being close to her.

Even after such a long day, Neely still smells amazing—like the sugar cookies my mother used to make.

Mom always tells me not to let disagreements get in the way of a relationship, either friendship or love, and I've always taken her advice. It's why no one can stay mad at me—I won't let them. It's not always an apology that's necessary, but putting in a little bit of work.

Making an effort. Showing some interest.

"Have you forgiven me for not telling you about *The Suitor* show right off the bat?" I ask Neely, giving the outside of her knee a quick rub with my thumb.

"There's nothing to forgive," she says stiffly.

"No? Good. So I can go back to being angry with you for leading me on."

"Angry—me? I never led you anywhere?"

"Seriously? All those smiles with the golden eyes. You have eyes like a lion, you know that? I guess a lioness would be more appropriate. They're amazing eyes." Neely doesn't say anything. "You can say thank you now if you think that was a compliment. Because it was."

"Thank you," she says in a soft voice. "I wasn't trying..."

"I hope you were," I interrupt. "You just about broke my heart when you danced with Dawson for the last song. Do you remember back in grade school, the last song at a dance was always the most important? It set the stage for the next week. I got most of my girlfriends from that last song dance."

"You had a lot of girlfriends? That's not a question. I can tell."

"You can tell I'm good at being a boyfriend."

"If that's the case, what are you doing on a reality show to find true love?"

"Ouch." I pause, looking at the path of moonlight on the water. If I waded out, would I ever reach it, or would it be forever out of my grasp? "It's really beautiful here."

"I love it," she says. "We live right by the water so I spend a lot of time down here. I haven't been here this late in a long time."

"Did you bring your boyfriends here? For a little skinny-dipping."

"No." From one simple word, I get resentment and regret. There's a lot more to Neely than what she lets on, and for someone who lives their life on social media, she seems very private.

I guess I can say that about myself too.

"I don't have problems meeting women," I say quietly as I start walking to the edge of the water, Neely still perched on my back. "I never have. They see me and they think I'm out for a good time, a bit of fun. I know that's the impression I give them. I've been told I'm afraid of commitment, afraid to try, and they're right. My father left my mother when I was thirteen." I pause there, wait for a comment, but Neely only smoothes her hand down my arm. "Because of that, I have been afraid to try. I saw how broken my mom was, and I've never wanted that."

"You're not your father," Neely says, hanging over my shoulders, her fingers pressed into my bicep. "And you're not your mother. You're you, and you shouldn't claim their mistakes as your own."

"I know that—now. From the sounds of it, you don't think that much of the show, and I don't blame you. There's a lot wrong with the premise. But I do know that it really helped me. The producer who was assigned me acted like my therapist when I was on. She was basically a psychologist, just a few credits shy of her degree, and she got me talking about everything. It's funny, because while I told Anya everything, I couldn't open up to Chrissa the way she wanted me to, and that's why she sent me home. I still talk to Anya," I add. "We're good friends now. She's the person who got me to admit that I need to try with a relationship. You have to try to make it work, not coast through like I'd been doing."

"Smart lady."

"She's great. I think you'd like her. She's strong like you, not afraid to give her opinions."

"Is that how you see me?"

"You may look like an angel, Neely, but you're one tough cookie. At least, on the outside. I think there's much more inside that you don't let out."

"So is Anya the reason you're going back on the show?" Neely asks, neatly sidestepping my observation.

"In part. Even though I didn't open up enough to Chrissa, I tried harder with her than I ever have before. I don't know if it was because it was all so condensed, like a surreal bubble that was about to pop, or that it took place on TV, but I really wanted it to work. I thought maybe if I had a second chance, I could figure out how to do it right."

"You don't need a reality show for that."

"Maybe not," I say with reluctance. "I don't really have a choice now."

For the first time, I find myself grateful that Chrissa sent me packing. And right now, with Neely perched like a monkey on my back, I regret ever hearing about the show.

Chapter Nine

Neely

G RAYSON CARRIES ME THE final leg across the beach and I can't help comparing the ease in which he makes his way along the sand. Dawson would be struggling, the sand dipping under his feet and making it difficult to hold my weight. Grayson seems like he could walk for kilometres with me on his back.

I want to ask if he works out regularly, but that would be construed as flirting and I don't flirt.

I like how he told me why he's going on the show. It doesn't help with the disappointment, but I understand better.

I know the concept of instant fame is alluring to many. I see it happen—social influencers who have their social media blow up, with thousands, millions of followers and seeing how those strangers can determine their own self-worth.

They don't think they're important until others are watching their every mood. And I have to admit, I thought Grayson was like that too.

"Where to?" he asks as the sand becomes firm and dark from the spray of the waves.

"To the water." I point, resting my arm on his shoulder.

"And then ride *over*?"

"You shouldn't have to carry me all night."

"What if I like it?"

"What would be the point of liking it? All you'll get is a sore back."

There's no point in me letting those wisps of interest for Grayson grow; no point letting them dig themselves deeper. He's more than surface-level. He has layers that, in a different time, I would like to peel back.

In a different time, Grayson might well be the one to force me to go back to thinking of Dawson as simply a friend, before my feelings for him ruin our friendship.

But there's no chance of that. The only thing this commitment-shy man can offer me is a few days and nights of fun, and then a quick goodbye while he moves on with his life, leaving me in the same boat as I've always been in.

Or it could be a different boat.

Grayson sets me down and I groan as my heels sink into the sand, leaving me tottering. "I hate these shoes!"

"Hang on." In a flash, he kneels beside me, untying the straps so I can step out of them into the sand. My toes flex with relief. "Those are some shoes," Grayson says as he stands up, now towering over me by several extra inches.

I glance down at the sandals, the straps dangling, looking innocently incongruous. "I did like them."

"You could do some damage in those heels."

"To my feet, yes."

"They look like ballet slippers," he offers, slipping off his own shoes, perfectly polished loafers that wouldn't fare well in the sand. "With the straps and the heels. Like, what are they called? Toe shoes."

I nod, because that's the reason I fell in love with them. Now, the love is gone because I won't be able to look at them without remembering how much my feet ached wearing them. Sort of like my real toe shoes, bundled into a box in my closet.

"What's the story with you not dancing?"

I stare out over the water, the waves lapping at the shore and leaving little piles of debris. I danced tonight—I performed tonight—but it already seems so long ago. But I smile ruefully when I remember the lift. "Car accident," I say slowly, the memories of the night it happened hazy but still overshadowing my happiness of tonight.

I don't remember where we were coming from, but Shae and I had been belting out a Black Eyed Peas song, with Dawson shaking his head at how bad we were. Shae was in the back, and I kept snapping at her to keep her seat belt on because she kept leaning forward to talk to us.

If I hadn't done that, she might have died in the crash, thrown out the window like a rag doll. That thought kept me awake for days after it happened—what if Shae had died?

"That's a real shame," Grayson says. "You've got some serious talent."

"I did," I agree without a trace of conceit. I know I had talent. In another life I could have danced on the stage, but then I wouldn't have done other things. If there's one thing I've learned from Shae, it's that regrets are never worth the energy you put in. "I had a concussion and it damaged my inner ear, which affected my balance. I could dance, but not like before."

Shae had been fine, but I wasn't.

"It was an accident," I say slowly. "The other driver died, so there's no one to blame. I can't help but think it's my fault—my body's fault—because it couldn't handle a hit to the head."

I've never admitted that to anyone.

Grayson chokes back a snort and I step back with disbelief. "I'm not laughing at you," he assures me. "Really, I'm not. It's just that I've heard Emmett say the same thing about his injury. And I understand it, because my body gave out too." He swings his arm, makes a motion like he's throwing a ball. "It sucks. You work at it for so long, get so strong, and then one little thing that you have no control over goes and ruins it. And now you've got a pretty pair of shoes that you won't be able to wear again without remembering how it felt to dance."

I stare at the shoes in my hand. He's right. There's no way I'll ever be able to put these on without remembering the ache in my feet that matched the one in my heart when I danced again. A swell of kinship sweeps through me. Dawson and Shae have always been sympathetic, but I know they don't really understand the loss of my dancing. And it is a loss for me. It changed me. "What did it for you?"

"An eighty-four-mile-an-hour slider. I can—I could—throw harder and faster than that, but as soon as the ball left my hand, I felt the pop and just knew. Worst day of my life."

"Worse than getting your heart broken on television?"

I don't know why I change the subject, but the pain on Grayson's face makes my heart ache. And I really want to know what a broken heart feels like for him.

"That wasn't fun either. Why are we still talking about me? You're so much more interesting."

"I wasn't a major-league ball player."

"Do you follow baseball?" Grayson asks eagerly.

I glance sideways at him. "No. I know the Jays play in Toronto, and I know Aaron Judge plays for the Yankees."

"You know who Judge is, so that's a good sign."

"Not really, since he asked to meet Shae when we passed through New York last year."

"Too bad." He sighs heavily. "If you liked baseball, you might have been the perfect woman for me, what with the *Star Wars* knowledge."

"That's all you're looking for in a woman? I think you need to broaden your search parameters."

Suddenly I don't want to talk about Grayson going on the show to meet dozens of women, all of which will inevitably fall in love with him.

Another sigh. "You're probably right, especially as I'm not hopeful there will be many *Star Wars* fans like you trying out for the show." He gives himself a shake and it's like he's turned to a new chapter in a book. "So what are you going to do about those shoes?"

"There's not much I can do with them." I hold my shoe up to admire it in the moonlight. Curving instep, scissor-sharp heel and strips of satin-soft leather to lace up my calves.

Beautiful shoes. Expensive shoes. And I'll probably never wear them again.

"They're not exactly practical for hiking in the jungle," I continue. "I'm more of a sturdy shoe or flip-flops type of girl now. I'll put them in a box with my other wedding stuff." A dried flower from my bouquet, a few of the diamante pins from my hair, the handwritten note from my bomboniere. The same things I kept from Davis's wedding.

"I think you should purge them. Set them on fire," Grayson suggests.

"I'm not setting my shoes on fire," I say firmly.

"They did it on one of *The Suitor* dates," he explains. "I wasn't on it, but Chrissa and one of the other guys had this bonfire and they threw stuff in it, like old letters and photos."

"We don't have a fire, although I'm sure Shae will be making one soon. And I'm not sure burning shoes would be good for the environment."

"Throw them in the lake," he suggests. "Signifying the hold dance has on your past. Let go of all the pain and hurt and let yourself just dance when you want to, not because you have to."

I look at Grayson, surprised with how insightful he sounds. Grayson is a lot of things—great-looking, funny, easygoing—but I never would have expected insightful. Or perceptive, which he must be if he can understand dancing still has a hold on my heart. It's the only thing I've ever failed at, and even though it's not my fault, I can't quite make my heart believe it.

"Did you do something like that with baseball?" I ask. "Did it help?"

"No. But I think it's a good idea," he adds. "I can't even watch a game without wishing I was playing. And that includes helping coach Rufus's team. Teaching the kids how to pitch is pretty painful."

I have a feeling calling it painful is an understatement.

Without warning, I step into the lake, the waves pushing the hem of my dress against my legs, and heave one of the shoes into the lake. It doesn't go very far, and I hear the *plop* as it hits the water. I hand the other one to Grayson. "You can use my shoe. Take all of your hurt and pain about giving up baseball and put it in my shoe. And then throw." It goes a lot farther than mine. "Feel better?"

"Kind of."

"Me too."

Without talking about it, both of us turn and begin walking down the beach. The sand is cold between my toes. It's a welcome relief but I can't believe that I didn't think of how I'm supposed to get home without my shoes.

It's very unlike me not to plan every move.

This far from Queen Street, only a few lights are visible, the rest blocked by the maple and oak trees along the street, and any sounds of vehicles have faded into the night.

The last time I'd been on a beach this late was in Australia where we had been invited to a bonfire on Mandalay Beach. And that night I watched Dawson walk down the beach, arm in arm with a girl he'd just met.

There had been so much pressure on my heart, I had to check to make sure my chest wasn't sinking into my body.

I blink to push away the image of Dawson in his baggy cargo shorts, becoming smaller and smaller, his footprints from his bare feet vanishing in the waves, wondering if it's my exhaustion that makes it hurt so much tonight.

Shae likes to give the impression with her posts and vlogs that our trips are all late-night parties, but it's not true. I pack so many activities into our days that we need to be awake too early for many late nights. There isn't much downtime, but I make sure we all get enough rest.

"I want to know what you're thinking about?" With a start, I realize the question, as with his Superman comment, must be one of Grayson's signature lines. It lets him be considerate and understanding.

I remember him using it on the handful of episodes that I watched. I'm absolutely not going to tell him how many—it's bad enough that he made me admit that I tuned in at all.

I can't believe I didn't recognize him from the show at the church, but then again, I never would have imagined my brother would have any reality show stars at his wedding.

"What are you looking for in a woman?" I ask, rather than telling him my train of thoughts.

"Why? Feel like putting yourself into the running?"

"I am not about to go on a reality show that forces imaginary commitments."

Grayson winces like I slapped him. "Tell me what you really think. No, really," he insists. "Do you think it's possible for me to find someone to love?"

"I have no idea." My voice is stiff at the image of Grayson in love with someone.

"I think it's possible," he says.

"That's all that matters. Because if you're to do it, you better believe it's going to work. You'd never go out to the mound without believing you could strike out every batter, right?"

"So I should believe it's possible for me to fall in love with every woman on the show?"

"Maybe not all at once. And you won't like everyone."

"I like most people."

"You need to narrow your search parameters."

"Who am I looking for?" Grayson muses. "I think I want someone who's smart, and sharp. Funny and knows how to laugh at themselves; passionate, not just like in the bedroom, but feels passion for things, so she'd know how it was with me and baseball. Beautiful, of course." He smirks and gives me a sideways glance.

"Sounds like me," I say lightly. "Except for the laughing at myself. Shae always tells me I have a problem with that."

"You guys sound pretty tight."

"She's my best friend." It's a matter of fact, like there can be no other way. It's always been like that with Shae, since the first time I picked her up in the playground. She's my person, and I'm hers, despite everything.

"What about Dawson?" Grayson asks. "How does he fit into your tight little twosome."

"What about him? He's my friend, my best friend."

"Are you in love with him?"

Grayson

NEELY INHALES SHARPLY, BREATHING through her nose like my question gives her a sharp pain, like a bad paper cut. I expect her to deny it, tell me I'm being foolish, or laugh it off. "I don't want to be," she admits in a quiet voice.

I wonder why she doesn't sidestep the question.

She glances over her shoulder to where the others are halfway down to the water and her shoulders seem to slump with relief. "I didn't mean to fall for him. It just happened one day. And I don't want to be. I don't want to be in love with him."

"Then don't be."

"It's not that easy. I have no idea why I'm telling you this."

"It's easier to tell things to strangers. Why can't it be easy? If you don't want to be in love, don't be. I got over Chrissa."

Neely smiles tightly and I see the exhaustion in her eyes. I'm not sure if it's from the long day or Dawson. "It's not that easy. You left the show and never saw her again. Plus, I can imagine you had lots of help getting over her."

"True," I say, without going into detail about the women I met who had been very eager to help me get over Chrissa. If I start naming names or numbers, Neely will take off. She already looks like a deer caught in the crosshairs. "It's got to be pretty hard with the guy being around all the time. Being in love with your best friend has got to suck."

She gives an almost imperceptible sigh. "It's not pleasant."

"But on a good note, apparently being friends first develops into the best kind of relationship. I wouldn't know, of course, since I don't have a lot of female friends."

That perks her up. "Really? You've never been just friends with a woman?"

"Anya, from the show, but I'm definitely not her type. And Pepper, but she's my sister so it thankfully limits any of the will-we-or-won't-we stuff." I shiver. "Every other female friend, we've ended up in the *we're- going- to* stage"

"Ah. That might fall into the too much information stage if I didn't just confess my deepest secret to you."

"Your deepest secret? Part of me thinks maybe you should do more to get a better secret, but I kind of like how I'm the only one who knows it."

"You're not, so get over yourself," she says drily. "And what's wrong with that being my secret? What's your deepest, darkest secret?"

"Oh, I don't know if I should tell you," I tease.

"Why not? After everything I said!"

"I didn't ask you to spill the beans."

"But you asked—"

I laugh before Neely can take a swing at me. "I'm kidding." Now I look over my shoulder to make sure Pepper is far enough away. "Of course I'll tell you."

"What is it? Please say you didn't kill anyone, or hurt a puppy. I don't think I could forgive you for that."

"Just a puppy? What about a cat?"

"Any animal. Any living thing. But I guess if you had a good reason…" She trails off with a worried expression, which makes me laugh.

"Relax. It wasn't that bad, although I don't like that you automatically jumped there. One of my deepest, darkest secrets has to do with Emmett's sister. Your new sister-in-law."

"Ew."

"What's ew? I thought you liked Ellie."

"I do, but if you and her, and then you and me—never mind," she says quickly. "Forget I said anything. What happened with you and Ellie?"

"No, no, I quite like where your mind was going there." I smirk, convinced her cheeks are pink in the dark and wish I could see the colour.

"If you say one more word about it, I'm going to tell Emmett."

"Beat you to it. I told him yesterday. He was not impressed, but I think he took it better than Pepper will, if I ever get around to telling her. They used to be friends."

"And now they're not?"

"Not like they used to be. You know girls—they grow apart."

"Shae and I have never grown apart," she reminds me.

"Well, the two of you are pretty special."

"Or something happened with Ellie and Pepper."

Something did happen. This would be the perfect time to tell Neely about the reason why Ellie and Pepper broke apart—the realization that their playdates and sleepovers were nothing more than excuses for our parents to hide their affair.

No one knows how long it had been going on for, or when it started. All we know is my father left in the middle of the night without a word. The only way we found out he wasn't coming back was because Peter Pike called, because his wife had a left a note.

It should be easy to tell Neely all of this, but I can't. The words are blocked in my throat and Neely finally turns away.

"That's your deepest secret? That you and Ellie…"

"For a whole summer." The words spill out in relief. My clandestine affair is so easy to talk about compared to the destruction of my parents' marriage. "Peter, Emmett's dad, gave me a job on the farm and Ellie used to make these silly excuses to come and see me."

"Oh, so you're saying it was Ellie's fault?"

"Totally! She's my best friend's little sister. There are some lines you can't cross."

"But you did cross it," Neely reminds me.

"Well, yeah…"

"But it's okay because it was her fault."

"Yeah." I pause. "No. That doesn't sound right."

Neely chuckles. "That's some secret. Is that the reason you can't be friends with a woman now? You're going to blame that on Ellie too?"

"No, that's all me. I like women."

"Your Insta account can attest to that."

"Are you stalking me?"

"I don't need to. You're all over the place. And it only took a couple minutes to find out lots when Shae and I were in the bathroom at the reception."

I don't know how I feel—pleased that Neely took the trouble to look me up, or half-ashamed that she thinks I'm no better than a player.

"I have friends," I begin before Neely cuts me off.

"That you want to move beyond friendship with."

"That's not wrong. Like you. I think you're great, and I'd love to be friends with you, but I'd always be wondering what it would be like to kiss you."

The word hangs between us like a thread. Neely looks up at me, her head cocked to the side. "Well, why don't you do it and get it over with?"

"Seriously," I choke. "You want me to kiss you?"

"It's not like I haven't thought of it," she says in a sly voice that makes me puff up with pride. "I think part of my problem with Dawson is that I won't let myself find someone else to take his place. I think you might be that person, but now that you're committed to the show—"

"I haven't signed the contract yet."

"I would never ask you not to."

"What are you asking, Neely?"

She bites her lip. "You found others to help you get over Chrissa. Maybe it would do the same for me."

"And you want me to be the one to distract you?"

Chapter Ten

Neely

"**F**ORGET ABOUT IT," I say, surging ahead of Grayson, my cheeks warm with embarrassment. "It's not a good idea."

"No, spending time with you is definitely a good idea," Grayson argues, tugging my hand to slow me down. "But I'm not sure why *you'd* want to. I mean, I know I'm great, but there's not much chance for a future."

"I don't want to fall in love with you. I'm not talking about that."

"What are you talking about then?" He raises his hand to touch my cheek, his thumb gentle as he brushes sand off my face.

Something knots in my stomach. "I don't know," I admit.

"Want to come on the show?" he asks. "I can make it happen." I shake my head but can't help my smile at the hopeful expression on his face before he groans and pulls me against him. "Why couldn't I have met you a year ago?"

"A year ago, I was in Australia." I rest my head on his chest, more comfortable being held by him than I would have imagined. His arms circle my back, firm but not clutching. He could hold me much tighter, but this is a good start.

A good start for what? There's no hope for either of us. Grayson will be the Suitor and find love with countless women; I'll go on trying to talk myself out of being in love with my best friend and not doing a very good job of it.

"What if I'd met you on a beach in Australia? During the day instead of the middle of the night. With you wearing a kick-ass bathing suit, with little cut-off jean shorts that make your legs look endless."

I pull away so I can stare at him. "What?" he says defensively. "Everyone has a fantasy girl? I just happen to know what she'll be wearing."

"I'm not your fantasy girl."

"Who says? You've got the hair, and those eyes..." His voice trails off as he stares into my eyes, and I admit, I get goose bumps. "They look like gold, but there's more brown than I thought, and these green flecks."

"I know what colour my eyes are."

"But you don't know how I see them. You have no idea how I see you."

"How do you see me?" But before Grayson can answer, something washes in with the waves, right across my foot, and I back away with a tiny scream.

"It's just a ball," Grayson says, laughing as he bends to pick up the rainbow rubber ball. "Hey, Emmett!" He turns and hurls the ball towards where Emmett and Shae are clearly about to have a moment.

Moment spoiled as Shae splashes through the water to grab the ball. For all of us.

After the riotous game of dodgeball, Shae makes a fire. And then my dear brother suggests we head to Pain au Chocolate. I agree, only because I'm already tired of seeing Pepper pressed against Dawson's side at the fire like she's known him for months rather than a few hours.

"Does Adam usually hang out at work after hours?" Pepper asks. She and Dawson crowd into the back seat of the Honda Civic the Uber driver picks us up in, giving the taller Grayson the passenger seat. We leave the even smaller compact car for Shae, Emmett and Adam.

"No," I say shortly, staring out the window so I don't have to see Pepper leaning against Dawson's arm resting on the back of the seat.

"It's a good bakery," Dawson says. "Good coffee."

"It's a patisserie," I correct. "Pain au Chocolate patisserie. And it's great—good coffee, good pastries and Reuben, who works with Adam, makes the most amazing gourmet cupcakes."

"What's the difference between a bakery and a patisserie?" Grayson wants to know.

"I have a bakery," Pepper announces. "I make breads and cakes and some sweets and pastries. A *patisserie* focuses on sweets. You can only call yourself a patisserie when you have a *maître pâtissier* working there."

Dawson blinks at how easily the French term rolls off Pepper's tongue. "Whoa. I didn't know all that. Do you think M.K. is this mater person?"

Dawson has never been good with languages.

"I've no idea, but I'm sure she knows the rules," I say firmly. "Reuben might have the designation."

"Reuben is awesome," Dawson adds. "He looks a little like Hagrid—"

"Or one of the dwarves from *Lord of the Rings*, only taller," I cut in. "But the beard—"

"His beard goes to here." Dawson slaps a hand to mid-chest. "Looks like a biker dude, but a seriously good guy."

"And a great baker."

There's a pause in the car, Pepper's gaze flicking between Dawson and me. Natasha used to complain about the quickness of our conversations, which leaves little room for others to join in. She might have a point.

"That means you're the *mater patiserer*, Pepper." Grayson mangles the French term even worse than Dawson. "She makes the best bread ever. Your cheese bread is to die for, and the rye-sourdough mix with the flecks of caramelized onion is my favourite." He grins over his shoulder at his sister.

"How long have you owned it?" I can't help but be impressed.

"I bought it two years ago. It's been tough, but I'm doing okay. I worked there all through school, so it's like a second home."

"I think we should go to Ashbury to pay a visit and stock up on bread." Although the *we* he uses suggests I'm included, tonight Dawson only has eyes for Pepper.

My eyes suddenly prick with unshed tears and I quickly turn to the window. I got rid of Natasha only to have her instantly replaced by Pepper.

The problem with that is I like Pepper.

When we arrive at Pain au Chocolate, the lights are already ablaze and Adam enters like he owns the place, rather than only the second keyholder. Although his hours have remained the same, Adam lost most of his kitchen responsibility when Reuben started working there. Which is good for everyone, since Reuben is truly a fabulous baker, and Adam's skills lie more as a barista than making pain au chocolate.

As Adam makes much-needed coffee for us, Pepper vanishes into the kitchen with Reuben, and Dawson takes the seat beside me, leaving Grayson to sit across from me. I watch him surreptitiously, memorizing his face to compare it with Dawson.

I know Dawson's features as well as I know my own. The thick shock of black hair, super straight and unruly; the thin nose slicing down his face; the greenish-brown eyes turning darker when he's sad or very happy.

They're fully brown now, with purple shadows of exhaustion. I wonder if I look as tired as he does. I know Shae does, which worries me.

I'm always worried about her. Keeping up Shae's strength has been my mission in life since she confessed the truth about her diagnosis.

I was the first one she told, even though she waited a full three weeks before telling me. Keeping something like that from your best friend can be disastrous when you're fourteen. I had known something was going on with Shae, and her refusal to tell me had hurt deeply. Of course I'd had no idea it was so serious—I'd thought it was something about her father, who had passed away a few months earlier, and who Shae was having difficulty grieving for with her mother's almost comatose behaviour.

"I'm dying," Shae had burst out one afternoon as we were standing on the driveway between our houses. I had been nagging her since we left school, lots of passive-aggressive comments designed to annoy her enough to fill me in.

I hadn't wanted it to be anything like that.

But once I got over the shock of the possibility of losing my best friend, I snapped myself out of it, berated myself for being selfish and thinking of myself, when Shae deserved my attention and energy. Since then, she's been my first priority—dropping everything to travel the world with her, fitting in university courses between trips. Thinking of her before anyone else, including men.

Now, as I watch her with Emmett, I wonder if she'll soon have someone else to take care of her. Where does that leave me?

Beside me, Dawson yawns, his leg brushing against mine under the table. There's the usual shock from his touch, but this time it only makes me tired.

I'm tired of loving him and him not knowing it. So tired that, for a moment, I picture opening my mouth and telling him.

I'm in love with you, Dawson. I don't want to be just friends anymore.

I see it so clearly in my head, and I grow cold, thinking of his reaction. The look of confusion, the horror on his face when he thinks of all the time we've spent together. The pity when he realizes how long I've felt like this.

I clamp my lips together just in case a word slips out. Not going to happen.

The table grows quiet as tiredness seeps in.

It's been a long day. It's been a long week—nonstop events in Thailand and then the long flight home. It's Sunday morning; only three days ago I was on a different continent.

The thought makes me even more exhausted and I pull out my phone to call Uber, finally putting an end to the night.

After we say good night to Reuben, who is most likely glad to see us go, I pull Grayson aside as we wait for the cars.

"About what we talked about on the beach," I begin, unsure of how to start.

"We talked about a lot of things."

"The thing about the *person*." I let my gaze skitter sideways to where Dawson is talking to Pepper, still excited from her tour of the kitchens. "That I want to change."

Grayson chuckles. "Cryptic is not a good look for you. The D-man. Got it."

"I thought it might be a good idea." Grayson knows enough about me already, so there's no point in beating around the bush. "A third party might be an effective way of changing things. Plus, it might be good if you had someone to practice your lines with. You can't go on the show with only that Superman line."

"Neely," he groans. I see the conflict in his expression as clear as if he said *I don't know what to do here.* "I can't offer you anything. Not now..."

"I don't want anything but your attention," I say. "Enough interest to distract me."

"Oh, there's interest. How much of it do you want to be real?"

"When do you start filming?" I ask instead. Grayson's question makes me uneasy, like I'm doing something wrong. Pretending to be interested in an attractive, decent guy to help me get over someone who doesn't know I exist in that way? Is that wrong?

"Six weeks," he says. "But I have to sign the contract in ten days. After that, they say I can't be involved with anyone romantically."

I glance over to the others in time to see Dawson hugging Pepper, and the knife twists into my stomach again. "Let's see what we can do in ten days."

Grayson

I LEAN MY HEAD against the back of the seat of the Uber, watching as the taillights of the car ahead blink out of sight around the corner.

Neely is on her way home, so tired that she's not making sense. I have no idea what I agreed to. It sounds like she wants to pretend to be interested in me? After that, it gets fuzzy. She's not trying to make Dawson jealous, which would be the logical outcome if he shared her feelings. It sounds like she wants to make those feelings for him go away, and I'm the target.

Sounds good, but I don't have to pretend. I'm interested in Neely, which means this isn't going to end well.

Which means I can't say no to her. When she looks at me with those strangely hypnotic golden eyes, I'm ready to give her the world.

Why am I afraid that she's going to take my heart along with it?

Pepper is curled up beside me, and if the drive back to the hotel is much longer, I think she'll fall asleep. I poke her leg. "Wake up. I'm not carrying you up to your room."

She mumbles a curse and sits up. "But you'll carry Neely, won't you?"

"That was different. She had sore feet."

"I have a sore head because I'm so tired. Plus, I'm your sister so that should account for something." She shifts in the seat to look at me. "What's going on with you two, anyway?"

I shrug because if I'm not exactly sure what I signed up for, how can I explain it to Pepper?

She wants a distraction, someone to help her get over Dawson. I'm good with that—perfectly fine with it. I've always said the best way to get over someone is to meet someone else. The only problem I have with this...arrangement...is the time line. I've committed to *The Suitor*, and before tonight, I was excited about it.

Now?

I wasn't lying when I told Neely I wished I'd met her a year ago. I think she's amazing, and if the timing were different, I think we could have something special. But because of the show and her feelings for Dawson, it doesn't seem possible. So this would be a pretend relationship—we'd go on pretend dates. Would I pretend kiss her?

I'd rather the real thing, not pretend.

"Are you interested?" Pepper presses.

"Have you seen her? Who wouldn't be?"

Pepper tosses her hair. "The long legs, blonde, gorgeous blue-eyed look is overrated if you ask me."

"Jealous," I cough into my hand. "And her eyes are golden, not blue."

"Why wouldn't I be jealous of her? Just because she's tall and beautiful, been all over the world, is smart and funny, and did I mention absolutely gorgeous?"

"Are you sure *you* don't want to date her?"

"Ha ha. I don't think I'm her type. Actually, I didn't think *you* were her type either. I think she's into Dawson."

"What do you mean, into Dawson?" The way Neely explained it, I'm one of the only people to know about her and Dawson. But is it obvious to others? Does everyone know?

Oh, Neely would not like that.

"I think she has feelings for her friend Dawson," Pepper says slowly, enunciating each word.

"I don't think so. Even so, it doesn't mean she can't be interested in me as well."

"No, but it might put a damper on things, as will you showing up to wherever they film *The Suitor* to meet all your girlfriends. You can't start anything, Gray. You know that, right?"

"Yes, Pepper."

"Because that's in the contract. You really need to read that."

"I'll get right on that." The hotel comes into view and my tired body sags with relief. I think I'm too old to stay up all night. "What about you and Dawson?"

"What about it? He's a cool guy. We're going to hang out this week."

My heart hurts for Neely to hear that but sings for me. It will be easier to distract her, as she calls it, if Dawson has made no secret of his interest in my sister.

"It's kind of funny how we all met someone tonight," Pepper says before her face creases into a yawn. "You and Neely, me and maybe Dawson...Emmett and Shae..."

In the front seat, Emmett's head jerks at the sound of her name. "What about Shae?"

"You like her," Pepper teases in a singsong voice.

I'm glad to hear Pepper teasing Emmett. For many years, even before Emmett pined for his lost love, Alex, my sister pined for my best friend. So when Neely talks about not wanting to be in love with Dawson, I can understand, because I was witness to Pepper's unrequited love for my best friend. But unlike Neely, Pepper actively planned ways to win over Emmett. Even days before the wedding, she had talked about dancing with Emmett, and what he might look like in his tuxedo.

I'm glad that's over. I owe Dawson one for that.

Chapter Eleven

♥

Neely

S HAE FALLS ASLEEP AS soon as the Uber pulls away from Pain au Chocolate, leaving Grayson with Pepper and Emmett headed in the opposite direction.

Shae and Dawson have the unique ability to fall asleep whenever and wherever they want, which leaves me responsible for the late-night driving shifts, or to stay awake on trains to make sure we don't miss our stop. I've never been able to drop off easily, needing my mind to quiet before I can fall asleep.

Even as tired as I am, I know it will take a while for me to find sleep tonight.

Shae's head lolls on my shoulder as I fight not to glance over at Dawson.

My plan on getting over him starts now. Stop looking; stop thinking. Carve him out of my heart and replace him with Grayson.

That's what I have to do.

And it should be a piece of cake. There hasn't been a man who has caught my attention like Grayson for a while. My stomach tingles happily as I think about his smile, how he made me laugh.

Plus, his hands on my legs while he was carrying me was pretty exciting as well.

It shouldn't be that exciting, Neely. You need a man.

The quiet voice of the driver's podcast thankfully drowns out the voice in my head and is the only sound in the car. Adam takes the passenger seat, for once quiet. This early in the morning means the roads are clear of cars, the sky a dusky orange as the sun readies itself for its appearance. The glowing light of the radio clock reads five seventeen.

I stare out the side window because the sky is quite beautiful, and looking at it means I don't have to think of anything else. No Grayson. No Shae.

No Dawson.

"I can't believe what time it is," Dawson says in a quiet voice. I sigh, because I can never truly stop thinking about him. "We haven't stayed up this later since we—"

"We graduated," I finish, turning to see him watching me. My stomach gives the usual twist when his smile is directed at me.

"Shae wanted to watch the sun rise."

"She insisted." I glance down on the head still propped on my shoulder. Shae gives a snort slash snore, like she knows we're talking about her. "And then you both fell asleep lying on the beach."

I don't like thinking about that night because even after almost ten years, the thought of it still embarrasses me.

The night itself was fine. Fun. It had been one of the few high school parties we went to, and everyone there behaved themselves around Shae. As the night wore on and the tequila bottle emptied, Shae came to the conclusion that we *needed* to be on the beach to watch the sun rise. We were graduates, and therefore had no curfew.

I wish someone would have told Mama that.

But no one thought of parents as we found a good spot and settled in, the cool sand molding under our bodies. Shae and Dawson promptly fell asleep.

Dawson lay between Shae and me, with both of us curled into him. I'm ashamed to admit that I took advantage of his being asleep, running gentle fingers over his chest and stomach, being careful not to wake him.

I kissed his shoulder. *A lot.*

I'm not proud of it. Thankfully Dawson slept through my embarrassing gropefest. As the sun was beginning to break over the horizon, he woke up to my prodding, none the wiser.

"I remember it being a good sleep," Dawson says with a smile. "No guy would ever complain about falling asleep between the two of you."

I smile faintly, confused, because Dawson has never once said anything like that before. Our friendship is based on his refusal to acknowledge that Shae and I are female. He's well aware of the fact, having seen us through PMS and cramps and racing to find tampons in foreign countries, but he never comments on our *woman-ness.*

"I'm surprised she's not awake and watching now." Dawson points out the window at the pink-orange glow. "Do you think we should wake her?"

I shake my head. "Let her sleep. She needs it."

"So do you."

"Are you telling me I look exhausted? Thank you," I say wryly. "It's what every woman wants to hear."

"I think you look beautiful." His voice is quiet as to not wake up Shae. "You always do."

I glance up sharply. It's not the first time Dawson has told me I look beautiful, but it's the way he says it. But before I can ask, or comment, or say anything, the car pulls up in front of the apartment building where Dawson lives with his mother.

"Guess this is my stop." After he unbuckles the seat belt, he leans over and kisses the top of Shae's head. Then he looks at me with a smile, touching my cheek with the back of his hand. "Get some sleep."

"You too. 'Night, Dawson," I whisper.

"'Night, Neely. See you Adam," he adds as he hops out of the car.

"Later, bro." Adam gives a sleepy wave.

I watch him walk up to the building's entrance with his easy, loping stride.

From the front seat, Adam heaves a tired sigh. "The two of you would be so good together."

"I know, right?" Shae mumbles, her head still resting on my shoulder.

I shake my head, still watching as the car pulls away.

A few hours later, freshly showered with my blackened feet scrubbed clean, I open the door to Emmett, his father, brother, and Rufus right at nine a.m.

Unlike his friend Grayson, Emmett is punctual. Points for him.

"Neely." Emmett greets me, doing his best to hide his smile, like we haven't spent the entire night together.

"Emmett." I mimic his nod.

"How do you look so wide-awake?" He looks understandably rough—unshaven with dark circles under his eyes, almost like he spent the night drinking rather than walking along the beach.

"It's my little secret."

My secret was that I haven't been to sleep yet. Mama had already been awake when I came out of the bathroom, my hair wet and wrapped in a towel. "You're late," she said, her voice still tinged with Messina, Sicily, even though she came to Canada when she was six.

"I told you I would be."

"Late means *late*, not out all night."

"Mama..."

She waved away my protests. "Yes, yes, I know, you're a grown woman, have travelled the world. Your brother is a man. But still, I worry. It's a mother's gift. You'll know someday. Now, get dressed and come help me with breakfast." Without another word, she made her way down the stairs, hitting the third step exactly right to make it creak loud enough for the house to hear.

My mother. She lives to prick at my guilt and remind me I should have a bundle of babies by now. "I had four children at your age," is her never-ending lament. "Stop poking into foreign countries and stay here and meet a man."

She also lives to feed others, which is why she invited Emmett's family for a post-wedding breakfast, which despite the lack of sleep, she expects me to help with.

"Will Shae come for breakfast?" Mama asked as soon I reached the kitchen. The rich smell of coffee fills the room, making up for the flour and eggs and mixing bowls waiting for me.

"I'm sure Shae will be sleeping, Mama. You said family."

"Shae is family."

Between the two of us, Mama and I have breakfast ready when our guests start arriving, the sausage and egg casserole steaming on the stove, the lemon ricotta pancakes thick and fluffy, zucchini fritters crisp and crunchy.

"So—Shae." I hand Emmett a cup of coffee as we wait for Ellie and James to arrive.

"So—Grayson."

My cheeks heat up at the mention of him, my skin pale enough that every embarrassment shows. Over the years, I've fought to control it; mind over matter, like everything else, to no avail. "Are you going to call her?" I ask bluntly.

Emmett's face finally cracks into a half smile. "I think I need more sleep for this conversation."

"I haven't been to bed yet. I think you should call her."

"Emmett, you're here." Mama emerges from the kitchen to engulf Emmett in a warm hug like he's been family for decades. "You look tired." She frowns, holding him at arm's length.

"I didn't get much sleep." Emmett gives me a sideways glance and I fight to hide my smile.

"My Neely didn't get home until dawn. I suppose you were with her?" Mama shakes her head. "I told her I don't want to know what you were doing."

"But of course you do." I drop a kiss on Mama's head. "It was all very innocent. Adam took care of us all."

Mama gives an unmotherly snort. "Your brother can barely take care of himself. It would be better if Emmett took care of you." She smiles hopefully at him.

"No, Mama," I say automatically, knowing exactly where this is headed.

"Yes, Neely," Mama argues. "So perfect. Your brother, your sister." She brings her hands together with a satisfied smile. "Isn't my Neely beautiful?"

"Ah..." Emmett looks like he's a mouse caught at the cheese by the cat, and I laugh.

"No, Mama. I've going to show Emmett pictures of *Shae*," I say, ushering him away from Mama and into the living room with the hope Mama gets the message. If not, I'm sure Adam will tell her. "Sorry about that," I apologize to Emmett. "She tries."

"Don't all mothers?" He's standing in front of the wall of photos hung on the living room wall. The room is evidence of how much Mama cherishes her family. There are pictures of us everywhere. The shelves on either side of the television are full of baby pictures of the four of us, as well as the generic school photos with evidence of my brothers' Mama-inflicted haircuts. Framed eight by ten photos hang on the wall instead of art, with Davis' family, i.e. grandchildren, beginning to overshadow the rest of us.

Emmett stands before one of many pictures of Shae, Dawson, and me on the wall. Mama considers both of them family.

"Italian mothers are a breed unto themselves," I say ruefully, avoiding looking at the family picture of twelve-year-old me beside it. "So, about Shae. You're going to call her, aren't you?"

"I got the impression that if she'd want to see me, she'd magically appear."

"She would," I concede. "Shae is...Shae. Jana-Shae, actually. Did she tell you her full name?"

"She did." He glances away from the picture. "Are you surprised?"

"Shae's an open book about a lot of things, but there are a few things she won't mention and refuses to talk about. Just be warned."

"Like what? A little help, please."

I shake my head with a smug smile. "I'll let you figure it out on your own."

"I thought we were on the same side!" Emmett protests. "I introduced you to Grayson."

"I would have met Grayson quite easily on my own."

"Yes, but I brought him to the wedding."

"Do you want a pat on the back for that?"

"Food will be ready in a minute," Mama calls from the kitchen. "And Dawson is here."

I whip around to see Dawson standing sheepishly in the doorway to the living room. "What are you doing here?" My rude tone masks the leap of happiness from the sight of him.

"Mama S. invited me?" His voice rises like it's a question. "And Adam told me to stop by last night. Shae not here?"

"Sleeping. I think it's better that way." I turn to Emmett. "Shae doesn't do well when she doesn't sleep."

"Who does?" he mutters. "I don't know how I'm going to get through breakfast. I almost fell asleep after your mother fed us yesterday before the pictures."

"Italians show love by feeding you," Dawson says. "I gained like ten pounds when I started hanging out with Shae and Neely."

"I think I did that yesterday," Emmett groans.

Mama calls us to the table just as my cell phone rings. There's a thrill of something—whether it's excitement or fear, I'm not sure—when I see Grayson's name.

Before we left the diner last night, he programmed his number into everyone's phone, complete with smiling picture.

"Hello." I turn away from Dawson, because he's looking at me expectantly, probably thinking Shae is calling.

"Why is Emmett there and I'm not?" Grayson demands.

"Good morning to you, too."

"Ah, yes, still really early. Why are you up?"

"I can ask you the same thing. But we're having a family breakfast with Ellie and James before they head to the airport. And Emmett is family, so that's why he's here."

Emmett is already at the dining room table, but Dawson lingers in the living room. I want to wave him away to let me talk to Grayson, but telling Dawson to go away is never an option for me.

"You could invite me. I could be there in five minutes."

"Not unless you want to get a speeding ticket." I think of Mama's reaction to Emmett. "Trust me, you don't want to be here."

"But I'm hungry!"

His childlike whine makes me laugh and Dawson looks at me with surprise. "I'll send Emmett home with leftovers for you."

"You better." There's a pause and I stand there awkwardly, not knowing if that's the end of the conversation.

It's not. "I think we should start things by going out on a date," Grayson announces. "Pretend or real, your choice."

"I thought this was—" I catch myself when I notice Dawson still watching me with a frown. He turns away, but stays in the living room.

"So that's a yes? I'll set everything up, just be where I tell you, when I tell you."

My stomach twists in a knot at the thought, one I don't have an idea how to untangle. "I think I need a bit more advance notice than that."

"Wednesday. Early evening. That enough?"

"Okay." I sound shy and quiet, which isn't me, but I just got asked out on a date. I'm ping-ponging between doing a happy dance and running scared.

"And I promise I'll make it worth your while." I hear the smile in his voice, which makes me smile, relaxing me. This will be fine. This will be fun.

I look at Dawson from the corner of my eye. This is necessary.

"Neely! Come!" Mama calls, her voice adding the *Now*.

"You're being called," Grayson says, overhearing her. "Better go, because I don't want to get your mother mad at me before you've even had a chance to introduce me."

"Okay, see you...Wednesday?"

"Wednesday. And wear comfortable shoes."

I give the phone an incredulous glance before I slide it back into the pocket of my jeans.

"Was that Grayson?" Dawson demands. My breath leaves in a surprised huff. "Moves fast," he mutters.

"Is there something wrong with that?" I ask sharply.

Dawson shakes his head, his shoulders slumping. "There's nothing wrong with anything, Neely. Mama S. called. We better get in there."

I follow him to the table, as confused as I was in the Uber earlier.

Grayson

"**Y**OU ALREADY CALLED HER."

Pepper is waiting outside the hotel room as I take a last look around. It seemed a waste to pay for a room which I didn't get back to until the sun was rising, but I sweet-talked the night clerk into giving us a late check-out, so both Pepper and I were able to catch a few hours sleep before we drove back to Ashbury.

Still, Pepper looks rough, with unwashed wedding hair pulled up into a bun and an old St. Louis Cardinals jersey over leggings.

"Of course I called her," I say with a grin as I check that the door locks behind me. "You don't think I should have?"

"Have you ever heard of playing hard to get?"

"I don't do games." And I don't. Women know exactly what they're in for with me—usually short-term, no real commitment, and I do my best to let them down gently, and before I move on to the next. It's one thing I'm proud of—I never string a woman along and I've never cheated on anyone.

It's come close a few times, and some of my breakup texts aren't the most sensitive, but I can confidently say that I'm a one-woman man.

"I didn't think she was your type. Too nervy. Intense," Pepper says as we walk to the elevator. I take her bag and sling it over my shoulder.

"She is that. But I think there's more to her than she lets on."

"What do you think of her and Dawson?"

"What is there to think about? They're just friends. But more importantly, what do *you* think of Dawson?"

"Cute," she says non-committally.

"When was the last time you were interested in anyone?" I wonder as the elevator doors slide open.

"I had a date last year."

"Last *year*," I scoff.

"I'm busy. Dating has never been a priority."

"Anyone ever tell you that you work too hard?"

"Yes, big brother. You. All the time. I can't imagine how those three just pick up and run off all over the world. It just seems—wrong. Frivolous."

"Look at it like it's their job. The three of them are social influencers and that means influencing people to go to these places. I think it sounds like fun."

"It would be but..." she trails off, and I know she's thinking of her responsibilities to her bakery, as well as her ambitions for the place. I know she wants more for it, and is slowly but surely making a name for herself in the world of sourdough and sweet pies, but she's not ready to take the next step.

I've told her I'd help her financially with whatever she needs, but my sister is as stubborn as our mother.

"Anytime you want to take off to travel around the world, you know I've got your back," I assure her. "I can look after your place."

"And watch it crash and burn—burn to the ground? When is the last time you baked something?"

"You have people for that," I protest. "Besides, if I tried to make something myself, you'd push me aside, tell me I was doing it wrong, and do it yourself."

"Because you *would* be doing it wrong."

"I'm a better cook than you are. My steaks are first rate."

"That's barbeque. It doesn't count. Speaking of food, I'm hungry."

"You just ate," I tease, even though my own stomach is feeling empty, "six hours ago."

"We can have elevenses." Pepper grins at the thought, or the word, taken from *The Hobbit*, which Mom read to us over and over again when we were young.

"Sounds good. Want to ask at the front desk what's good around here?"

"Or we can try to find that patisserie?"

"To steal more recipes?"

"Something like that."

Chapter Twelve

Neely

B Y THE TIME I help Mama clean up the kitchen, I'm dead on my feet.

At least I have Dawson to help. Mama is a traditional and old-fashioned sort of woman and doesn't believe a man's place should ever be in the kitchen. My brothers have always taken full advantage of that, leaving me as both the cooking and cleaning assistant to Mama. I know it's a lost cause trying to get Mama to change her mind and jump into the twenty-first century when it comes to division of labor in the home, so I've long stopped trying. And I have to admit I've learned a lot from helping her in the kitchen.

I leave the desserts to Adam. At least for him to bring something home from Pain au Chocolate. It might be a French patisserie, but Mama loves M.K.'s pastries.

Reuben's pastries now.

"Go—shoo," Mama says to Dawson as he carries a stack of dirty plates into the kitchen. I'm elbow-deep in soapy water, with more to wash, but she still tries to escort Dawson out of the room. "No men in here. Go sit with the boys."

"If I don't help you clean up, Mama S., my mother will never forgive me," Dawson says, scraping the plates clean. "You go sit with the boys. I can help Neely."

I stare at Dawson, not used to anyone defying Mama.

"No, no," she mutters, scowling as Dawson begins to load the dishwasher.

"Sorry, Mama S." Dawson smiles over his shoulder at her. "But look at everything you've done for this wedding, and with Neely not around to help you? Cleaning up after you fed me the best breakfast ever is the least I can do to make up for her being away."

Luckily, Adam calls to Mama, and she walks off with an ominous mutter, leaving Dawson and me alone in the kitchen.

"Wow," I say with admiration, rinsing the casserole pan. "I haven't seen that before."

"I've wanted to do that for years," Dawson admits with a sheepish grin. "My mom always asks if I help with the cleanup when I eat here, and I hate telling her Mama S. never lets me. It just took a little time to get my nerve up."

"I'm impressed."

"It must drive you crazy that your brothers get out of helping." Dawson picks up the frying pan to dry it.

"You have no idea. There's no way I'd ever let my husband or kids sit there while I did all the work like she does. But she likes it that way," I finish ruefully. "*I* don't, but she's perfectly happy with the system. While I keep living here, that's how it will be."

"James is in for a rude awakening with Ellie."

"Definitely. I think she'll teach him a thing or two."

"Two thumbs up for a sister-in-law?"

I nod. "Much better than..." I trail off, giving Dawson a sideways glance. Davis's wife Aubrey is as pretentious as he is, and I can't be in their company for longer than an hour without wanting to add several tablespoons of sugar into whatever she's drinking to sweeten her up. But even though Aubrey has never stepped foot in the kitchen when there are dishes to do, she has given my mother three grandchildren and therefore can do no wrong in Mama's eyes. "Christmas might be bearable now."

"Or you can always hang out with Ellie's family, now that you and Emmett are so tight."

I frown into the sink full of bubbles. "Emmett and I aren't tight."

"If things work out with him and Shae you will be."

"I think I've made it clear that I don't have to be close to whoever she's dating. Or you."

Dawson shakes his head with a smile. My fingers brush against his when I hand him another dish but there's no flash of electricity when we touch.

It could be because my hands are wet and a jolt of electricity might end up electrocuting both of us, but still, it's a good sign. And bodes well for my reaction for when Grayson took my hand last night.

"You really never liked Natasha, did you?" Dawson asks, completely oblivious to where my thoughts are.

"Do you blame me?" I ask bluntly. Some of Shae has rubbed off over the years, the part that you don't speak ill of people behind their backs. At least not much, so we kept our criticisms of Dawson's girlfriends to a minimum. But Natasha is no longer Dawson's girlfriend. "She was only around to get her fifteen minutes."

"Yeah," he admits with a guilty grin. "I realized it a while ago, but it's hard to break up with someone when you're half a world away from home. I felt bad dumping her in Thailand."

"So it was okay to make Shae and me miserable while you kept her around?"

"You're never miserable, Neely. It's what I love about you."

"I think you're confusing me with Shae," I say with a forced laugh, even though my insides are quaking at his casual *what I love about you.* Of course he loves me—I'm one of his two best friends. But still, it's always nice to hear.

"No, you. No matter what, you deal with it, push through it. You never let anything get you down. It's admirable."

"I'm admirable. Good to know."

"You know what I mean," Dawson pleads.

"I really don't."

"Like the way you deal with my girlfriends. It can't be easy."

I freeze, my hands submerged in the water, gripping the prongs of a fork so hard that it starts to embed into my hand. What does he mean? Does he *know*? After all these years, has he known that I love him the whole time? "Why do you say that?" It's almost an impossible feat to keep my voice steady, but I manage.

"Well, like Natasha. It couldn't have been easy for you and Shae to deal with her."

I choke back a sudden sob of relief, somehow making it into a laugh. "That's what friends are for."

For once I can't wait until Dawson leaves. The kitchen is Mama-standard spotless when he goes, but I'm still shook, and escape up to my bedroom.

I've hid my feelings for Dawson so well over the years. I kept the expression of pain off my face the first time he kissed a girlfriend in front of me, never letting on how my heart crumbled when I saw him with someone. How the longing gets unbearable when I see him hug a woman, or hold their hands, and I react with snide comments to hide my hurt.

It hurts loving Dawson, so much that I wonder if there's something wrong with me that I can't get over it.

I've tried.

Years ago, I convinced myself that Dawson would never feel the same way for me. He's told me so many times that Shae and I are his best friends, as close as sisters to him. That's how he sees me, how he lumps Shae and me together.

He only sees me as an extension of Shae, just like the rest of the world.

I am the sidekick: the Watson to Holmes, the Sallah to Indiana Jones, the Duckie to Andie.

Dawson loves the movies of John Hughes, and *Pretty in Pink* is one of his favourites.

Because there is no hope in changing Dawson's feelings, I've tried to change my own.

I've visualized hardening my heart. I've made countless lists detailing things I don't like about Dawson. I've tried to keep things as impersonal as I can with him, which usually lasts all of ten minutes.

The best thing for me to do would be to keep my distance, but that's impossible. To distance myself from Dawson means I'd lose Shae as well, because I could never make her pick between us. With everything she's dealing with, that wouldn't be fair to her.

So I grin and bear it, hiding my feelings from the world so I don't lose either Dawson's or Shae's friendship and, for the most part, I handle it.

Some days are worse than others.

The worst was the morning after the night... When we...

I deserve an Oscar for that. Shae, Dawson and me had spent the summer working in Tuscany, back-breaking work tending to the vines of a family-run winery, with a group from all over the world. We made friends, learned languages, and ate mountains of pizza. I learned a lot about wine. We drank a lot of it too.

Every Friday night, we met on the far terrace behind the house to eat pasta and drink wine late into the night. There was flirting and there was drinking and at the end of one night, somehow there was only Dawson and I left sitting under the stars.

And the next morning we got up to do our chores in the vineyard like nothing had happened. Nothing was said, but the awkward glances and uncomfortable silences were enough.

To this day, I have no idea if I told Dawson how I felt that night. I'm pretty sure I showed him.

The fact that nothing in our friendship had changed even after making love suggests I didn't let on; or if I did, Dawson did not feel the same and dealt with it by ignoring it.

I know he doesn't feel the same, because Dawson still treats me the same way he always has, giving no indication that he has seen me naked.

I guess he saw me naked when we went zip-lining that last morning in Thailand. No change after that, either. It's like I'm not even a woman to him.

When I finally told Shae what happened between me and Dawson, a terminally long three days after the fact, she'd been in shock. Not about Dawson, but that I could have kept such a thing from her. We told each other everything—first kisses, first periods, first times.

"I was processing," I had explained. "It was an accident. A one-time thing. It didn't mean anything." I stayed calm throughout the whispered conversation among the vines. Emotionless. Stone-faced. No one, not even Shae, could have known that inside, my heart was crumbling like stale bread.

"How do you know it didn't mean anything to him?" Shae demanded.

Because it had been three days, and Dawson had not said a word. There was no way he could love me.

"Because he would have said something," I said. "And I'd know if he felt the same way as I do."

"How? You can't know everything about him, Neely!"

"But I do," I said simply. "I always have. I know that he loves dogs, even though he's allergic. I know being around the water makes him happy. I knew senior year when he was in love with

Miriam before he did, and I knew she would break his heart. I know Dawson."

Which is why that the possibility of Dawson knowing how I feel catches me off balance, like I'm on board a ship that is rocking over the waves.

I need to get over him. I need to get him out of my heart, except for the safe spot reserved for friends and family. For Dawson to remain my best friend, I need to stop loving him.

I fall asleep before I can figure out how to do that.

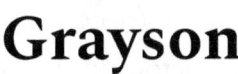

Grayson

I FEEL LIKE AN old man, creaky and grouchy, when I finally open my eyes at eleven thirty Monday morning, but it's been a long time since I've pulled an all-nighter. And to have one after a wedding was definitely unexpected.

My phone still lies on the pillow beside me. I fell asleep watching videos of Neely, Shae, and Dawson.

They lead quite a life.

When I played ball, I got to see a lot of ball parks, in a lot of states, as well as across Canada. Even though I rarely got to see any of the city other than the inside of a bar, I was proud of being what I call, 'well-travelled'.

Neely has seen a lot of the *world.*

South America. Eastern Europe. West Africa. All of Australia. After scrolling through their Instagram, clicking on at least a dozen videos, I can't tell where Neely hasn't been.

Her passport must be impressive, unlike mine. This Canadian has only been to America, as well as Mexico for a family vacation when I ten.

I get a sense of just of how impressive Neely is from watching the videos.

Shae is clearly the star: always with a big smile, laughing, talking to strangers, making everyone—from the shopkeeper in the market, the waiter in the bistro, or a random couple on the street—feel welcome and part of her world.

It's a gift. Shae is warm and friendly. Open, but not too much. Caring and considerate, generous and giving. I can learn a lot from watching Shae. I don't want to change for *The Suitor*, but it might help to adapt to the life of a reality show, which is a lot like Shae's life.

I reach for my phone, still thinking of Neely.

While Shae is the star of their vlog and Dawson is the foil, the butt of jokes and teasing from both girls, Neely is a solid presence in every one of the videos, albeit in the background. After watching a few, I notice how it's Neely who plays point as well as brings up the rear. She steps back for Shae, arranges everything that can be done to make her friend shine.

She's selfless and amazing, and I get to spend time with her because she wants to fall out of love with Dawson.

The screen of my phone is peppered with text notifications from my sister, Emmett, and several from Neely. I check those first.

> NEELY: I need to know more about this "date"
> What are you planning, and can I do anything?
> I think it should be low-key. Don't go to any trouble
> Maybe this isn't a good idea. You have other things to
> do.

These aren't from the amazing girl in the videos. Neely obviously has many sides and layers to her, and for the first time I let myself wonder if I know what I'm doing.

I have ten days before I sign the contract to become the next Suitor. After that, my life will be whatever the producers tell me to do, to step up and improve my social media visibility and likeability.

It's a process, and there's a lot that happens even before the camera start rolling. Neely will understand.

What I don't understand is what she wants from me.

After spending nearly twelve hours in her company, I like Neely. But the timing couldn't be worse. And I don't know much about what she wants out of this.

Time to find out.

> ME:When I am planning a date it means I am planning a date
> Thanks, but no need for help. It's a surprise .

It has to be a surprise because I have no idea what to do and now I've gone and raised Neely's expectations.

Great.

Neely must be on her phone because her response is instantaneous.

> NEELY: I don't like being surprised

ME: Who doesn't like surprises?

NEELY: I don't like being surprised. It's different

ME: Can't see how
You're up early

NEELY: 4 am. I'm still on Thailand time, plus I slept most of Sunday.
You must be rested if you're only getting up now

ME: How can you tell?
Do you have a secret way to see into my bedroom?
I'm still in bed btw. Do you like that image?

NEELY: Bedhead, bad breath, not to mention sleeping male smell?
You forget that I have brothers so just-woke-up image doesn't do it for me

I give a bark of surprised laughter.

ME: You wound me

NEELY: Get over it

But Neely adds the emoji with the tongue sticking out.

ME: How was family breakfast? Did Emmett behave himself?

NEELY: Too much food as always. And Emmett was good enough for Mama to try and set us up. Awkward

ME: Did you fall for his wickedly charming ways?

NEELY: I thought you were the wickedly charming one?

ME: I taught him everything he knows

NEELY: Somehow I doubt that

ME: Do you miss me already?

NEELY: I don't know you well enough to miss you

ME: Oh, you will. What are you doing now?

NEELY: Updating the vlog

ME: Where do you do that?

NEELY: In my room. Why does that matter?

ME: I'm a very visual person.
Does that mean you're in bed?

NEELY: Sitting on it. Why?

ME: What else do you do there?

NEELY: Re: above–I don't know you well enough to answer that

That gets a happy face from both Neely and I.

ME: That about to change.
Tell me something that no one else knows about you.

I settle back under the covers, keep asking questions, and she keeps answering, until I've got a good understanding of her. I find out she's planning on going back to school next month, to finish her business degree. I get Neely to admit Adam is her favourite brother, pink her favourite colour, and how she loves frozen pasta dinners more than her mother's cooking.

Occasionally I drop a personal tidbit, but I'm the king of the step-around and over the years I've found that women love to talk about themselves.

ME: What else are you up to for the rest of the day?

NEELY: Organizing James's wedding presents and watering his plants.
Basically hanging out at my brother's today.

ME: Are you the nosy type? Do you go through his
things?

NEELY: Of course not! Are you? Do you read your
sister's diary?

ME: No diary.
Really good recipe collection though
Need to shower but tell me one more thing nobody
knows about you before I go.

The ... tells me she's thinking of something good to tell me.

NEELY: Clay Loughton kissed me in fifth grade but
I told him I wasn't interested because Shae liked him.

I wonder if she always puts Shae first.

ME: Shae and Clay?
You should have kept kissing him

NEELY: Maybe. Have to run. Go have your shower

So now I leave her with thoughts of kissing as well as me in the shower. It's a good start to the day.

The smile is still there when I finally reach the kitchen, the lack-of-sleep fog vanishing after a long shower.

"He emerges." Mom sits at the little table in the corner of the kitchen when I wander in to see Pepper in full control of the rest of the room.

"Why aren't you doing that in your bakery?" I ask. Flour and eggs and other ingredients are strewn across the counter. Pepper has been baking since she was five years old, but since she bought the bakery in town a few years ago, she does most of her baking there, bringing the remnants home to us.

Except for new recipes. Pepper likes to perfect them before letting anyone other than Mom and I taste test.

Pepper flips the switch for the mixer and doesn't hear my question. Or she's ignoring me.

"Do we know what she's making?" I ask Mom, pulling open the fridge to find the orange juice. It'll be cold cereal for me this morning, since there's no way Pepper will let me within three feet of the stove.

"Cupcakes." Mom flips the pages of an old cookbook, one of Pepper's greatest inspirations and sources of recipes. Mom is an amazing baker, but with Pepper's Pies and Pastries taking over so much of our life, Mom's cakes and cookies have taken a back burner to Pepper's.

But Pepper has focused on bread in recent years, experimenting with flavours and flours, the discards from her sourdough starter helping her create scones and flatbreads.

For a thirty-two-year-old former pro-baseball player, I know way too much about how to make bread. However, my knowledge has impressed one or two women over the years, so I don't regret the hours spent with Pepper going on and on about feeding her starter and how you can't over knead the dough.

So why is she making cupcakes this morning?

It takes me a moment to see the connection between Pepper's bakery and cupcakes but then the light bulb goes on. "Ah. A little friendly competition is it?" I ask over the noise of the mixer. Pepper had chattered about Reuben and her tour of Pain au Chocolate all the way home yesterday.

"I can make cupcakes as good as he can," Pepper says, her tone fierce, and giving me no argument that Reuben is behind her frenzy.

"I'm sure you can," Mom soothes, turning another page.

There has never been one thing that Mom didn't think Pepper and I could succeed in. In all my years working with Ashbury sports teams, I've never met a more supportive parent. And not the scary intensity of those parents who push and push to try and make their kids live out their own, never-forgotten dreams, but a strong, unwavering belief in her kids. When I told her I wanted to play in the major leagues, she signed me up for summer baseball camp and found a set of second-hand catcher's gear and crouched in our tiny backyard and caught my pitches for hours. When Pepper announced she wanted to be a baker, Mom talked to the owner of the bakery and arranged for Pepper to work there mornings before school, as sort of an unpaid internship. Mom drove her there each day.

It worked out for Pepper; Ruth, the owner of the bakery, sold the place to Pepper when she retired rather than a large bakery chain.

I've often wondered if Mom is so involved in our lives because it's just her. After our father abandoned us, it turned Mom from a really good mother, into an amazingly terrific one.

She may look like a delicate flower, with her cloud of white-blonde hair and big blue eyes, but as Pepper and I—as well as countless grade six students can attest—she's one of the strongest women I've ever met.

She had to be to pick up the slack that my father left.

Taking my juice and stealing an unfrosted cupcake from the counter, I sit down beside Mom and pull out my phone to send another text to Neely.

I wonder what Mom will think about Neely.

I think she'll like her.

Chapter Thirteen

Neely

I T ISN'T UNTIL WEDNESDAY that Grayson tells me anything about our date.

Not that he says much.

GRAYSON: Wear sensible shoes

ME: I need more than that. What kind of "date" is this?
Casual? Fancy? What am I supposed to wear?

GRAYSON: I need you to stop putting quotes around the word date

That stops me cold. I won't let myself think of this as a real date, the kind people go on when they're interested and attracted.

Even though I am.

But for me, Grayson is only a means to an end—to help me get over Dawson.

And it's not like he's completely one sided. I can help him too. From our text string of the last few days, I can tell Grayson is fun-loving, charming and sweet. But I know nothing *real* about him, like what happened when his parents broke up, and how it must feel not to play baseball anymore.

Even from the little he told me on the beach, it's easy to tell there's so much more to Grayson. What was it like being on *The Suitor*? Has he ever had his heart broken? I can tell all sorts of things from Googling Grayson Grant, especially about his baseball career, but nothing about the real person.

And he needs to learn how to share himself, or he's going nowhere on *The Suitor*. I can help him with that. I should be helping him, but he side-steps everything I ask, and to be honest, for once it's nice having the attention of someone like Grayson.

Even if we're only texting.

> ME: This can't go anywhere so why call it something it isn't?

Maybe I do want to get to know him, but I have to keep reminding myself that he's firming up the plan to meet and date twenty-five women in a matter of weeks.

> GRAYSON: This is a real date for me.

You can call it whatever you want

I'm not sure what to call it, so I don't answer. And I don't know what to call the tingles that erupt when I read Grayson's text.

And reread it.

I'd really like to talk to Shae about what's going on—that I asked Grayson to distract me enough to get over Dawson, and it seems to be working.

This is new territory for me and I don't like it the not-knowing.

I haven't seen or heard from Dawson since he helped me with the dishes after the breakfast. Radio silence isn't unheard of when we come back from a trip, especially after the added hours we spent together after the wedding, but usually I would text to find out what Dawson was doing, who he was doing it with, like some masochistic stalker type.

Instead, I spent the time texting Grayson.

I don't even realize Shae has disappeared; the plan was for her to visit Emmett's farm on Monday and shoot a short video for the vlog. I look at being an influencer like a business—we constantly need fresh content, there's marketing that needs to be done, as well as networking with sponsors. And while Shae is definitely the face of ExpiryDate vlog, and Dawson is the IT guru, I work the magic behind the scenes.

With no trips planned in the near future, we still need steady content, and the idea to showcase Pike's Farm was a good one, plus it would push Shae closer to Emmett.

And it seems to work, since Shae didn't get home until Tuesday.

Wednesday is the first day I'm able to get together with Shae and Dawson. I hate to admit my heart beats a little faster when I see him already settled on the couch in Shae's living room, so caught up in his *Fortnite* battles with Shae's step-grandfather, Mike, that he barely looks up when I get there.

Yet another reason for me to get over him. I can't stand video games.

When I log onto the vlog, I see that Shae has already uploaded the video of Pike's Farm. Seven minutes long; some of the editing is a bit choppy, but the stats look good. I busy myself with answering a few of the comments while Mike and Dawson fight to the death onscreen until a text interrupts.

GRAYSON: What are you calling it?

I can see my reflection on the screen of my laptop: soft eyes, biting my lip and trying not to smile. Grayson is...persistent.

For a moment I let myself wonder what he'd be like if there was no *Suitor* for him to rush into.

ME: I don't know

GRAYSON: I have some options—visit, woo, epoch, consort with, tryst, assignation.
My fav is rendezvous. Say it in with a French accent and it sounds sexy

Dawson looks up at my laugh. "You heard from Shae?" he asks, fixing his eyes on the screen where his avatar blasts away with a machine gun bigger than he is.

"She'll be up soon," Mike assures him, before letting out a crowing battle cry.

ME: Everything sounds sexy with accent. I like epoch

GRAYSON: That's the least sexy of all!

ME: That's me

GRAYSON: I sincerely doubt that.
Are u excited for the upcoming rendezvous?

ME: You make it sound like we're doing something illegal?

GRAYSON: When's the last time you did anything illegal?

It's been like this for the past three days. I don't know exactly what Grayson does with his days, but he seems to spend a lot of time on his phone. I make a mental note to ask him tonight.

Against its better judgment, my stomach gives a pleasant squeeze at the thought of seeing him tonight. I'm happy that it's almost as intense as the quick thump of my heart when I saw Dawson.

Definite progress.

Thanks to Grayson's constant comments, I don't get much done on the vlog while I wait for Shae to wake up. Mike's worry over Shae's missed doctor's appointment spreads to me and I block off Friday morning in case she needs me to take her. I've always strongly disagreed with Shae's refusal to go see her doctor, but she's a grown woman and able to make up her own mind. Plus, despite her size, Shae is as stubborn as a muskox when she sets her mind to something. And she really doesn't like being reminded that she's going to die.

Which I find out in the kitchen later.

Shae is only moody when she's not feeling well or when she feels guilty about something. After a quick question about Emmett, it's not hard to tell which one it is today.

"Shae messed things up with Emmett again," I report to Dawson like it's an everyday occurrence. Dawson has followed us into Shae's kitchen, which smells of coffee and freshly baked muffins, with the sound of Mike still battling in the next room.

"Already?" Dawson groans, grabbing one of Mike's muffins. "I like him."

Once again Shae has made a point of ruining a potential relationship. She refuses to tell Emmett about the disease, and instead, ran full-speed away from him when he told her about his wife. It's frustrating to hear, to say the least.

"I'm not about to keep someone around just because you like him," Shae says defensively.

"I like him better than Grayson," Dawson mutters.

"Not surprising," Shae says in a low voice.

Where does that come from? "You don't even know him," I say in an icy voice. "He's smart, funny and considerate and—"

"He's the Suitor." Dawson's tone is full of disgust.

"What's *that* supposed to mean?" I can only gape at him. Instead of backing me, and trying to talk some sense into Shae, he decides to badmouth Grayson? When did this conversation become about me?

"You went on and on about Natasha only wanting her fifteen minutes of fame—what do you think Grayson is doing?" Dawson demands, his hands balled into fists, one clenched with part of his muffin inside. Crumbs scatter onto floor but for once I don't try to clean up the mess.

"He's trying to meet someone!"

"He just met *you*! Isn't that enough?"

How can I tell Dawson that as much as I've enjoyed the text strings of fun, flirty banter over the last few days, there's no future with Grayson? How can I say that although it feels like I'm being wooed, seduced via FaceTime and Instagram posts, this thing with Grayson is going nowhere?

And that's because of Dawson.

"Have you seen the guy?" When I hear the bitterness in his voice, so very unlike Dawson, I feel unbalanced again, like the Earth is out of orbit. "Are we talking about the same Grayson? Really good-looking guy, seems cool, and hey, he was a professional baseball player? What reason could he possibly have for going on a reality show to fall in love?" Dawson spreads out his hands looking more upset than I've seen him in the longest time. "And if that's what he's really doing, what's wrong with him that he has to have women picked out for him? Can't he meet someone on his own? You jumped right into his lap, didn't you?"

"What?" I whisper. I quickly glance at Shae for support to find her slumped against the counter, smelling her coffee cup.

"And where is that going, anyway?" Dawson continues, his voice rising. "Waste of time if you ask me. You've got better things to do, Neely. Stuff for the vlog, looking after Shae. What do you need him for?"

I can only stare, shocked into silence at Dawson's outburst. "You don't have an argument for that, do you?" he presses.

"I don't need to argue because it's none of your business!"

"It's my business if he hurts you because he's trying to get famous!"

And then, just as quick as it began, Dawson gave a little shake and turned to Shae, leaving me with a quick-rising anger that has me storming home.

An hour and a half before Grayson told me to be ready, Shae pushes into my house.

"Dawson is still playing *Fortnite* with Mike," Shae says as she sets my laptop on the table before me. "Want me to fetch him to go over this stuff?" Like always, she's managed to shake off her moodiness, letting her emotions slide off her back for others to deal with.

I don't know if it's that fact, or Dawson's attack that makes me snap back. "No." I open my screen to find the vlog stats that I was looking at earlier and stare unseeing at them. I don't see anything but Dawson's angry face.

"Oh, goody, you're mad at him, too." Before I can respond, Shae ducks into the kitchen like she knows Adam brought a cupcake home from Pain au Chocolate for her.

When she returns, the cupcake has been cut in half. "I need to share with you."

"Is that because of your little pity party?"

Shae sighs, her gaze on the cupcake before her. Even cut in half, it's a thing of beauty—white cake sliced with ribbons of caramel, a slick of buttercream frosting with a pecan and apple crumb top. But I can tell the sight of it isn't the reason for Shae's solemn expression. "It's gets tough sometimes," she admits in a quiet voice.

My heart gives a tug. I may get frustrated at times, but I love Shae enough for it to easily blow over. "I know," I whisper. "But you've got this."

"I know you know. That's why I save the pity parties for you." She looks up with a small smile and I reach for her hand to give it a squeeze.

She squeezes my hand and visibly pulls herself up. "Tell me about Grayson."

That's how it is with Shae and me. We don't bemoan her fate, shaking fists at the sky in anger. We just deal. It's the only way.

"There's nothing to tell—yet."

"Right. So, is this thing with Grayson to make Dawson jealous?"

"No!" How can she think of that?

"You sure? Because I think it might be working."

I shake my head enough to push the thought away so it won't take root in my heart. There's no reason for Dawson to be jealous of anyone in my life. "He said I don't have time for him."

"I don't think that's what he meant," Shae says slowly. "But have you really thought this through? Two things that concern me." Shae holds up a finger covered with a smear of frosting and pops it into her mouth. "One—Dawson. You're kind of hung up on him."

I stop myself from commenting by take a bite of the cupcake.

"Two," she continues. "Grayson is going to be the next Suitor. Both reasons are not great when looking at beginning a new relationship." She looks at me expectantly.

There's no hesitation. I knew I would tell her as soon as I had the chance. "There's not going to be any relationship."

Shae looks confused. "So is this, like, just a hookup?"

I understand her confusion, because unlike Shae, I don't do casual. "Grayson is a distraction."

"From what?"

"From Dawson," I say heavily.

"I don't understand."

"Grayson knows how I feel, but I asked if he would somehow distract me. We'll spend some time together before he goes on the show. He's nice...nicer than I expected...cute..."

"A little bit." Shae smiles, but I see I haven't convinced her.

"Grayson can't start a relationship because of the show. Even if he could, it wouldn't be fair to him for me to start something, knowing I'm still...whatever...with Dawson. Not that I'm with Dawson. I'll never be with Dawson."

"You might." The hope in Shae's voice hurts my heart.

"I've resigned myself to the fact that it's never going to happen. Even if it wouldn't destroy our friendship, I'm clearly not his type. Hopefully Grayson will work whatever magic he thinks he has and get my mind off Dawson. Then Dawson will never have to know I've been hopelessly in love with him for years."

I can tell from Shae's expression that she's torn. Yes, it's a practical decision because my love for Dawson is a ticking time bomb for our friendship. But I know she's always hoped the two of us would end up together.

I've stop hoping because it takes a lot of energy and I'm using it all to keep Shae alive. I just want out.

"What if you fall in love with him?" She asks. "With Grayson. I mean...look at the guy. He's pretty hot. And that's what happens in fake relationships, or whatever you think this is. They fall in love."

"This isn't a love story," I say, ignoring the pang in my heart. What if it was? What if it was me and Grayson, without any of the past and present? What if it was just now?

Would I fall for him?

"It's just—I need to fall *out* of love." My frustration bubbles to the surface, my hand fisting where it lies on the table. "I'm not worried about anything else right now. I can't do this with Dawson any more. The only option is to stop being around him, and that means stop being around you, too. I would never make you chose between us."

Shae notices, laying her hand over mine until it relaxes. "I can't let that happen," she whispers. "Sorry, not sorry. I need you in my life too much."

That brings a slight smile to my lips. It's nice to be needed. Plus, it takes my mind off the fear that if I made Shae choose, she might not pick me.

"Okay," she says reluctantly. "But...it's sad."

"A lot of things are sad," I agree. "And I'm tired of being one of them."

Grayson

WHEN NEELY OPENS THE door with a shy smile, some of my own nerves fade. I didn't realize I'm tense until I walk up to her front door with all these thoughts racing in my mind, about Neely changing her mind, or being as cold as she had been in the church, or the worst—Dawson opening the door.

"Hi," she says. She looks amazing in a blue dress with tiny shoulder straps and— like I suggested—comfortable shoes.

"Neely, who is at the door?" Her mother pushes her way past Neely to stand before me. To say that a five-foot-three woman, with a tea towel in her hand, wearing a black-and-white-striped soccer shirt over yoga pants is intimidating sounds absurd, but it's very true.

"Mama, you remember Grayson from the wedding? He's a good friend of Emmett. And Ellie," Neely says, looking like she wants to be anywhere else but standing at the door with her mother.

"It's nice to see you again, Mrs. Scalzo," I begin, but Neely's grimace stops me.

"Mama S.," Mrs. Scalzo corrects in a no-nonsense voice. "That's what you call me."

"That's what I call you," I repeat.

"That's what you call me. Why are you here?"

"I'm going out with Grayson tonight," Neely says. It's amazing how submissive her tone becomes when she talks to her mother. I wonder if she realizes it.

"With Shae?"

"No, not Shae, just—"

"This a date?" Mama S. turns her scowling gaze from Neely to me. It's been a while since I've met parents when picking up a date. I forgot how terrifying it can be. I feel like I'm back in eighth grade picking up Lori Davidson to take her to the school dance.

"Yes, Mama." Neely sighs. "It's a date."

Glad to hear it verified, especially after my mix-up with Chrissa. "You look great, by the way." I smile appreciatively, but not too much because her mother is still right there. "But you might want a sweater."

"Where are you taking her?" Mama S. asks, sounding like I'm planning on kidnapping her. It's no wonder Neely hasn't had many relationships if this is what she has to go through every time she goes on a date.

Then it strikes me that I know nothing about Neely's past relationships, only that she's in love with her best friend, which is why I'm here.

"It's a surprise." I paste the smile on my face, despite the fact that a tiny Italian *mama* practically has me shaking in my boots.

"Neely doesn't do surprises."

"Mama! I'll go get my sweater," she says to me with a worried expression. "It's upstairs…"

"I'll be fine," I assure her, even though I'm not too confident about that. I fix my smile on Mama S., who frowns.

"Be right back." Neely disappears, leaving Mama S. blocking the door, complete with arms folded across her chest.

"That was a nice wedding," I begin. "Ellie will be very happy with—with...your son." I completely blank on his name. James. *James*! "With James."

Mama S. sniffs. "Of course she will." She studies me like I'm a bomb ready to go off and I shift my feet nervously.

How to break the ice wall between us... Wedding, weather... "You like soccer?" I ask, gesturing to her shirt. "Is that—?"

"Juventus Football," she says proudly, her accent nearly undecipherable. She finally unfolds her arms to tug down the hem of her shirt. "My *Bianconeri*. My team."

"It's a good team," I say, hoping that is the case. "I'm more of a baseball fan—"

"Baseball," she sniffs again. "Give me one player that can go up against Ronaldo."

"That would be difficult since they're two different sports—no one," I finish quickly. "No one can touch him."

They must be the magic words because Mama S. finally breaks into a smile, just as Neely rushes back.

"Okay, let's go," she says, dropping a kiss on Mama's head before stepping around her. "Bye, Mama."

"Nice to see you again, Mrs.—Mama S." I'm quick to follow Neely down the steps of the porch. "Go Juve!"

Her second smile is less convincing, so I'd better quit while I'm ahead.

"Sorry about that," Neely apologizes. "I told you it's better if I meet you wherever we're going."

"If I told you, then it wouldn't be a surprise. Do you really not do surprises? Am I on strike two before we even start? Or yellow card, if you're a soccer fan like your mom?"

Neely laughs. "Mama loves her soccer. There was a game on this morning—or last night in Italy—hence the shirt."

"I never imagined your mother as a fan of anything, but especially not soccer," I say as I open the door for her. "From what you told me, I thought maybe cooking shows?"

"She does like *MasterChef,*" Neely acknowledges. "She was furious when they cut Mike when he was on." Thanks to the hours of texting, I know Mike is Shae's grandfather who helped raise her after her father passed away. "But she really loves her soccer. Apparently, she used to spend summers in Italy when she was a teenager, and she went out with this soccer player. Giuseppe Bergomi. He played for Milan, but after he broke up with her, she refused to cheer for the team ever again."

"I hate to admit I'm not up on my soccer players. I can tell you the lineup for the Toronto Blue Jays 1980 to 1989, if you care to know."

"Thanks, but I'm okay without knowing that."

I slap a hand over my heart. "You don't like baseball?" I gasp. "I don't think we can do this."

"I never said I didn't like it, just that I don't need the trivia. But you'll have to get used to explaining things, because I doubt there will be many of your *Suitor* girls who know much about baseball."

"Are you kidding?" I laugh. "They'll be studying up on it. When I found out Chrissa was the Suitorette and that she rode horses, I made it my business to find out as much as I could about them."

"That would be a good idea," she admits. It's not until I pull out onto the street that she looks sideways at me. "Did you read up on dance?"

"Of course. I pride myself on my research. I watched ballet videos, as well as hip hop and something called Acro. Plus, I've checked out the last few seasons of *Dancing with the Stars*. What have you got?" There's a challenge in my voice, and I'm happy to say that Neely rises to it.

"What was it like striking out Bryce Harper?"

To hear Neely mention one of the proudest moments of my career makes me—I can't think of the words of what it makes me.

It's so cool and very impressive.

"Point for you," I tell her.

"It's not a competition," she says, then laughs. "Maybe a little."

"You are on. Why don't you tell me about eating the cockroaches when you were in Peru and one of them was still alive?"

We go back and forth as I drive to our destination, with lots of smiles and laughter. I'm surprised how easy it is with Neely, like I'm hanging out with Emmett or Pepper. Never before have I relaxed enough with a woman to just be myself.

Neely looks around with surprise when I pull into the parking spot under the tree. "High Park? We're going to the park?"

"I thought we'd spend some time here," I say in a vague tone.

"But you're not from Toronto. How do you even know about this? It's a good park, but it's not like it's famous, like Central Park."

I smile widely as I turn off the car. "Like I said—I always do my research."

"Point for you," she says, looking impressed.

Taking her hand, I lead her into the park, off the paths and onto the grass, far enough from the parking lots that I can't see the gray of my car, nor hear the sound of the streets bordering the park. It's nice here; a little bit of nature in the middle of a busy city.

At first, I wasn't sure what do to with her on this fake date. It needs to be special, because Neely is special and I have to live up to my end of the bargain and get Dawson out of her thoughts.

She needs to focus on me tonight, and I didn't want the distraction of a fancy restaurant or show.

Plus, from the way Neely's face softened when we were down at the beach, I thought that she needs to get out of the city once in a while when she's between travels.

"This is the spot," I say, stopping suddenly.

"Here?" Neely looks around, seeing nothing but grass and trees. A group of teenagers play Frisbee nearby, their laughter drifting over to us.

"Here." Taking the blanket out of the bag, I spread it over the grass and then unpack the bag, setting our dinner out. Bread and cheese, thinly sliced prosciutto rolled around spears of melon, olives and nuts, with a bag of grapes.

"A picnic," Neely says with awe.

"Do you like picnics?" I ask with mock suspicion.

"Who doesn't like picnics?"

"You'd be surprised. I dated a girl once who was deathly afraid of ants. Going anywhere outside the house with her was a challenge. I remember when she found an ant *inside...*" I trail off with a shudder.

"I don't have a problem with ants. I've even tasted them."

"That doesn't surprise me."

"This does." Neely cocks her head as I gesture for her to sit down. "I would have pegged you for the indoor dining type."

"I do like a good restaurant," I admit.

"I was thinking of you more with a basket of wings and a beer." She laughs.

"Only when I'm out with Emmett. You better hope Shae is into hot wings and Budweiser."

"This is much better. You didn't have to go to all this trouble," Neely says as she unties her white sneakers and slips them off.

"I make an effort on all my dates."

"I guess you have to make it look good. I need a reason to fall for you, after all."

"Oh, I don't think you'll need a reason. It's all natural." Neely grimaces at my smirk, which makes me laugh. And then she laughs.

I like watching her laugh. It sounds nice too—very pretty and melodious, but even better is how her face lights up. Her cheeks flush for an instant and her eyes turn golden.

They're more hazel-brownish when she's upset or thinking about something.

How do I know so much about her already? A long night together, countless texts, and my list of things I know about her is already growing.

I might know more about Neely than I knew about the last girl I dated.

"So this is Pepper's best-selling bread," I say as I set the triangle of Brie on the lid of the container beside the baguette. "It's usually sold out."

"I'll be sure to give you proper credit for this," Neely says so sarcastically I stop, plastic container of olives in my hand.

"I don't want credit," I tell her, serious for once. "I want to give you a good time." Our eyes meet, and the romantic in me feels the flicker.

"For pretend." But this time there's a note of uncertainty in her voice.

"For real. This—" I sweep my arm out to encompass the blanket and everything on it. "I'd do this for any date. But wait." I scramble in the bag. "I got something extra for you." Neely watches with wary eyes as I pull a shoebox out and present it to her with a flourish. "In case your feet start to hurt."

"You got me a pair of shoes?" After she opens the lid, she sits back with her hand over her mouth, the delight evident in every angle of her face. There's a rumble of warmth inside me knowing I put that look on her face.

"Technically, they could be slippers, but I looked for the most comfortable ones I could find. And pink. I had to get pink."

"Of course, pink," she says with a bubble of laughter. "It's my favourite, but I never wear it because it clashes with Shae's hair."

"Tell her to dye her hair a different colour."

"You even got the size right." She lifts a shoe out as tenderly as if it's Cinderella's glass slipper rather than a pair of TOM's slip-ons.

I shrugged. "I checked before I chucked your shoe in the lake. It's the least I could have done."

Neely hugs the shoes to her chest. "Thank you. That was very considerate of you."

"I'm a considerate guy." As Neely tries them on, I rummage in the bottom of the cooler bag. "Oh...darn..." I mutter.

"What's wrong?"

"I forgot the knife to cut the bread."

"That's fine." She grabs the baguette and tears off the heel, pulls out a bit of the soft white inside and pops it in her mouth. "We eat like that all the time when we're travelling. Knives are frowned on in your suitcase so we got used to eating with our hands. I remember one of our first trips, someone told us to bring a jar of peanut butter because it was easy to get bread and then we'd save money looking for snacks. All three of us brought those little jars but no one thought to bring a spoon, or even a fork. We'd use our fingers to eat and even spread it. My fingers smelled like peanut butter for the whole trip."

I smile. "I'm picturing you sitting like this digging into peanut butter."

"I did it more than once."

"What's the worst thing you've ever eaten?"

Neely shivers. "There were a few things that I wouldn't touch again, especially in some countries in Asia and South America. Shae always insists we try as much as we can. Dawson's always the first to grab something new, and some of the things he's eaten, I can't stomach. But fish eyes have never been a favourite, and I tried these crackers made from cricket flour that didn't do it for me." She shivers again. "What about you?"

"I'm much less adventurous than you. I had hot wings that nearly took off the roof of my mouth once." She smiles and I can't help but wonder if she's comparing me to Dawson. "What's the best thing?"

"I had this pasta once in Verona. Mama makes pasta all the time, so you'd think it would be something else, but this was so delicate, like nothing I've ever tasted. Angel hair pasta with olive oil and lemon...baby artichokes and I think anchovies...so good. Mama always makes heavy sauces." She spears a piece of Brie and adds it to the crust of her bread. "I never eat like this when I'm home. Mama insists on big dinners and even bigger lunches, so there's always so many bowls and platters of food."

"What does Mama do?" I notice her smile at my use of Mama.

"She cooks for us, and anyone else she can find. I think she might have worked in a food store before we came along, but she's been home with us since then. Since you've met her, I think you can understand why that's both good and bad."

I think about growing up with Mama S. overseeing everything and hide my shudder. "I can imagine. My mother is a teacher so what we lost out on by her working full-time, we got back in spades because Pepper and I were at the same school as she until grade nine. Fun. What about your dad? You never mention him."

"Mama sort of takes over," she says vaguely. I wait because I sense there's more she's not saying. I know fathers.

Or at I least I know what my father was like with his ability to leave us.

"My father," Neely begins. Her forehead is wrinkled like she's thinking hard, and her gaze won't meet mine. I prepare for evasion. "My dad is a good father but a lousy husband. He's been having an affair with a woman for years."

I never expected us to have that in common.

Chapter Fourteen

Neely

"**I**'VE NEVER TOLD ANYONE that."

I didn't realize how hard it is to keep a secret until you tell someone, like tying an over-inflated balloon. When a bit of air escapes, it's so easy to let it all go. And with Grayson, with his concerned expression and understanding eyes, I let it all go.

"Not Shae. Not Dawson. Not even my brothers. Davis knows, but that's it. He was the first one I went to, which is silly, because Adam is the one I go to with everything else, but Davis is the oldest and..." My words burst out, running faster and faster until I realize I'm speaking too fast to be understood. I take a deep breath, feeling foolish.

"How did you find out?" Grayson asks gently.

"I saw him at Starbucks, of all places."

I remember the day like it was yesterday. It had already been a bad day; I had picked up Dawson, only to be forced to watch him leave his apartment hand in hand with Emily Burgess, an acquaintance from high school. Since it was eight-thirty in the morning, it was clear Emily had spent the night.

The way Dawson kissed her goodbye and the grin on his face confirmed it.

We had gone to Starbucks instead of Pain au Chocolate and I left Dawson in the car texting. I noticed my father standing at the cash right away but didn't recognize the woman.

When he leaned down to kiss her, he caught sight of me over her shoulder.

"His face." I shiver with the memory. "He knew he'd been caught, and all these emotions were going across it—anger, regret. Fear. I never imagined my father could ever look so scared. It was my dad..."

"So what happened?"

"I walked out of there, went to the car and drove away. It took him four days to come talk to me. Four days...I love my father, but I lost most of my respect for him then."

It still hurts to admit that; that I saw my father as a coward, not only for cheating on Mama, but his inability to confess and explain things to me.

"I have no respect for my father," Grayson says flatly.

"When he finally came to talk to me, he didn't even apologize." I swallow the ever-present lump in my throat that I get whenever I think about that moment. "Didn't once say sorry for being unfaithful. He just told me he wanted to explain; that the woman I saw him with was very special to him. He said he had been in love with her for quite some time, but he wanted to keep their relationship private to protect the family."

"He asked you to lie for him?"

"No. He said I could tell Mama if I had to, that he would understand. It was up to me. He let me decide if I was going to blow up my family or keep his secret."

Grayson presses his hand over mine. "That's so not fair."

"It's not. It really isn't. And there are days still that I wonder if I did the right thing. I let him get away with it. I know Mama can be difficult, and they've never had the perfect marriage, but they took vows! We're a family!" I choke on the words, furiously blinking back tears. "I probably shouldn't have said anything about it. You don't need to know about my family's dirty laundry. It's—"

"My father left us when I was thirteen," Grayson interrupts, seeming to be more comfortable with true confessions than I am. "With Emmett's mother."

"Excuse me?" That information pulls the rug out from under me.

Grayson gives a rueful shrug. "Emmett and I have been friends since kindergarten—our parents were friends. And then they were more than friends, at least my father and Emmett's mom. No one has any idea how long it was going on because one night they were just gone. Without a word or a note...no phone call telling us they were sorry. Nothing. I doubt they're sorry." The bitterness in his voice masks any note of concern that had been there with my bombshell.

"You haven't seen your father since you were thirteen?" At Grayson's sad shake of his head, my mind starts whirling like Nancy Drew faced with a mystery. "Do you think...?" *Do you think they're dead*, is what I want to ask, but can't bring myself to say the words.

Grayson seems to know what I'm asking. "I have no idea. Some-times I wish they are so there's a reason why they never got in touch with us. Is that bad? How can you just disappear from your family?"

"No," I say softly. "It's not bad to think that."

"My father called once, on my birthday about a year and a half after they left, but I didn't talk to him. I couldn't think of what to say other than *why*, and I knew the answer to that. He didn't love us enough."

"That's not true." My protest is quick because being the daugh-ter of a father who has strayed, I know how guilt plays with your mind.

"Oh, I know." Grayson's smile isn't as wide or white as it usually is, but somehow it's more real. "My mom made Pepper and me talk to someone a couple years after he left. I'd be a real mess if I hadn't. Not that I'm perfect." Another rueful shrug. "I'm going on *The Suitor* to find the love of my life. Anyone with half a brain would say that's crazy."

"Then why are you doing it?" It's something I've wanted to ask Grayson since I met him. I don't understand how anyone could open themselves up like that, inviting criticism and critiques and comments of all kinds.

Maybe I should understand, seeing how for the last nine years, the majority of my life has been wide open on the vlog.

"I honestly don't know." Taking a few slices of cheese and a hunk of baguette, Grayson stretches out, propping himself up on his elbow. My gaze drifts down the length of him almost against my will. Long and lean, and the way his shirt has pulled out of the waistband of his pants has my fingers itching to pull it up to see if his stomach is as tight and taut as I imagine.

Not that I've been imagining...I have. It's hard not to. My unrequited love for Dawson has put a damper on any romantic endeavors, but there's been a few men along the way that I've let distract me. Not many, but a few. None have been as appealing as Grayson, though.

Looking at him, I let the constant conflict over my father's secret life drift away. For a moment, I pretend it's just Grayson and I having a picnic, without the spectre of Dawson or the constraints of the reality show. Without the baggage of our fathers.

What would it be like if we were just two people, with no issues or responsibilities, just enjoying each other's company?

I wonder what it would be like to kiss him.

"I've always been a romantic." I yank myself back away from the study of Grayson's lips and to his words. "And I've had no luck in the romance department. At first, I thought it was because baseball was a priority, but then I stopped playing. I had girlfriends—"

"I'm sure you did." He smiles, thinking me sarcastic, but the reality is that it suddenly hurts to think of him with anyone else.

It's going to hurt to see him on the show.

"But no one was serious," he continues, with no inkling of what's going on in my mind. "Or maybe, no one took me serious." The way Grayson's brow furrows has me wondering if this is the first time he's admitted this, maybe even to himself. "I'm fun Grayson, like Fun Bobby on *Friends*, always ready for a good time, but nothing more. Women don't want conversations with me, at least not about anything important. I've never told any of my girlfriends about my father," he finishes, with a flush of pink brushing his cheeks.

"Thank you for telling me."

"I feel like I can be myself with you," he admits with a hint of surprise. "Like you would take me seriously, and still want to have fun. Are you sure you don't want to come on *The Suitor* with me?"

"I don't think I'd be a good fit for a show like that," I say stiffly, not wanting to think about the idea of him with twenty-odd women, all fighting for his love and attention.

And what kind of women will that be? Women like Natasha, trying to get her fifteen minutes of fame, or do they truly want to find love? How do they think it's possible to fall in love with the world watching?

"I'm worried about what kind of women would be a good fit," Grayson muses like he's reading my mind. "Are they there for the right reason? Are they serious about finding love, like me? Will they take me seriously, and really take the time to get to know me?"

"In six weeks?" I ask skeptically. "Can you really know someone that well?"

I've known Grayson for five days, and I think I know him very well.

"Twelve," he corrects. "And I know it seems like a long shot, but the best thing about it is that there's nothing to distract me."

"Only twenty-five women."

"I'll narrow them down, but there's no work or responsibilities or cell phones"

—Grayson picks up his phone on the blanket beside him and waves it at me— "to look at. When does anyone have an opportunity for that?"

"I guess you're right."

"It's not the best idea for everyone, but I think it might work. I'm looking forward to it."

"I hope you find what you're looking for," I say honestly.

If I was truly interested in a relationship with Grayson, his words would devastate me. Even though we're both pretending, his words are still a slap in the face. A weak slap, like from a playful kitten, but kittens have claws.

"I can't believe I'm talking about this while I'm with you." Grayson gives himself a visible shake and sits up. "I'm so sorry, Neely."

"It's fine." I wave off his apology and take out the mosquito buzzing by my ear. "We both know what's going on here."

"What if we didn't? I mean, what if there was no Dawson and no show. What would happen, do you think?"

The question does a funny thing to my insides. There's no way I'd ever admit that I'm having the same thoughts, but it eases the sting of the kitten slap, knowing he's thinking about it too.

What would happen—I would kiss him. Even with Dawson on the edges, if Grayson wasn't in line to take over the Suitor's bouquet of roses, I would push him down and kiss him until we both couldn't see straight.

Grayson holds my gaze for the moment to change from just a look into something more. Something that makes me lean forward, picturing the moves I need to make, my focus flickering from his blue eyes to his mouth, full and, for once, not smiling.

What would it be like to kiss him?

"There's no sense what if-ing," I say, hating how prim I sound. "Nothing can really happen between us, not anything serious. I mean, it could—we could..." My eyes flick to his mouth again. Could I? Could I lose myself with Grayson for a night? For an afternoon? For an hour?

Can I forget about Dawson enough to let Grayson get close?

It's tempting.

But then Grayson pushes his hair off his forehead, and it all comes back—whatever I might begin to feel for him, whatever this is between us is going to be over in a few days when he goes off to meet a group of beautiful women and become a reality show star.

And fall in love with one of them. That's his plan and I don't have a part in it.

I take a few olives from the container to have something to do with my hands. "But you're committed to the show. And honestly, as good as you may look, I'm not about to do that to myself."

"I actually haven't signed the contract yet," he muses.

"But you're going to."

"Unless I have a really good reason not to." He smiles at me and I can almost feel his lips under mine, tasting of olives and cheese. And there's a spot on his neck, right under a curl of hair. I imagine it would smell good, the true essence of Grayson.

The silence stretches between us, with me fighting the urge to kiss him and him waiting.

If I kissed him, would that be enough of a reason for him to give up his dream? Because if I do this, and he still goes ahead with it...

I give an almost imperceptible shake of my head; not telling Grayson no, but cautioning myself.

Grayson sighs and the moment passes. "Tell me about Dawson."

Coward! Shae would have done it. Why can't I? What's stopping me?

"You met him." There's a note of irritability in my voice—directed back at myself, not Grayson. "You don't need to know anything else."

"I think I'd like to know what he's got that keeps you hanging on for years, and never giving another guy a chance."

"I give guys a chance!"

He cocks an eyebrow. "Really? You're not giving me a chance."

"Do you blame me?"

For a moment Grayson has an expression that is exactly like Shae's when she dares me to do something, whether it's take the step off the ledge attached to a bungee cord, or to push myself through a crowd to meet Jason Momoa. There's so much more I can do when someone looks at me like that.

But I'm not doing this. Even an hour with Grayson would hurt too much when it was over.

"It's difficult with the travelling." I sound like Shae and I don't like it. "Relationships have never been a priority for me."

"That's a real shame," he says lightly. "But I want to hear what got you hooked on this guy so we can unhook you. When did you fall for him?" His voice is matter-0f-fact now, all business. It's like I imagined the soft sigh of disappointment.

Maybe it wasn't even disappointment. Maybe it was nothing more than relief that he wouldn't have to put in the work untangling my baggage?

I have no idea what Grayson is thinking. I don't even know him.

I turn off the emotion and give the facts, like I'm giving a presentation. "Shae and I met Dawson halfway through grade nine, at some party. We stopped going to parties soon after, because they got weird for Shae. I was never into the party scene, but Shae liked them, so I tagged along. Anyway, Dawson was there with some friends. I'd seen him around school—"

"And liked him?"

"I thought he was cute." I had, but Dawson hadn't been who I thought was my type. I thought I needed muscles instead of brains, a big group of friends instead of a solitary walk down the halls, and the ability to throw a ball instead of code a computer program.

In high school, I would have been very interested in Grayson.

"But at the party, Shae got to him first," I continue. It's been so many years ago since that night, the bitterness has faded from my tone. I'm stating facts, reporting how it happened, nothing more. "I had been talking with another group when she came to find me, she and Dawson, both of them laughing like idiots. She asked if I was ready to go, and Dawson walked us home. They told me what happened—they were talking, and one thing led to another and they kissed. I think Shae kissed him...not sure. Anyway, they kissed, and it didn't go well, and when Shae pulled away, she laughed."

"She laughed at him?" Grayson asks with disgust.

"I think it was probably more of a nervous giggle. Shae would never do anything to hurt anyone's feelings. And luckily Dawson didn't take offence because he laughed too. One minute they were kissing and then laughing, and they've been best friends ever since."

"But that's Shae and Dawson," he prompts.

"I'm getting there. We said goodbye to him, and they were still laughing. I felt...left out?" I pose it as a question even though the rush of resentment is still there, like a tomato sauce stain on a white sweater washed countless times.

"I'm sure you did."

"Shae hugged him and said something about it being a bad kiss. I don't really remember. But Dawson laughed. The self-confidence he must have had." I shake my head, remembering the image of a fifteen-year-old Dawson. Once I saw him up close, it was obvious that he was cool—there was no other word for it. Smart and just a little geeky, and with a confidence that I'd never seen before. I heave a sigh before continuing. "And then he turned and hugged me. 'I knew I should have kissed you instead of Shae,' he said. I have no idea if he was serious or joking, but something inside me..." I trail off, not able to find the right word.

"Exploded?" Grayson suggests. "I've been in love a couple of times," he adds when I nod.

"And that was it. I've been hooked ever since."

"Did you ever...did anything ever happen between the two of you?"

I keep my gaze on my hands twisted in my lap. I've said enough tonight, opened up like I'm a corpse on an autopsy table, letting Grayson poke at everything.

Time to close up.

When I finally look up, Grayson is watching me with a shrewd expression. "I say yes, but that's for next time."

"That's it?" The relief I should feel about not having to say anything more isn't there. Instead, I'm disappointed.

"No way." Grayson smiles. "It's time for the second act of our date-that's-not-a-date-but-is-a date."

"A date," I echo stupidly.

"At least I think it is."

Grayson

I CAN'T THINK OF tonight as anything *but* a date.

I've never had problems with attracting women; never had issues with women not willing to open up to me. Usually, problems and complaints rush out of them like Pringle Creek, and I only need to ask a question or two.

Neely is no exception, but for the first time, I'm the one who wants to tell her things.

I can't believe I told her about my father, but how could I not when the opening was right there.

"Let yourself be vulnerable." I can still hear Chrissa's words that night of the rose ceremony when she sent me home. Is that what I did? Is that why I'm shaking like a stray dog out in the rain?

It's good that the picnic is over, but the look of disappointment on Neely's face props me up. We've only begun and already she doesn't want tonight to be over.

Dawson, who?

After we clean up the remains of the food and Neely changes her shoes to the new ones I bought for her—a stroke of brilliance on my part, if I do say so myself—I lead her to the path to the amphitheatre.

"Where are we going?" She looks around with suspicion. The sky has transformed from the bright blue late afternoon sky to the dusky orange of the sunset, all in the length of time it took for me to fall completely under Neely's spell.

There's no sense trying to convince myself that I haven't. Everything about her pulls me closer as if she's a magnet and I'm a stickpin.

I don't know what I can do about it.

"Still trying to surprise you," I say, taking a firmer grip on the cooler bag so I don't reach out and take her hand. If I hold Neely's hand, it would be easy to put my arm around her, and if I put my arm around her, it's only a step away from kissing her.

I really want to kiss her. Before, I thought maybe—just for a second, there had been a look in her eye, and a glance at my mouth, but then she stopped herself.

I wish she hadn't.

"What if I told you I really don't like surprises?"

"I'd say you're really impatient, and that's something else I now know about you. Hang on for another minute and we'll be there."

"Where? We're walking on a strange path in a dark park and no one knows where I am. You've gone from romantic leading man to possible serial killer in five minutes. That might be a record."

"Don't you like horror movies?"

"Actually, no. I've watched too many over the years. Dawson is a huge movie buff and he—" She stops with a shy glance at me. "I shouldn't talk about him when I'm with you."

"I brought him up before. You can talk about him if you want to, but it does kind of defeat the purpose of our evening. A better thing to do would be to think of all the times he forced you to watch scary movies, and then compare that to me, who would never put you through that. I'd invite you to sit through a *Star Wars* marathon."

"But I'd like that."

Another glance from her has my chest puffing out like one of Emmett's roosters. "I know. We have so much in common, don't we?"

We step into the clearing before Neely can answer and her gasp of surprised delight is better than anything she can say.

"I've heard of this, but I've never been here," she says, golden eyes shining as she pulls out her phone. "I need to take a picture."

The rush of relief makes my shoulders sag. I'm still not sure where Pepper came up with the idea for me to take Neely to the outdoor theatre. I had a feeling she might have asked Dawson, which means he's already been here with Neely, or knows her well enough to know she'd like it. "You want a pic for the vlog?" I ask.

Neely gives me a sideways glance. "For me too."

"You want memories of tonight? Think you'll forget about me?"

"Oh, you're definitely unforgettable," she says dryly and I laugh.

I don't remember the last time I laughed so much on a date.

I lead her to a spot on the far side. The seats are slabs of concrete in tiers set in a half moon around the stage at the bottom. Ashbury has nothing like this; the green spaces around the village all belong to someone, or are chock-full of playing fields.

We settle on the seats, the blanket giving enough cushion on the hard steps. Neely keeps looking around with a smile of delight as the sky darkens.

"Do we have to wait until it's dark?" she asks.

"I don't think so. The tickets said it starts at eight."

"What are we seeing?"

"That's a surprise."

"I'm not much for surprises," she says with a frown.

"Yes, I know, which is why it stays as a surprise." I've already recognized Neely is someone who needs to be in control at all times. It's fun to take it away from her.

My sister is the same way. I've noticed similarities with the two of them, which might not bode well for Pepper, if Dawson's not interested in Neely.

How can he not be interested in Neely? To be that close to a woman like her and never take the chance?

I watch her face as the dancing begins. Pepper told me about a contemporary dance troupe that performs in the park. But as the dance goes on, Neely's expression changes from one of excitement and delight to one of sadness, almost like she's in pain watching.

I never thought of that.

Leaning over, close enough I can smell her faint perfume, I whisper in her ear. "You must miss it." When she meets my gaze, there's a moment when it looks like she's about to cry. Instead, she bites her lip and nods. "I know what that's like. Not dancing," I quickly add. "As you can tell, I'm not much of a dancer."

"You're good," she protests and some of the sadness leaves her face.

"Not like you. For me, it's baseball. I miss it every day, but sometimes it really hurts, like an ache. It's like I'm missing a part of myself."

"It's like a phantom limb." At my confused expression, she continues in a hushed voice. "When people have arms or legs amputated, sometimes they still have pain where the limb was, like it's still there. Sometimes my feet ache like I've been dancing all day, but all I've been doing is sitting on the couch watching a movie. I haven't put on my toe shoes in years, but my feet still cramp up at times. It's strange."

"My arm aches, but not when it rains like with arthritis." I hunch over like a wizened old man to make her laugh. To make myself laugh, so I won't think about how this conversation is hitting home. I never talk about how much I miss playing baseball with anyone, not even Emmett.

"I'm glad you don't have arthritis."

"Me too. There's enough wrong with my body now."

She lowers her eyes and gives me an appraising gaze. "It doesn't look like there's much wrong with it to me."

I raise an eyebrow. "So glad you approve. Can I say that your feet are the loveliest feet I've ever seen on a former dancer? I've heard that ballet dancers' feet are...well, kind of scary."

She stretches her legs out before her and wiggles her feet, now wearing the new shoes I bought for her. "Mine were hideous. It's taken years of pedicures and pumice stones to get them looking like this again."

"Nice work." I lean closer again and brush my shoulder against hers. "Can I say the rest of you is pretty nice as well? I don't want to offend you again, like at the wedding," I trail off with a winning smile.

"Ugh," she groans. "Don't remind me. I was rude to you."

"Little bit," I concede, not even attempting to hide my smile.

"But in my defence, you annoyed me by being late," she says. "I have a thing for punctuality."

"I got that."

Neely makes a rueful expression. "Am I that obvious?"

"No, but I have a sister who is a lot like you. Pepper was so mad at me that we were almost late for the wedding, even though it was partly her fault."

"You were late. There's no almost about it. We were ready to walk down the aisle."

"Still. We made it in time. Pepper likes to be on time, she's a super organizer, likes to be right, and if she doesn't know something, makes it a point to find out, and then tells me she's right about it."

"It sounds like you're talking about me." She opens her mouth like she's about to say something but shuts it before she does.

"What were you going to say?"

"Just that we have Dawson in common too, but I don't want to talk about him. There's no place for him here now."

I'm very glad she says that.

We watch the dancing in silence. I can't help but appreciate the graceful moves, the way the dancers tell a story that even I can follow. I've never been an artistic person, but seeing how in control they are of their bodies, the precision and dedication that goes into every step is impressive.

Midway through, Neely leans over. "When does your arm ache? You said it wasn't when it rains, so is it other times?"

I swallow the sudden lump in my throat. "When it's a beautiful summer day," I admit in a low voice. "Because those were the ones that I was always at the ballpark. From dawn until dusk sometimes, especially when we were kids. Emmett and I would practice and then we'd help other kids, other teams before we had a game. By the end of the day my arm would be so sore that I could barely move it. But it was a good ache, you know? Because I loved it, plus I was helping others."

"I do know," Neely whispers. And then she slips her hand into mine.

We watch the rest of the performance like that.

From the upright lamps scattered throughout the amphitheater, there's enough light that I can see the smile on Neely's face. Maybe it's the light, or her happiness, but there's a glow about her. It's so pretty.

I did this. I made her this happy. I give her hand a squeeze, and she looks up with soft eyes. "You like?"

"I like."

Her eyes look like caramels, sweet and shiny. My gaze trails over her face, tracing the gentle curve of her cheek to her chin and falling on the pink of her lips, parted slightly as she looks up at me.

Sitting so close together, it would only take a slight drop of my chin to press my lips against hers. To claim her mouth, tangle my fingers in that long, blonde hair...

The want is like a vibration buzzing through me, and holding my breath, I lean forward—

"I think that's my phone," Neely whispers.

With an apologetic smile, she pulls it out of her bag. I sit up straight and wipe my suddenly damp hands on the legs of my jeans.

This just got real all of a sudden.

But then Neely's smile is gone like a wayward smear of jam wiped off a counter.

"Everything okay?" I ask, trying to see her phone, wanting to know who interrupted what might have been *the* moment of the night.

She drops the phone back in her bag like it burned her. "Fine."

"Okay..." Can I pick up where I left off? Is there still a chance to rekindle that split second where everything was going my way?

"We should get going. It's late."

And...no. Moment gone.

Chapter Fifteen

Neely

I QUIETLY LET MYSELF in the house, hoping Mama is already in bed. She would see the disappointment on my face and there would be questions. I don't want to answer questions. I don't even want to talk. All I want is quiet to mentally rebuke myself for being so utterly stupid to let the night end like that.

So caught up am I in my thoughts and with the expression of resignation on Grayson's face when he dropped me off, that I let out a soft shriek when Adam rears up from the couch as I tiptoe by.

"Ooh, you're home! Did we have *fun*?" Adam hangs over the back of the couch with an expectant smile.

"I don't want to talk about it."

"That doesn't sound like fun. Was Grayson a bad boy?"

"He was a perfect gentleman."

"Also not fun. What happened, then?"

"I said I don't want to talk about it."

"Ask me if I care." Adam's face is set and serious, his talking face. "What happened?"

My shoulders sag as I swing around to sink into the couch with a tired sigh.

I am tired; so tired. It hasn't been a week since we got back from Thailand and my sleep patterns are still out of schedule.

I'm not even sure what a normal sleep pattern is like. The trips for the vlog have been nonstop for the last three years, like Shae is trying to cram in as many adventures and experiences as she can. I know that's what she's doing, which is why I don't question it, but for once, the thought of hopping on another plane isn't appealing. Being in one place, being quiet and still, enjoying Mama's cooking and getting to know my new sister-in-law...that sounds nice.

Getting to know Grayson would have been nice too.

All this goes through my mind as Adam watches me with an expectant expression. "Nothing bad," I say. "It was good. Nice." I give him a quick recap of the picnic, of the dance performance, and Adam clasps his hands to his chest.

"But that's perfect! The perfect first date for you."

"I know," I groan. "And it was great. We held hands, I told him about—I told him things and we talked about my dancing and his baseball. I really didn't think we had much in common until we started talking and then..." I trail off, not wanting to let anything slip about our father. "We have a lot in common."

"You like him."

"Shae texted the group chat to ask Dawson how his date went," I confess like it's a dirty secret. "I guess he was with Pepper tonight. I didn't know."

Adam groans with disappointment. "I want to say why does it matter, but it clearly does. Neely, come on!"

"I know." My head droops as low as my spirits. I thought maybe Grayson would be the one who got me out of love and into reality, but one mention of Dawson's love life and the reminder that I'm not part of it send me spinning back in time, forced to watch Dawson with a new girlfriend.

"You've got to get over him."

"I know."

"Well, do it!"

"It's not that easy," I snap. "I'm with him all the time, and when I'm not, I'm talking about him or thinking about him, or seeing pictures of him and other women—" My words finish with a staccato of breaths, usually a good indication that I'm about to break down in tears.

I hate crying. I'm not good at it at all. Instead of pink and pretty, my face turns red and blotchy, with a snuffling nose like a toddler with a cold.

"Poor Neely." Adam scoots over beside me and throws his arm around my shoulders. "I only want what's best for you and unrequited love is clearly not for you."

"Is it for anyone?"

"I wouldn't know because everyone always falls desperately in love with me," he says archly.

I thump his leg. "Not nice."

"No. My bad. And it's your bad to fall for the wrong people." Despite his teasing words, I see the empathy in his eyes. "So how did Dawson say his date was?"

"I didn't read that part. I only saw the part of the text where he asked me how *my* date was and I just..." My head drops to the arm of the couch and I stare sideways at my brother. "The only reason he would ever ask about how my date was if he has absolutely no interest in me outside our friendship."

"That's because Dawson doesn't know there's a possibility of something outside your friendship," Adam reminds me in a gentle voice that somehow makes me feel worse. "He has no clue how you really feel, because you refuse to say anything."

"I can't."

"You can, but you're scared to. The very thing you keep accusing Shae of. Kind of hypocritical if you ask me."

"It's different."

"And how?"

I don't answer Adam because I know he's right. I've never told Dawson how I really feel because I'm afraid he won't love me back. Not what it would do to our friendship, but what it would do to me. I've never been rejected before, nor do I want to be, so it's better to keep things as they are. Even the night we spent together...

I jump off the couch before my mind heads there. There are times when I let myself relive that night, but I'm not about to do that in front of my brother. "I thought Dawson might take notice if I was with someone like Grayson." It's only because I let the exhaustion creep over me that I even admit that.

"What, someone tall, hunky, and hilarious? Seriously, sister, you could do worse."

"Then why can't I get over Dawson?"

"Maybe if you get *under* Grayson...sorry, sorry," Adam hastens to add when my face falls. "No jokes. Maybe you're not meant to get over Dawson. Maybe he's your ride-and-die, your lobster."

I smile at the mention of Adam's favourite Phoebe episode of *Friends*. Then my face falls again, and I feel tears prick in my eyes.

"Don't you think he'd figure it out by now if he was?" I head for the stairs before I can embarrass myself even more tonight.

"He might if you fight for him," Adam calls after me.

Grayson

I WAKE UP ON Thursday with the same regret gnawing at my stomach—I should have kissed Neely.

There had been the perfect moment, but there were others that I missed out on. While we laughed on the blanket. Walking in the darkened path on the way back to the car. And even when I dropped her off; Neely had said a curt goodbye and gotten out and I had *let her go.* I sat and watched her disappear into her house instead of walking her to the door and going in for the kiss then.

Stupid. So many missed shots.

It doesn't help that I had assigned myself homework that day—to go through old episodes of *The Suitor.* For hours, I sit on the couch and watch women in bikinis and ball gowns with impeccable makeup that is never kissed off make moments with guys in great suits, and I kick myself that I let my moment with Neely slip away.

As I watch, it's easy to see why viewers flock to this show. Not only is it the possibility of romance that draws them in, but there's plenty of drama and back-stabbing conflict as the contestants prepare to fight to the death for their true love, even though they barely know the person.

I was never a big fan before I got picked as one of the contestants, so these are never-before-watched episodes for me. I've met a handful of past Suitors over the last year and it's fun to watch them on screen.

I take a special interest in the episodes where the Suitors get vulnerable to the ladies.

I opened up to Neely last night and it seemed to bring us closer. Thanks to my therapy sessions as a teen, I know it's not healthy to keep things inside, but it's easier said than done, especially when you're looking into the eyes of a beautiful woman, with more than being vulnerable on your mind.

But in all the past seasons I fly through that day, despite the vulnerability and bold actions I see, out of the eight Suitors, only two of them have had a happy ending.

They all end up with their person at the end of the season, but only two remained in a relationship. The odds are...not good.

Like twenty-five percent not good.

It'll be different for me. But as I keep watching, my confidence begins to ebb. How will it be different? I'll be faced with twenty-five women, and everyone says the process depends on what contestants are selected. I get my first look at their profiles on Friday, so I'll feel differently then.

I hope. Because I can't stop thinking of Neely and wondering if a twenty-five percent chance is worth giving up the possibility of winning her over.

Closing my laptop with a decisive click, I go for a run to clear my head from the romantic cobwebs that clutters it today.

Several kilometres later, I find myself outside Pepper's shop in downtown Ashbury, sweaty enough to hesitate going in. Like always, the sweet smell of her pastries pulls me in through the door.

The tables are filled, and a short lineup waits to make their purchases, which means another good day of business for Pepper. Since she bought the bakery five years ago, she's been trying to make it into more of a coffeeshop, adding tiny round-top tables and brightly painted chairs as well as a high-tech coffee maker that looks like something from a sci-fi movie.

The coffee maker doesn't fit with her collection of kitschy salt and pepper shakers that line the counter, wide window frames, as well as the shelves on the wall, but it makes a darn good coffee. She also painted the cream-coloured walls a cheerful blue, replacing the generic fruit paintings with black-and-white photos of the town and paintings by local artists.

I'm happy and proud that she followed what she loved and made a success out of it, but at the same time can't help the twinge of envy.

I had the career I loved and lost it. Who knows if I'll get as lucky a second time? But to decide that, I need to decide on a second career.

And that is a question for another day, another run.

"How was the date?" Pepper calls from behind the cash. Unlike Pain au Chocolate, Pepper doesn't have many employees working for her. Mrs. April, the retired nurse who helps out most mornings, a high school student on weekends, and Mom pops in some days after school, but for the most part, Pepper runs the place by herself.

Helping out Pepper would be the perfect job for me, if I was any good in the kitchen, and if I wasn't scared that working for my sister would forever damage our relationship. I like Pepper but I have a feeling she wouldn't like me if we worked together for any length of time.

"Date was good." It's not conceit that makes me think every head in the place turns to hear my answer, because they do. I know what the town thinks of me—the playboy ballplayer who changes girlfriends in time for the weekly *Hockey Night in Canada* game. And I admit I don't do much to change their perception.

They're going to love seeing me as the Suitor.

"New girlfriend, Grayson?" I recognize the woman in line before me as one of the mothers of a kid on Rufus's ball team, but I can't remember her name. From the way she's smiling at me, I can tell she'd really like me to.

"New friend," I correct. I've had my fair share of stories told about me over the years, so I'm well aware of how fast gossip flies in Ashbury. Pepper often comes home irritated with fending off countless questions about my love life.

"She's from the city." Jena Markov, a sort-of-friend of Pepper's turns from her spot at the cash, the disdain in her voice evident to all within hearing distance, which is the entire shop. Jena's had a thing for me since she insisted on having sleepovers with Pepper, complete with pajamas better suited for the catwalk of a Victoria's Secret fashion show than for a fifteen-year-old with an overbite and pimples dotting her forehead. Back then, she liked to sneak into my room in the middle of the night. Thanks to that habit, every time I bump into her, I'm hit with the unease I felt faced with a nearly naked girl crawling into my bed.

It kind of spoils things.

"She is from Toronto. She's Ellie's new sister-in-law. I met her at the wedding." Jena hadn't been invited to the wedding. She's gotten better looking over the years but developed an unattractive nasty streak so I don't feel bad about the subtle dig.

"Neely is great," Pepper says enthusiastically.

"Nice wedding?" The woman before me asks.

"Beautiful," I enthuse. "I'm sure they'll be very happy together."

The team mother, who informs me she was a couple years ahead of Emmett and me and remembers Ellie well, keeps me answering questions while Pepper gets Jena's order without her usual good humour. By the time I get to the counter, the scowl is fixed on her face.

"I can't stand her," Pepper mutters. "She gets worse every year."

"Jena, or Colin's mother?" I ask, studying the glass display case. "Cupcakes look good. You've been practicing."

"And they taste great," she tells me. "I think I nailed Reuben's recipe."

"Good for you."

"What's up? You're running. You only do that if you're bored or thinking about something."

"Both, I guess." She raises her eyebrows and I know she's thinking that she doesn't have time today for my issues.

She listens to a lot of my issues.

"*The Suitor.* I should do it, right?"

Pepper heaves a sigh. "We've been through this enough; both when you went on the first time, and when they asked you to come back. You are the perfect person because you believe in romance more than anyone I know, and you're in the perfect position in life to do it now. So, yes. Go sign the contract."

"I don't know..."

"Neely will be there after the show is over," Pepper says bluntly. "If that's what you're worried about."

"But will she?"

"From what Dawson says, she's not going anywhere."

"What's that supposed to mean?" I snap.

Pepper looks at me with unease. "It means that he doesn't think she's looking for a relationship."

"How would he know what she's looking for when he doesn't even notice her? If he had half a brain in his head, he would have grabbed her years ago."

As soon as the words escape my mouth, screaming across the counter like one of my fastballs, I know I've done a bad thing.

"I knew it!" In her delight in being right, Pepper even does the arm pump. "I knew she was in love with him. It's so obvious." Then her face fades into bewilderment. "Why did you go out with her if she's in love with another guy?"

"I didn't say anyone was in love with anyone." I back slowly away from the counter because Pepper will pounce with any quick movement or retort.

"Grayson," she warns.

"Pepper," I mimic. "She's a nice girl. I'm allowed to date who I want."

"There will be enough drama when you get on the show," Pepper warns. "Don't go looking for it now. And don't get your heart broken before you even meet any of the women. Neely's great, but it's not a good idea."

"I think I know when something's a bad idea, and this isn't it." I reach the door, almost falling out as a customer opens it behind me. "See you at home," I call to Pepper, escaping before she can call me out for being a liar.

Chapter Sixteen

Neely

S HAE ISN'T AT FRED'S when I arrive for lunch on Friday, which isn't surprising. I know she had her doctor's appointment this morning, which will put her in a mood.

She can join me in my mood.

I'm still fighting to understand what happened Wednesday night with Grayson. How could a night that began so well end up with me in tears, alone in my bedroom?

The door swings open and my breath catches as Dawson walks in. "Hey," he says with his easy smile. He sits across from me, pushing his glasses up his nose in a move that's as familiar to me as my own face.

How can I not be in love with him? I've felt like this for so long. Who will I be if I'm not pining for Dawson?

I don't pine. I don't obsess either. I just love him.

"How was your date with Pepper?" There's never any beating around the bush with me.

Dawson blinks with surprise. "Uh—" Another push of his glasses. "It wasn't exactly a date. I went to see her bakery in Ashbury, and we grabbed something to eat after. Cute little town," he adds, flipping over the menu lying on the table.

"I haven't been there. Yet."

"How was *your* date?" he asks slowly, gaze still on the half page of hot sandwiches offered for lunch.

"Great." My voice is firm, confident. "You seem to have a problem with that."

"Maybe I have a problem that *you* don't have a problem with it. The reality show part of it."

"That's my business."

"It's not like you, Neely. This guy is obviously a player and you..he's not your type."

"And you seem to know exactly what my type is?"

"You need a man who respects you."

"Grayson respects me! He's good and kind, and decent. He's funny and smart and—"

"Okay, okay, I don't need a grocery list of what's great about Grayson."

"I'm not giving you a list. I wouldn't give you a list. That's...not me."

"I know." He looks down at the menu again. "Did you ever tell Shae?"

"Tell her what?"

"About what—about us?"

All the breath seems to be sucked from my body like a giant vacuum has hoovered me up. Dawson has never once mentioned that night, ever. Never. "No...details..." I stammer. "But, I think she knows."

I know she knows because I told her. But I don't want to confess that to Dawson.

"It's okay if you told her," he assures me in a quiet voice. "I would have said something, but it felt...awkward. You know?"

"Very awkward," I agree.

"You think it was awkward?"

"You just said it was!"

"I meant, telling Shae would have been awkward. What happened...wasn't really."

What am I supposed to say to that? For the first time in my life, I'm speechless.

Of course Shae takes that as the perfect opportunity to show up. I only have a moment to compose myself, to still my brain racing with questions and theories and *omigod* spurts like bolts of electricity before she sits down beside Dawson.

I swallow audibly. "Hey," I say, my voice too loud for the table. "How was the doctor visit?"

"I went," she says, stacking her cutlery set out on the napkin. "Love being a human pincushion. He wants to run some tests. I wasn't there long." I notice that she seems overly distracted by the fork and knife on the table before her and have to fight the urge to grab her hand to stop her from fidgeting.

Mabel, the daytime waitress, brings her a Pepsi. "Good to see you back," she says, squeezing Shae's shoulder. She's older and slower than Dee, but much sweeter.

"We were here the other night," Shae tells her, looking relieved to have the subject changed. I want to tell Shae I'm not finished with her. "But it was a bit late for you."

"I heard about that." Mabel lifts her religiously plucked eyebrow. "You brought boys here."

"We bring Dawson here all the time, and he's a boy." Shae's grin helps, but her eyes still look heavy, almost like she's fighting sleep. Or a headache.

"Well, next time, make sure I'm working so I can have a boo at him. They ordered for you, you know. Grilled cheese, extra pickle." She gives a wink and heads back behind the counter.

"Thanks," Shae calls after her.

"I'm a little scared to have Mabel check out Grayson," I say under my breath.

"I don't blame you." Dawson leans his elbows on the table. "It's bad enough coming in here alone, and I've known her for years. I think she checks out my bum."

"Of course she does," Shae teases. "It's a nice bum."

"If you're not saying anything about the doctor, then what about Emmett?" I ask. "Mama said he stopped by earlier. I assume that was on the way to your place."

"I thought you didn't want to hear about my *me me me*." Shae raises an eyebrow.

"*You you you* is more interesting than my life, especially with Denzel swooping in to whisk you away. We'll get to that in a minute."

"Emmett caught me with a headful of hair dye. And then I dropped the strawberries he brought me. Not my finest moment."

"But...?" There's more. There has to be more.

"But I'm going to Rufus's baseball game tonight, so I'll see Emmett." She smiles ruefully, and I feel a swell of victory. "And we're going to talk."

"Talk about what?"

"I don't know, maybe about the weather." Shae grins at my exasperation. "I have no idea what I'm doing with this, so help, please. I need it."

"Don't ask me. I went out with Grayson Wednesday and I still don't understand what happened." I glance sideways at Dawson, who is still staring at his menu.

"If you don't understand it, maybe you're doing it wrong." Shae laughs. "What's wrong, Dawson? Afraid of being stuck in the room beside them? We had to put up with you and Natasha—"

"Why are we talking about my sex life?" Dawson asks angrily, unusual for him. "I didn't say anything about either of you."

Shae stares from Dawson to me and back to Dawson. "No more talk of romance today," she decides. "You're being weird about it."

Dawson quizzes Shae about her meeting with Denzel and I tune out until Shae mentions Antarctica. Another trip.

"I thought we were waiting a few months before we took off again."

"I know, but we could cash in on the Denzel concert going viral and—"

"I told you, I'm back at school for the summer."

"I didn't know about that."

"Yes, you did, because I clearly remember having the conversation."

"Okay. I think that's great," Shae says. From the sound of her voice, I can tell it's not okay.

"We could do something in the fall," I suggest. "Or maybe we'll make it short and go before school starts."

Dawson clears his throat. "I may have a job."

"A job."

"Look, Shae, we've been doing a lot—Thailand, and right after Costa Rica." Dawson glances at me, and I nod with encouragement, even though my heart sinks at the thought of missing out on that time with him. "It's been nonstop and I think it might be catching up with you. I know it has for me. It might be a good idea for all of us to get some downtime. You look really tired," he finishes.

"I'm beginning to get a complex, because that's all you say about me now. I'm still jet-lagged," she protests. "It takes a while."

"We're well aware of that. We're going through the same thing, but unlike you, we sleep. Take care of ourselves. I'm worried about you." I frown, studying her face that has suddenly turned pale. Maybe it's the new hair colour. "You don't look good."

"I'm fine. I don't need the two of you ganging up on me."

"Have you been taking your vitamins?" I demand. "Because I know you're not sleeping. Your eyes give it away."

"I don't need your pity."

I bite my tongue. Shae is so positive despite it all, but her refusal to accept sympathy is not one of her best traits. "Since when have I ever shown you pity? This is concern for my friend. You should be used to it by now."

"I know." The ding of the bell signalling our order pushes Shae to her feet. Running again. "I'll help Mabel with the plates."

But then I change my mind as Shae bumps into a table. She seems wobbly, unfocused. Almost like she's drunk. "Are you okay?" I jump up, willing my feet to move faster, because I think—

"Shae!" Dawson shouts as Shae pitches forward, her head hitting the table with a sickening thump as she falls to the floor.

"Shae!" The scream rips out of my throat as I shove the table aside to get at Shae, lying limp, half under the table. "Oh my God—Dawson! Shae!"

Dawson gets to her as quickly as I do and kneels beside her. "She's breathing," he cries.

"Of course she is!" Panic grips me around the edges, pushing ever closer. "She can't—she's not—"

"Call 9-1-1," he instructs, his hands feeling her neck.

"Don't move her!" I shriek, fumbling with my phone. It's the only first aid training I can remember.

"I know, Neely." Dawson had been a lifeguard, I remember; more training than I had.

I don't remember what I said to the 9-1-1 operator, but it got an ambulance to Fred's in record time. And then both Dawson and I climb into the rig beside Shae, still unconscious.

"She can't die," I whisper like a mantra as the siren shrieks and the traffic along Queen Street miraculously moves out of the way. "She can't die. She can't die."

I take back every criticism of Shae that I've ever made. I take back every word I've uttered when I was jealous or annoyed and in a bad mood. I didn't mean any of them. Shae is my best friend and she needs to be okay.

She can't die before I tell her how sorry I am, for every slight I've made, every time I was too busy to spend time with her.

She can't die.

Dawson meets my eye and I choke back a sob, because yes, Shae can die.

He grips my hand like a lifeline.

Grayson

Before me, the table is cluttered with photos of beautiful women, but all I keep thinking is that none of them can hold a candle to Neely.

"You see, we've got a wide variety of types," Ria, one of the producers, says, and I wrench my mind back from Neely to the task at hand, the final veto of contestants for the show. I've never met any of these women, but I'm allowed to give them a firm no if I can't find anything attractive about them.

"They look great." Blonde, brunette, red; tall, short, curvy, athletic—seriously, there's something for everyone, and lots for me.

"It's easier when you start to get to know them," Ria says in an encouraging voice, like she knows I'm about to be overwhelmed with the process. Being one of the contestants was easy—I showed up with my suitcases filled with suits and bathing trunks and prepared to have fun for a couple of months. That's all I wanted; meet a pretty girl, hang out with some cool guys. But it quickly got real when I met Chrissa. It also didn't take long for me to fall for her.

Was I in love with her? I certainly thought so, and from the thousands of messages that flooded my inbox on Twitter and Insta, viewers thought so too. But now that time has passed, I'm not too sure.

"She looks a lot like Chrissa." Raoul, the second producer, tosses a picture at me and it drifts onto the pile. Angie. Same glossy brown waves, same honey-kissed skin. But this girl has an innocent look to her that Chrissa lacks. For all her beauty, Chrissa is tougher than she looks.

"Pretty," I say and push the picture aside.

"Is she your type?" Raoul asks.

"I don't have a type." Today, my type seems to be tall, cool blondes with golden eyes and a talent for dancing. Tomorrow, it may be different. "This is going to work, isn't it?"

Ria chuckles sympathetically. "Getting a little anxious, are we?"

"Wouldn't you be? This is worse than being set up by your mother."

"Does your mother set you up with women?" Raoul reaches for a clipboard that hasn't been out of reach since I first met him. "That's good. Mama's boy—we haven't used that for a while. She could show up, help you make choices—"

"My mother is not coming on the show," I interrupt firmly.

"She will when you bring the girls home to meet your family," Ria reminds me.

"That's fine, but there's no way she's going to be helping. And no—I'm no Mama's boy, so you can stop right there." To distract them, I pick up a random picture. The girl had a cascade of red hair, so gorgeous I chalk it up to Photoshop. Really, some of these women have such beautiful hair that it's a wonder why they're not doing shampoo ads. "She's pretty."

"Ireland," Raoul supplies, even though I'm capable of reading the name on the sheet. "Grayson and Ireland?" he muses. "Doesn't flow." He moves to take the picture, but I slap my hand over it.

"I said, I like her. This is *my* choice, isn't it?"

"We're here to help in any way we can," Ria soothes.

In the end, I deselected two girls—one has a long, narrow face that resembles a fox; pretty, but I knew I'd start calling her Foxy and that would get me into trouble. The other has an uncanny resemblance to Pepper.

"There's no way I'm going to be able to kiss her without thinking of my sister," I explain.

"Let's just take out the possibility of any *ick* factor," Ria says. I was told I'd be spending a lot of time with Ria and Raoul, that they'd be my go-betweens to those really in charge. And it's good to get to know them. I even warm up to Raoul after they sweep me off to the nearby pub for a necessary beer.

"So you really want to do this?" Raoul asks, dipping a chip into the bowl of guacamole.

"I signed up, didn't I?"

"You can still get out of it. You haven't signed the final contract yet."

He doesn't need to remind me. The thick stack of papers is still sitting in my bedroom. I tried to go through it the other night, only to fall asleep not ten pages in. "I'll get to it."

"Is there a reason you're not signing it yet?" Ria asks. The way she looks at me with narrowed eyes reminds me of Anya, the producer than had been assigned to me during my first go-round on the show. Anya could always cut through the waffle to get to the main point.

I shrug. "It's a big decision."

"Have you met someone?" Raoul demands.

"Well, yeah, but she has nothing to do with it. She doesn't mean anything. I mean, she does." I give myself a shake. "But I'm not stopping this for her."

"Why not? Is it a sure thing?"

"Not even close."

"So what happened?" Now it's Raoul who gives me the look. Is this something they learn in producer school?

"Is that important? It's not really part of the process. I mean, Neely isn't part of this."

"We just need to be in the know in case this girl suddenly turns up with your love child, or something like that," Raoul asks with a lack of emotion that gets my back up.

"It's not like that. There was a date. End of story."

Ria looks at me suspiciously. "There has to be more than that."

"If not, we're in for a boring show!" Raoul laughs.

"Seriously, that was it." I'm flustered by the way both of them keep staring at me. "I didn't even kiss her," I blurt out. "Definitely regretting that now."

"Have you thought of inviting her onto the show? If there are unresolved feelings, maybe we can work with that if you don't have a strong connection with anyone else." Ria asks in all seriousness.

"Or even if he does have a strong connection," Raoul adds. "Like on Peter's season of *The Bachelor* when they brought Hannah B back?"

"That was television gold," Ria agrees.

Even though *The Suitor* is a completely different show, *The Bachelor* is held up as a what-to-do example. And every time the producers make a comparison, it reminds me that this show isn't just to help me find love—it's to catch the attention of the viewers and keep it. To do that, they need drama, and lots of it.

This is what I signed up for.

"I don't think Neely would have any interest in coming on the show. Although she does want to interview me for her vlog."

"She's an influencer?"

"No—well, not really. Actually, I have no idea. She runs a travel vlog with her friends. They go all over the world, do all these adventures...ExpiryDate. I think that's what it's called."

"You met Shae?" Raoul asks in an excited, high-pitched voice. "I follow her. The stuff they do is amazing!"

"Neely," I correct. "I met Shae, too, and Dawson—"

"Dawson!" Ria giggles. "He's cute."

"Do you think *they'll* come on the show?" Raoul interrupts.

"I doubt it."

"You're going to be ratings gold," Ria promises. "The baseball history, Chrissa breaking your heart, and now this. I can't wait."

Suddenly, I find myself willing to wait a long time for this.

Chapter Seventeen

Neely

I CAN'T LET GO of Dawson's hand.

It's like he's a line tethering me to shore. If he didn't hold on to me, I'd drift away in a mess of tears because my best friend is lying in a hospital bed, unconscious, and I don't even know if she'll wake up.

And that brings me to the worst thing I've ever felt—relief.

Not for me, but Shae. If she is dying, then the last thing I want is for her to suffer. Watching her waste away into a skeleton of herself would be a horror no one needs to experience. My head, the rational part of me agrees that going quickly and painlessly would be best, but my heart is screaming no. Fight, Shae. Fight for as long as you can.

I've never been so scared in my life.

Dawson and I sit in the hall watching the curtain that surrounds the bed that Shae lies in. The nurse ordered us out but there was no way I could wait in the waiting room. I started by leaning against the wall across from her room, and then Dawson's legs seemed to give out and he sank to the floor and I've been right here with him for the past seventeen minutes.

I've watched each number change on my Fitbit.

"She should have woken up," Dawson mutters for the tenth time. "Why do you think she isn't waking up?"

"She hit her head pretty hard." I'm *not* about to voice my fear that she may never wake up. Saying it out loud might mean that Dawson takes it seriously, and if he believes it and I believe it, does that mean it will come true?

What will my life be like without Shae?

No fierce and fun best friend. No going on adventures that I had no interest in, only to find myself having the best time. No spontaneous hugs right when I need them, and even when I don't.

I drop my head onto my pulled-up knees with a choked sob, still holding Dawson's hand so tightly that his fingers must be asleep. "She'll be okay, won't she?" he asks in the voice that I remember from fifteen-year-old Dawson.

"She might not."

"How can you say that? She has to be."

I lift my head and turn to Dawson, nodding my head as I study his eyes, full of fear. I like the *she has to be*, because she does. Shae has to be okay.

"She'll be okay," I murmur.

"If we say it enough, it'll be true. She'll be okay."

"She'll be okay," I echo, feeling a single tear slide down my cheek. Dawson reaches out with his hand and wipes it away, and I lean my cheek against his palm. "What do we do without her?"

"We do the same thing we always do. I've got you."

"I've got you too," I whisper.

That's when the nurse opens the curtain. "She's awake."

Shae is confused and looks impossibly tired as we crowd behind the curtain, but I've never seen her look so beautiful. It brings tears to my eyes to see her, knowing this isn't the end, but not knowing when the end will be. It's hard to look at her with the constant tears dripping down her cheeks

Dawson leans forward and brushes his hand across her cheek. "Don't cry," he whispers, still gripping my hand. "It'll be okay."

"That's what I say." Shae's voice doesn't even sound like her. It's like she's transformed right in front of our eyes into a fragile girl who cries instead of laughs, whose pink hair is lank and tangled and whose eyes have lost all their sparkle. It's like she knows the end is here.

That's not Shae. She'll never give up without a fight.

"Now it's my turn." Dawson brushes the hair off her forehead with a smile that breaks my heart. "It's going to be okay because we love you, Shae."

Her tears fall faster, and she swipes a hand across her nose. "Don't say that."

"It's the truth." I reach forward to grip her hand. "And we're here for you. Always."

The doctor pushes through the curtain, followed by Shae's mother. Shae looks nothing like her mother—Cybil is tall and willowy like a tree, the kind that a strong wind will pull up by the roots. In all the years I've known Shae, I can count on one hand the number of times I've seen Cybil smile.

She's a very unhappy woman.

"How are you doing? I'm Dr. Patel." The doctor is young and handsome. Is he too young and handsome? Should I find an older, less attractive one to help keep Shae alive? Would it matter. And why is he smiling at her? How can anyone smile at a time like this, when Shae is dying?

"How long do I have?" Shae whispers, her voice hoarse.

He frowns. "Until you're out of here? We might keep you for the day, but there's no reason for—"

My anger swells at his ignorance. "You're letting her go home when she looks like this? She's dying. You need to help her."

Dr. Patel steps back. "She's dehydrated and it looks like she's severely anemic. Who said anything about dying?"

"She was diagnosed with Batten disease thirteen years ago," Shae's mother snaps and the doctor blinks with surprise. "It's a form of neuronal ceroid lipofuscinosis."

"Uh, yeah. I know what that is." He checks his clipboard with a frown. "I'm going to check my notes...run a few tests."

"Check with her doctor," Cybil demands.

That's when things get confusing.

They move Shae to a private room and take a lot of blood. And then we wait, this time sitting on chairs instead of the floor. Two hours move to three, and Mike is there, and his eternal optimism smoothes the edges of Shae's mother's sharpness.

Until finally, the doctor returns.

"I don't usually get to tell people good news in here," Dr. Patel says. "But it's right here. We did the test twice. There is absolutely nothing in your blood work to indicate that you have neuronal ceroid lipofuscinosis."

I stare at the doctor with anger. How can they say that? Is there something else wrong with her?

"Did I get better?" Shae asks because no one else can say anything.

"I don't think you were ever sick," the doctor says gently.

"How could there have been such a terrible mistake?" I cry. "We thought she was dying! For years, she's been dying. How can you just now tell us she's not?"

"I honestly don't know." The doctor looks at me. "There could be—you're severely anemic, so it's possible that the numbers for that affected something, or were misread..." He shrugs with a rueful expression on his face. "I'm so sorry. I have no idea what happened, but I can tell you with all certainty that you do not have Batten disease."

"She's not going to die?" Mike's voice is a gruff rumble.

"Not yet anyway. She does need to take care of herself. She's dehydrated, and her red blood count is very low, so I'm prescribing an iron supplement. As well, a diet with lots of iron-rich food, like red meat and spinach—"

"She needs spinach?" I demand with disbelief. "And to drink more water? But she's not going to die, because it was a mistake? That's what you're telling us, that someone made a mistake? What can we do about it? Can we sue? Can we—?"

"Neely." It takes a moment for me to realize that Shae is calling my name. "I'm not going to die."

"You're not going to die," Dawson echoes, a smile transforming his face.

"I'm not."

Is it...true? "You're not..." I choke, my mind spinning. What does this mean? "Not dying...oh, Shae!"

I throw myself into her arms. Crying has never been my thing, but it's like a lifetime of pent-up tears burst forth. The sobs hurt my chest and I try to apologize to Shae for lying on her when she starts to laugh. And then I laugh, and Dawson is there, his hand still clutching mine, but now he's laughing too.

"I'm not going to die!"

"Not for a long time." Dawson shakes his head like a Hawaiian doll stuck to a dashboard.

"Not ever!" I cry.

"Not without you," Shae whispers. "Not without both of you."

"Wait a minute." I swipe at my nose, wishing for Kleenex. "We're not doing some death pact for the vlog if that's what you're thinking. There's no way—"

I laugh and wipe my eyes with the corner of the sheet. "The vlog! Dawson, take a picture of the doctor! Hashtag #savemylife #hotdoctor."

Grayson

I'M AT THE KITCHEN table, watching Pepper make a mess of the kitchen when my phone buzzes. "Neely?" Jumping up from the table, away from the prying ears of my sister, I head for the tiny bathroom off the living room and lock myself in.

"Hi, Grayson."

"Hi. *Hi.* How are you?" An alarm shrieks in the background, and the sound of voices interrupts Neely. "Where are you?"

"At the hospital. We—"

"Are you okay?"

"I'm fine. I'm so good. It's not me, it's Shae, but now she's fine."

"What happened?"

"Shae fainted, but she's fine now." Neely's words tumble out, which along with the noise makes it difficult to understand. "They did tests and found out she's not dying—"

"Shae is *dying*?" I understand that word. "What do you mean, she's dying?"

"Not anymore." I hear the smile in her voice, as well as the deep breath she takes. "Shae was diagnosed with something called neuronal ceroid lipofuscinosis when she was fourteen. It's also called Batten's disease and it's nasty and it's fatal, so we thought she was going to die. We've thought she had a terminal disease. For years… if she really had this, she really wouldn't be alive now."

I sit down heavily on the toilet and force myself not to interrupt.

"That's why we do the travelling, and the vlog," Neely continues. "For Shae."

"ExpiryDate," I push in, unable to help myself.

"It started as Shae's bucket list of things she wanted to do before she died and grew from there."

"Okay…but you said she's *not* dying. I'm confused because I had no idea that she was ever dying. At least not any different than anyone else."

"She doesn't like to tell people," she says, still with the defensive note in her voice. "And it's not my information to tell, so I don't say anything."

"I think it's your information," I say slowly. "She's your best friend. But whatever. This sounds like good news, not something to argue about."

"It's the *best* news."

Hearing the excitement in Neely's voice makes me happy, whatever it is she's trying to tell me. I'm still confused.

"They ran some tests, and it turns out Shae *doesn't* have Batten disease after all."

"So you've been travelling with Shae and Dawson for no reason? Never mind," I add with a shake of my head. "She's going to be okay?"

"She's great! They made a mistake about the diagnosis and there's nothing wrong with her except she's anemic and slightly dehydrated and really tired. And oh, she's got a huge goose egg on her head from falling into the table at Fred's, but she's going to be fine. She's great." Neely gives a tell-tale sniff.

"You're crying, aren't you? Happy tears?"

"I can't help it. But, yes, very happy."

"Then I'm happy too. I think that's great that Shae is no longer dying."

"I wanted you to know," she says with a choked laugh.

"You wanted me to know, or you wanted to tell me?"

"It's the same thing."

"No, it's really not." It's clear in my mind that they mean two very different things, and I hold my breath, waiting for Neely to get it.

"I wanted to tell you," she says softly, and my heart bursts into a crescendo of singing, even though in reality, I can't sing a note. "And I want to apologize for how things got weird the other night."

"So it wasn't just me?" I keep my voice light and teasing, afraid to put too much emotion on an already vulnerable Neely. "I thought maybe I got weird and chased you off, but I couldn't think of anything I said or did, other than buying you the shoes. Do you not like the shoes?"

"I love the shoes. I'm wearing them now. It was me. I got..."

"Scared?" I suggest.

"I'm not scared," she retorts so quickly that I choke back a laugh. "I don't know what I am. But it's nothing but a fake relationship so I'm not scared of it. Why would I be?"

I've been called fake before. Shallow. I've never liked it, but never as much as I hate it now. "It's not fake."

All the photos of the women I looked at today vanish from my mind and it's only Neely.

It's just Neely.

"We don't have to decide what you are right now," I continue, talking slowly like I'm approaching one of the goats at Emmett's or a stray dog. "You're happy for your friend. That's great. But, Neely, I need you to know that whenever you're ready to think about something other than Shae, when you're ready to decide what you are, that I'm willing to do this for real with you."

Am I really willing to give it all up for her?

The phone is silent, and for a moment I want to take it all back. Even the background noises have vanished, as if Neely has locked herself in a closet or a room like I have. "I don't understand," she says finally.

"I don't either," I admit. "But we can figure it out together. You seem pretty smart."

"I am, but...you...you're going to—"

"I'm not going anywhere right now but Rufus's baseball game. I wish you could come with me, but we'll save that for another day. Deal with what you need to deal with, and then we'll talk."

"Talk," she echoes.

I give a hollow laugh. "For the first time I want to talk. And... do some other things," I say, thinking about that missed moment for a kiss. "With you."

Chapter Eighteen

Neely

A FTER I TALK TO Grayson, I return to my spot on the floor outside Shae's room, sliding down the wall to sit beside Dawson.

My shoulder brushes against his and I jerk away, wanting to put some distance between Dawson and me as much as I want to lean against him.

"What do we do now?" I ask quietly. I don't know if I'm asking about Shae lying in the hospital bed, newly recovered from what was going to kill her, or about what Grayson meant about talking. Talking about what? There's really nothing to talk about, other than I like him more than I should.

Shae was right about the falling for the fake relationship.

Shae's not dying.

Dawson stares at the wall opposite us, the scuffs and scratches of years of patients marring the white paint.

The background noise of the hospital fades away as he picks up my hand again.

With Grayson battling Shae in the forefront of my thoughts, my heart still gives a dolphin-like leap at Dawson's touch.

"Mike said he'd give us a ride home," he says turning to me, his dark hair mussed from running his hands through it. His eyes are wide and stunned. It hasn't hit him yet. "He's saying goodbye to Shae. Goodnight, I mean. Not goodbye."

Shae. This is all about Shae for him, and it should be for me too. Grayson and analyzing his need to talk can wait.

My best friend is no longer dying.

When I entered this hallway hours ago, I thought I was going to have to say goodbye to Shae. I thought it was time, but I wasn't ready, because how are you ever ready for that? Knowing it's the last time you are going to see someone?

There's no ready for that.

But now...no goodbye.

"I mean, what do we do?" I ask.

He turns to me with a look of confusion at my question. "We do what we've been doing. It's still you, me, and Shae."

"But things have changed." I glance down at my hand, still clasped in his.

"Nothing's changed," Dawson assures me. "Only thing is that we'll have Shae around for longer. Forever now."

Dawson's wrong about it not changing things. I've lived my life with a narrow focus—everything for Shae. Help her live her best life. She's come first for me, even putting my own desires in second place. Am I resentful about this?

Yes.

But it doesn't matter now because Shae is going to live.

The laser focus I've been living with abruptly shifts and opens—wide open. There's so much ahead of me now, now that I'm no longer living Shae's life.

It changes everything; I'm going to come first for once. No more feeling guilty about forgoing trips for school. No more doing only what Shae needs.

Me. No more sidekick. I'm going to grab the starring role in my life.

A strangled laugh escapes as I sit, the weight of Shae tumbling off my shoulders, stunned with what it all means. It changes everything.

"It's great, isn't it?" Dawson asks. He has no idea what's going on in my head.

"It is. Unbelievable, especially after everything she's been through."

"We. We've been through it too, Neely. This is huge for us, too."

Maybe he does get it.

"I called Emmett," I say. "He didn't know anything."

"But that's okay, because now nothing is wrong."

"I don't think he sees it like that."

Dawson and I turn in unison at the sound of footsteps. "You're still here," Cybil says in a stiff voice.

"Why wouldn't we be here?" A sudden burst of anger swells at the sight of Shae's mother, still with her usual pinched expression on her face. Her daughter just got the best news of her life and still that doesn't make her happy. "Shae's in the hospital. We brought her here."

"Yes, I'm well aware of that."

"You didn't even know anything was wrong with her," I burst out, my words halting Cybil from entering Shae's room.

I clamber to my feet, with Dawson still clinging to my hand, needing to stand up for this. "You're a nurse, and you didn't see anything wrong. You're her *mother*. You need to act like it for once."

Beside me, Dawson sucks in his breath. Cybil stands with her back to us, hand on the door, and the sight of it brings back memories of a young Shae left alone, left unloved by her mother.

I think of Emmett and the hurt in his voice when I told him Shae had lied to him by not telling him the truth. "Shae can't love anyone because of you," I say, my voice harsh and hurtful.

"Neely, don't," Dawson hisses.

"If I don't, no one else will," I snap. "I *hate* seeing Shae hurt good men who care about her, because of *your* inability to show love for her, or anyone else. You lost your husband, and that's sad, but you still have a daughter who needs you, and you've been ignoring her for years. And because of that, Shae's grown up thinking love is painful and hard and not worth it. You showed her that, and that's not right. I just had to tell Emmett that she's not dying, but he didn't even know she was sick! That's not right! You don't keep that from people—only Shae does, because that's what you taught her."

The door to Shae's room opens and Mike steps out. "We finished here?" His tone is mild but the concern in his expression speaks volumes.

Dawson squeezes my hand. "We're done."

"Nothing more to say, Neely?" Cybil turns and faces me. For the first time her face shows more than tight disappointment; her eyes flash with emotion, her lips quiver. She looks like she's about to cry.

Oh, God, what have I done? "I'm sorry," I say quickly. "I didn't mean—"

"You did." She straightens her shoulders. "I'm going to see to my daughter now." Without another word, she disappears into Shae's room.

"What the hell was that?" Dawson turns to me in horror.

"I don't know, I just—Mike, about what I said to Cybil—"

"Don't even think of trying to apologize," Mike says, looking infinitely more cheerful than when he interrupted my tirade.

I heave a relieved breath. "I wasn't."

Mike grins and some of the tension drains from me. "Of course you weren't. Look, whatever you or Shae think, I know Cybil loves her very much. Despite everything, she wants the best for her. I think this will change a lot for the two of them."

"I hope so. Shae deserves more."

"She deserves the world," Mike says. "And thanks to the two of you, she's seen most of it. You're a good friend, Neely. You always have been. She's lucky to have both of you." He hugs me then, and I sag in his arms, finally letting go of Dawson's hand. "Let's get you home. It's been a long day. You must be exhausted."

Exhausted would be an understatement. I feel drained, like a phone battery hovering around five per cent. I need to be plugged in, recharged, rejuvenated. I need sleep. "A little bit," I admit.

"It's been a long week," Dawson says, slinging an arm around my shoulders as we follow Mike down the hall. "Remind me again never to get on your bad side. You're pretty fierce."

"I am," I admit.

And it's time I start acting like it.

Grayson

I KNOCK ON NEELY'S door Sunday morning; for the first time I'm unsure of what the reaction will be. Neely's been surprising me since I met her, and today will be no different.

I haven't seen her since our date, but I take her call when Shae ended up in the hospital as a good sign. I spoke to her again yesterday and made her explain it all again and I'm starting to understand the dying-not-dying aspect of things.

Something in her voice suggested she needed a friend, which is why I'm at her door, unannounced, uninvited, and unsure.

The door pulls open without warning to reveal Adam with a grin on his face. "Well, hello, Mr. Grayson Grant."

My shoulders sag involuntarily with relief that it's not Mama S. "Hey, Adam. Is your sister home?"

"Neely!" Adam bellows, not stepping away from the door. "Got a visitor. Does she know you were coming by?" he asks, lowering his voice.

"No, but I wanted to see how she was after Shae...you know."

"Isn't dying? Pretty amazing, if you ask me. But...yeah." He adds a concerned twist of his mouth. "She's been...off since then and she won't tell me why. Maybe you—" His gaze rakes the length of me. "Maybe you have some special power that will make her talk, because I do not. And there she is." Both of us turn at the sound of Neely's footsteps.

My first thought is that she doesn't look off. She looks very on—a pair of pink shorts show off the most glorious long legs, with a tattered Roots sweatshirt and her hair bundled into a bun on the top of her head. For a sleepy Sunday at home, Neely looks radiant.

"Hey. Sorry to drop in like this." I'm boosted by how her confused expression keeps dipping into delight. At least I think the smile she keeps trying to hide means she's happy to see me.

"Is everything okay?" Neely asks, finally mastering the concerned expression.

"I wanted to ask you the same thing. How're you doing with everything? Shae and…stuff."

But before she can answer, there's a shout. "Neely? Who is at the door?"

"It's for me, Mama," she calls back and Adam can't hide his smirk. "You came all this way just to ask me if I'm okay? It's so far."

"It doesn't seem far when I'm with you."

Neely gives her brother a sideways glance and rolls her eyes. "That's cheesy."

I beam. "I'm very good with cheesy."

"You're going to need more to get anywhere with the *Suitor* women."

The *Suitor* women are the last thing I want to talk about. "Yeah, well, I'll be okay. Feel like joining me for a walk along the beach?"

She studies me for a moment, long enough to wonder if she's going to say no. "Let me get my shoes," she says finally.

"You can always go barefoot again. Happy to give you another piggyback ride."

Her mouth quirks into a smile. "I'll get my shoes."

Slipping on a pair of flip-flops, she leads me down the steps. The house is halfway down the quiet street, with the wide expanse of beach at the end. It's a different area from where we were last weekend, but the same boardwalk stretches into the distance. The day is cool and overcast, with a dampness in the air, but there are still clumps of beachgoers, from the dog walkers to the families with little children darting into the low waves, to the boisterous volleyball games taking place.

"This is great," I say, trying to look everywhere at once. "You're so close to all this."

"I love it here," Neely says simply, slipping off her flip-flops when we reach the sand.

I gesture to the sandals in her hand. "Those look more comfortable than the ones you had on the last time we found ourselves here."

She squints in the direction of the water, choppy from the constant wind. "I shouldn't have thrown them into the lake."

"It was a sacrifice. Had to be done to get your mind in the game." My hand dangles beside my leg, itching to take hers but she holds the shoes in her hand. "That's kind of what I wanted to talk to you about."

"I thought it was Shae," she counters. If I didn't know better, I'd say Neely sounds nervous. Or maybe it's just me. I've never had problems making decisions, even less putting big decisions on hold with a wait-and-see attitude. But settling things with Neely means settling things with *The Suitor*, which means my future, even past the months on the show.

This could give me the push to figure out what I'm going to do with the rest of my life, and it all rests with Neely.

No pressure.

"How's Shae?" I ask, kicking off my Vans and smiling as the cool sand squishes between my toes.

"Good. Great." The wind whips her long hair into tangles. "Not dying seems to agree with her."

"You wouldn't want it to disagree with you. What about you? Does this change things for you?"

Despite the threatening clouds, Neely heads towards the water's edge. "It's going to rain," she predicts in a voice tinged with sadness.

"Looks that way, but I'm not going to melt. Are you? Are you secretly the Wicked Witch of the West?"

Another sigh, deeper this time. "I feel like it today."

"Because you're not jumping for joy that Shae is going to live forever?" Her quick intake of breath suggests I might have hit the nail square on the head.

"That's not it," she snaps. "You don't understand."

I catch her arm to turn her to face me. "Then help me understand."

She worries her bottom lip between her teeth, her gaze tracking the waves over my shoulder. "It's not that I'm not happy. I am. I'm so happy. It's so good, and I'm so happy and I have no idea why I'm not." Her golden eyes finally meet mine full of worry and sadness, and the sight of them clutches at my heart.

I don't want to ever make her look like that.

"Even though it's a good one, it's a really big change," I start slowly. "Shae's your best friend. From what you've told me, you've put your whole life on hold to travel around the world with—" I pause as Neely winces. "Ah. No more travelling?"

"We haven't talked about it. It all started as a way for Shae to finish her bucket list and then got way out of hand. But it's been great. Really it has."

"Past tense."

"Maybe present," she corrects. "We have to sit down and see what Shae wants to do. I told her I wouldn't be able to go anywhere for a while. I'm starting school again for the summer."

I pick up the *what Shae wants to do* as if Neely had underlined it in red.

"How many credits do you need to finish your degree?"

"Six. If I go full-time, I can finish this time next year."

"Have you ever gone to school full-time?" I'm still not sure of what Neely's concern is but at least I feel like I'm getting somewhere with her. She shakes her head. "Because you've been travelling. Putting your life on hold to be with your friend."

"I don't look at it like that."

"But you could. Look, Shae is great, and I'd do anything I could if Emmett was in the same boat. I went crazy when he went to rehab because there was nothing I could do for him. It's tough to see them hurting and then all of a sudden come out on top. Like Emmett, really."

"This is nothing like Emmett."

"Isn't it? I've watched him hide himself away from the world for three years, and now all of a sudden he woke up with a girl beside him, and I didn't do a thing. I've done everything I could to help, but nothing worked and now he's all better. No thanks to me." My words are a revelation to me. I had no idea I felt like this—sort of pushed to the side. It's not Emmett's fault; none of this is anyone's fault.

"Maybe it's a little like Emmett," Neely murmurs.

I make a sweeping motion with my arm. "Now it's your turn to elaborate."

"I looked after Shae," she bursts out. "I took care of her and organized everything. She used to call me her babysitter, but it was more, you know. I looked after her. I had her back. And now, everything I've done seems...it's like it's wasted."

"It's not wasted."

"I don't know who I am anymore if I'm not looking after Shae." She lowers her voice as if she's afraid of being overheard . "Is that strange? And horrible? I've been Shae's best friend for so long, and now I don't know who I am."

"Pretty sure you'll still be her best friend."

"How do you know? She won't need me—"

"Shae isn't your best friend because she needs a babysitter. Anyone who sees the two of you together—the three of you—knows that she adores you. Geez, when I saw the two of you at the wedding, I could tell you were tight. She loves you, because that's what friends do, not because you make her eat her vegetables."

"Vitamins," she says reluctantly. "I tried to get her to take vitamins."

"They must have helped, even a little. Look, Neely, speaking as one who had the rug pulled out from under him a time or two, change is tough. But this is a good change. You'll still be able to be

Shae's best friend. But now you won't have to micromanage her life. Or maybe you still will."

"I don't—" She stops herself. "I guess I tend to do that."

"I've known you how long? Even I can tell you could effectively run a small country on your own. Maybe even a big one."

"That's funny you say that because I'm taking public administration."

"You're going to run for Prime Minister someday, and I'm going to be the first in line to vote for you."

"I don't think I'd go that far." But she's smiling now, some of the haunted light gone from her eyes. Friendship can be a complicated thing.

"I would." Finally giving in to the urge, I catch the hand not holding her shoes and bring it to my lips. "Do you have any idea how amazing you are?"

"Yes."

Her quick response throws me off guard. "You do?"

"Of course. Everyone knows I'm amazing."

I choke back a laugh and kiss her knuckles again. "I adore you."

"You do?" The self-confidence has vanished, leaving an expression of hopeful longing that makes my heart burn to see it.

"Of course I do." I hold her hand to my mouth, in the hopes that the touch of her skin will tide me over. Because I'd really like to kiss Neely right now—fake relationship or not.

It doesn't seem fake.

"You're not supposed to."

"Who says?"

Neely gives a choked laugh. "You did. You're the Suitor, remember? And I'm not one of the contestants."

"Do you want to be? We could do this for real."

"That's not fair."

"I really don't care."

"Grayson..."

"Neely. You want this to be fake, but why? Why can't we try it for real? I can help you get over him and you can—"

"What can I do for you?" she interrupts in a low voice.

"Anything I want, hopefully." She laughs, but I mean everything I say. Being close to her, looking into those golden eyes and letting myself think of a future is making me dizzy.

"I don't want you to break my heart."

The vulnerability in her tone stops me cold. As much as I want to promise that I would never hurt her, I can't. Until I fully kiss the opportunity of *The Suitor* goodbye, I can't promise her anything. Reluctantly, I draw away from her. "That's the last thing I want."

"Then we keep it simple," she says firmly. "Casual."

"Fake."

"Friends," she corrects. "For now."

"I can handle that. Friends for now." I can tell by her smile that the conversation is closed. There's so much more I want to say, but can't. For once, waiting to see what's going to happen might not work out so well.

For once, this might not work out the way I want it.

I wish I knew what I want.

This time, Neely takes my hand in hers as we set off down the beach. "You like living so close to the water?" I ask as the waves rolling over her bare feet bring a smile to her face.

"I love it. Something is missing if I don't see the water every day. I make Shae go to as many places near an ocean or lake as possible. She hates it because she's a horrible swimmer."

"Me too. I'm not much for the water."

"No?" I like to think a pang of disappointment colours the word.

"I like snow," I explain. "I took up skiing after baseball and I like that. I'm pretty good at it, too."

"You'll have to go with Shae. And Dawson. He's a great skier."

"Dawson doesn't seem the athletic type."

"He doesn't do much, but what he does, he's pretty good at," she says lightly, but if I listen closely, her emotions are right under the surface.

I want to grind my teeth with frustration. I never like coming in second, but with Neely talking about Dawson like that, it doesn't seem like I'm even in the game.

"So how are things with the two of you?" I tread carefully. I practically pour my heart out to Neely and this is what I get?

"There are no 'two of us,'" Neely says firmly.

"You know what I mean." I can't hide the sudden irritation in my voice.

"I don't know." Neely stops and kicks at the waves, sending a spray over her bare legs. I jump out of the way just in time. "It's hard to tell because of things with Shae. He held my hand all the time at the hospital," she confesses.

It's hard to tell whether she thinks that was a good thing or not.

I look down at our hands caught together. "Like this?" At her nod, I bring our hands up in front of us. "Did you like it with him?" A shrug. "What about me?"

"I like holding hands with you," she says carefully, looking out into the distance. "I think—look!" she bursts out, dropping my hand to rush ahead where a weak ray of sun hits something pink. "Grayson, my shoe!"

Neely's wedding shoe lies tangled in a mat of seaweed washed ashore. She picks it up with a grin. "What are the chances?"

"Well, it obviously floats, so chances are pretty good," I say sullenly, annoyed to be sidetracked once again. Neely isn't making this easy.

"I wonder if the other one has washed in yet."

"It's been a week. It should be gone for good."

But Neely insists, so we spend the next twenty minutes walking along the beach, poking through every pile of debris that washed up from the storm last night. "It's gone," I say finally. "Or someone has already found it and it's in the garbage."

"I'm going to keep this one," she says, hugging it close.

"You can't wear one shoe."

"But this one came back to me, so the other one might too. I don't like to give up."

I pretend she's talking about me. Maybe she's not, but it's easy to pretend that she's telling me she'll wait—wait for me to go through all the uncertainty and potential *Suitor* stuff and when it's all over, she'll still be there.

I like pretending that. It's the motivation I need to lean forward and brush my lips against hers.

Soft. But unyielding.

Heart heavy with disappointment, I pull away. Even I have to admit it's not much of a kiss. But Neely isn't expecting it, and her eyes widen with surprise. "Is that okay?" After a pause, she nods. "I've wanted to do that since I met you, you know."

Neely wets her lips with her tongue. "Me too," she says in a soft voice.

"Because you were jealous of all the kissing I did on *The Suitor*?"

She laughs and my heart lifts to hear the sound. "That," I say, cupping her cheek with my hand. Her skin is cool and damp from the breeze blowing off the lake. "I'll never get tired of that sound."

"My laugh?"

"It's gorgeous. My new favourite sound." She drops her gaze, running a toe through the sand. Self-conscious, I decide, and wonder why. "I'll wait as long as you need," I tell her in a soft voice. "As long as it takes for you to be ready for me to kiss you again. I mean, really kiss you."

"You're waiting for me?" At my nod, she laughs again. "Don't bother," she says, taking a fistful of my T-shirt to pull me close. "I'm ready now."

And then her lips are on mine.

Soft. So soft and full and sweet.

And then she turns up the heat and I never notice the waves pooling around my ankles, or that I drop my shoe in the water.

Chapter Nineeen

Neely

A FTER GRAYSON LEAVES, I float up to my room, my fingers touching my lips to make sure they're still on my face. Make sure Grayson didn't steal them, like he's in the process of stealing my heart.

He's a very good kisser.

Probably his time on *The Suitor* helped, kissing Chrissa every chance he got.

I'm sure that isn't the only reason, but it's the first time I acknowledge her.

I have never been a big fan of the original *Suitor* show, as watching twenty-five women fight over a man hits too close to home for me, but intrigued enough to tune in when the situation is reversed. And Chrissa, the third Suitorette in the franchise, struck me as strong and independent, rather than princess-in-the-making and waiting for the man to rescue her.

I'm of the Pretty Woman theory when it comes to rescuing—a man may come to a woman's rescue, but she's going to rescue him right back.

So I watched Chrissa's season and while Grayson came across as attractive and fun, he didn't stand out for me.

I probably shouldn't tell him that. It must have been me, because I've seen the fan pages and forums dedicated to Grayson's love life. I doubt he's seen them all because it's obsessive enough to make a person close their social media accounts. If he's going to be the next Suitor, it's going to be a popular season.

I watched the show, saw her make her choice that wasn't Grayson. I had been rooting for the less popular Luke to win her heart, the soft-spoken and sensitive cowboy from Alberta. But it was the sophisticated Aaron who had got the final rose, with his Quebecois accent and sexy confidence.

Grayson spent most of his time kissing Chrissa, so it's no wonder she wanted him to open up more. Take away the physical contact, like with me, and Grayson has no choice but to talk about himself.

Will that change now that we've had our first kiss? Will that be all we do from now on, moving from simple kissing to weak-kneed make-out sessions, to sleepovers and me keeping an extra toothbrush at his place?

There's no way Mama will ever let him sleep over here, not unless he puts a ring on it, and that's not going to happen for a very long time.

I'm getting ahead of myself.

Flopping onto my bed, I stare at my ceiling, at the glow-in-the-dark stickers my father put up years ago. My room is the smallest in the house; a closet really, barely big enough for my single bed and a dresser, and I've had to purge my clothes and toys every year. But the small space taught me how to be organized, plus it's all mine.

Adam has a slightly larger room, and Davis and James shared a room. Both gone now, Adam was quick to move into their room, but I stayed put.

I remember Daddy standing on my bed, affixing the stickers. I had been eleven or twelve, home sick from school. Mama had always insisted on full bed rest when we were sick. Because my room was so sparse, I didn't spend much time in it, and a day forced to remain behind closed doors made me fake being well more than most kids faked being sick.

At the end of the long day, my father had popped his head in after returning from work. I had been on my back reading—I don't remember the book, but I know there were stars on the cover. "How're you feeling?" Daddy had said.

"I'm perfectly fine. I don't know why I need to be locked up here for the whole day."

"A little bored, are you?" He came and sat on the edge of my bed. "Good book?"

"It's okay." Boredom had made me cranky, but like always, Daddy never complained.

He took it from my hands, looked at the cover. "Stars. I've always loved looking at the stars. You can't see enough of them in the city, but out beyond the lights, the millions of little lights are amazing. But sometimes it's hard looking at them because it makes you feel small, like you don't matter."

I caught my breath because that's exactly how I had been feeling all day. Mama had been so busy with housework and laundry that she'd barely come to check up on me. I heard my brothers come home from school, but no one had come to visit. Not even Shae had knocked on the door with my homework like she promised to do.

I felt alone, like I didn't matter to anyone.

"My father took me camping once." Daddy had smiled ruefully at the memory. "Horrible time. He knew nothing about camping. But he looked at the stars with me, and he told me that stars should never make you feel small. They should make you feel important, like you're a part of something amazing. You should always feel like that, Neely." He put a hand on my head then, almost like he was blessing me. "No one, not your family, or your school, or your friendship with Shae, should make you feel any different. She's sick at home today, too," he adds. "I bumped into her dad outside."

"She's sick?" I asked, my mood brightening, now that I knew she was in the same boat at as I was and therefore had a reason not to stop by.

"Sounds like it. I want you to remember, Neely, to always recognize how important you are. Amazing, actually. My incredible little girl."

That weekend, he brought home the package of glowing stars and put them on my ceiling. That memory is one of my favorites of my father, and what I come back to when I think of him being in love with another woman.

I've always wondered how he can love them both, like he says he does. I know he loves Mama in his tolerant, patient way, but sometimes I find myself thinking of the other woman. How did he love her? Was it intense, like the attraction I feel for Grayson, or was it sweet and gentle like my love for Dawson?

I love Dawson and I kissed Grayson, and I don't feel bad about that at all.

There had been men in my life that I let myself be attracted to enough to want to do more than kiss. Both had shown up when Dawson had seemed serious about someone.

I barely remember their names, because I never cared about them. I had turned to them for comfort, out of desperation to have someone beside me who wanted me.

To make it worse, neither had been particularly nice guys.

I wonder how Dawson had felt when he found out, or if he felt anything at all. Because I had felt the sharp sting of guilt, like I had been betraying Dawson when I let those men put their arms around me.

It's so stupid that I felt like that. What had been the point?

But now...there's no stab of guilt. My shoulders aren't heavy with the weight of the world. I kissed a boy, and I liked it.

As I stare at the stars on my ceiling, I wonder if that's because I'm finally getting over Dawson.

♥

Grayson

I MEET UP WITH Emmett Wednesday night at the pub in Ashbury.

There are four drinking establishments in the tiny village, which may seem like a lot for the population, but each have their own loyal clientele base. The farmers who own the land circling the town meet for late afternoon beer at The Waltzing Weasel, which means they're cleared out by eight. The hard-core drinkers and the GM and Hydro workers head to The Pen, a tired bar over on First Street which has been there longer than I've been alive and shows the evidence of the fist fights that break out on a regular basis.

It had been at The Pen that I had my first and last bar fight. No woman was worth the beating I took. The bruises on my face took forever to fade.

The hipsters in the area, which have swelled in number since it's become cool to live outside the city, congregate at Bollocks Bar and Grill and Fagan's Fish and Chips in the centre of the village.

I've been unofficially banned from Fagan's ever since one of my ex-girlfriends started a fight with one of my current girlfriends. Most of the men in the place thought it was great, but the owner happened to be another ex of mine, who apparently held a grudge.

I'm also not very welcome at Bollocks since I was kicked off *The Suitor*, because business dropped considerably after that night.

I'm sure it will be open arms and free drinks when it's announced I'm in for another round, but until then, Emmett and I claim a table at the Weasel.

"So what are you going to do about Neely?"

I look up to see Emmett staring at me. I had taken the opportunity while he had gone to the washroom to read my latest text from Neely.

"I'm not sure exactly what to do with her," I admit.

"I don't miss that." Emmett stretches out on the seat across from me, cradling his pint glass in his hands. "Never knowing what a woman is thinking or going to do or is trying to say. It's all confusing."

"You'd think we'd have learned something from having a sister."

"I think it made it worse. Now I know that women have all these complex layers. It's easier thinking they're like us."

"One-dimensional and boring? It's no wonder they don't want anything to do with us."

After the laughter fades, I squint across the table at my friend. "So...Shae."

"I thought we were here because you wanted to talk about Neely?"

"That was an excuse. This is an intervention, my friend."

Talking to Emmett is my attempt to help Neely. From our conversations, she seems concerned and frustrated with Shae's seeming inability to connect with Emmett.

"It's obvious they're perfect for each other," she had raged last night. "She's still afraid to try."

Since I find it easier to talk about Emmett and Shae than myself and my situation, giving Emmett a pep talk is a no-brainer. After all, I have a lot of years of him listening to me moan about my relationships to catch up on.

Emmett looks around. There is another group seated by the pool table, loud and boisterous and looking freshly legal to drink. Other than that, it's only us in the place. "Pretty lame intervention."

"Yeah, well, last minute."

"Thanks for the thought, but I don't need any intervention. There's nothing there. She's a nice girl. I wish her well." He won't meet my eye.

That's his tell right there.

I've known Emmett since the first day of kindergarten when we had a fight over whose turn it was to go on the swing. I've seen him deal with family crises and personal smackdowns—his mother, Alex and not getting resigned being the worst—and been with him during his best times. I know him as well as I know myself and there's nothing about Emmett Pike that can surprise me.

In all the years we've been friends, he's never outright lied to me. Until now.

I raise an eyebrow. "That's it? That's all you're going to say about her?"

"There's nothing to say." He still won't look at me, and his shoulders seem tied to his ears like he's got a bat strapped to his back.

"Then that, bro, is a crying shame. I saw the two of you together that night—it was pretty sweet."

"She lied to me," Emmett says into his glass.

"She didn't tell you the whole story," I correct. "And really, who can blame her? It sounds like it was a rough deal, definitely a conversation killer. And then she found out Alex died? Just think about what must have been going on in her head!" When Emmett doesn't respond, I lean my elbows on the table. "Just talk to her and see how it goes."

He lifts a shoulder in a half-hearted shrug.

"She'd want you to be happy."

This gets Emmett's attention. "How do you know what Alex would have wanted? You barely knew her."

"That wasn't my fault. The girl did not like me." When I first met Emmett's girlfriend, it had been a clear case of opposites not attracting. She made no bones about her opinion that I was a bad influence on Emmett. I wasn't, and never had been. In fact, growing up, Emmett had most of the good ideas that led us into trouble.

I gave it a good try with Alex, but it never got better. It was a shame, too, since the time Emmett spent with her was one of the few times things were distant between us.

"I know. I'm sorry about that."

"Why should you be sorry for that? I'm not for everybody and I'm cool with that." Although I say it in a light tone, it still stings. I don't like people not liking me.

I'm sure it has something to do with the fact that my father didn't like me enough to stay.

Lately, at least since my date with Neely, I've been thinking about my father more times than I care to admit. After pushing thoughts of him out of my mind for years, he's popped in enough times to annoy me. I've done fine without him this long so why now, when I have enough to figure out?

"Do you ever think of them? Where they are, what they're doing?" I ask carefully. I don't know how to talk about him to Pepper, so how am I supposed to bring up the subject with Emmett?

Should I talk to him about it? We never have before; we share everything except the mess of our families.

"Who?" Emmett's tone is guarded, like he knows exactly who I'm talking about, but doesn't want it to be them. He's reacting exactly how I worried he would.

"You know, my father. Your mother."

He leans back in his chair, his mouth a tight line. "We're not talking about them."

I rest my elbows on the table. "But do you ever think about them?" I demand. "It's been almost twenty years, and we've never heard anything about them."

"It's the way they wanted it."

"I wonder if they're even still alive," I muse. "I talked to Neely about it because she's in a similar situation; not the same, but her father has a mistress."

Emmett's eyes pop. "Seriously? He'd do that to Mama S.? I had no idea."

"She said she's the only one who knows. I wonder if that's worse than it is for us. It's right in her face—when her dad goes to work, it's got to be in the back of her mind whether he's going to see the other woman or not. For us, we know nothing."

"I think they're dead," Emmett says after a pause. "It's one thing for a father to do that to his kids, but a mother? How could a woman leave her children without a word?"

"They do, though. It sucks—probably worse than if a man does it. There are some good dads out there, yours included, but not enough. I'm going to be a great dad to my kids." I give a sharp nod of my head like I'm convincing myself. "Tell them I love them, spend lots of time with them, always be there. They'll never wonder about me because I'll always be in their face."

"May not be the best thing," Emmett says with a hint of a smile. "Remember after they left, how Dad was always watching over me? We used to tell him one thing and do the complete opposite?"

"Like when we took those girls down to the pond?"

"Or when we skipped school and hitchhiked to the Go station to get to Toronto for the Jays game?"

"Or when we stole all the beer from his case and then put the caps back on when we finished?" Emmett laughs at the memory.

"And he took the whole case back to the Beer Store and complained!"

Emmett ruefully shakes his head. "He never thought it was us. Still doesn't."

"I don't want to tell him! I love your dad. He's more of a father to me than mine ever was."

"Yeah. I feel the same about your mom."

Both of us are quiet, afraid to show any emotion. Women would hug after a moment like that, but not us.

It's nice though, to have a moment like that.

I take a deep breath and try to find my way back to what I came here for. "You know, if you get things settled with Shae and I figure out Neely, we can be dating best friends," I say. "That hasn't happened since eighth grade with Lily and Lyn-Beth."

"Ah, Lily." Emmett takes a nervous glance around since Lily Smith still lives in the area. "First and last time I ever dated a redhead."

"Shae has pink hair. That's close."

"It'll change tomorrow if she wants it to." He glances into the dregs of his beer. "I kind of miss seeing the colour change."

"Then do something about it," I urge. "Or at least listen to her when she comes to you. Because I know she will. At least, if Neely has anything to do with it, she will. Apparently, you're the best thing that's ever happened to her."

"That so?" I see the gleam of interest now that he's not trying to hide it. Emmett is good at the stoic, lack-of-expression face, but when he shifts it, he's as easy as a book to read.

"You deserve to be happy, you know." He only nods. "And it sounds like Shae knows how to make others happy."

"I wouldn't know anything about that," he says bitterly. "But if I listen to her, will that get you off my back?"

I lift my glass. "Case closed." Mission accomplished. I can't wait to tell Neely.

"So, what about you?" Emmett narrows his eyes, looking frighteningly like his father. "What are you doing about Neely? Or the show, I guess, because I think it has to be one or the other."

I roll my nearly empty glass between my palms, wishing I had a ball in my hand. "I've already asked if she wanted to come on, because that would solve everything."

"What'd she say?"

"Uh—no. A big fat no." I pause for a moment, debating. "She's in love with Dawson," I confess.

Emmett narrows his eyes. "You know that for a fact?"

"She told me. She wants me to help her get over him. That was the plan—take the couple weeks before the show started, spend some time together, have me work my magic. It's all fake."

"Is it?"

I lift my shoulders. "I don't know." For once, I'm ready to talk about my feelings, only I don't know what to say. "No. Not now. But what's the point? Even if I wasn't going on the show, she's in love with him. And how can I make sure he doesn't feel the same way and she leaves me for him, after all I give up for her?"

"You're thinking of not doing the show?"

I shrug again. It's been in the back of my mind for days, clogged by insecurities, so I can't visualize it. I need to see it laid out—plan it, figure out the steps I need to take.

It's how I used to prepare for a game. See the ball in my hand, see it float over the plate like slow motion, straight into Emmett's glove.

"What do you think?" I ask, leaning forward. "Neither is a guarantee. I don't know if the show will work, and I have no idea about Neely. I don't know what to do."

"I don't want to tell you. Dawson's a big boy," Emmett says. "He's known both of them for years. If he felt the same way, I think he'd have the balls to tell her."

"What if he doesn't realize it yet?" That's been my biggest fear with Neely's idea—what if me sniffing around was the kick in the pants that Dawson needs to get his head straight about Neely? What guy wouldn't want to be with her?

"I think you should stop thinking about Dawson and focus on your own problems. Besides, I thought he had a thing for Pepper."

He shakes his head. "Wild wedding, wasn't it? The three of us..." he trails off as I nod in agreement.

"Yeah. I'm not keen on being the rebound guy," I admit. "But going on the show...did I tell you Chrissa got in touch with me?"

Emmett cocks his head. "You did not."

"She did...I'm still not sure why. It was strange to see her."

"You *saw* her? Think that was a good idea?"

I grin. "Probably not. But I'm full of them, aren't I?"

"You mean bad ideas? Like the time we 'borrowed' your mom's car?" The way he uses his fingers as quotations marks makes me laugh and ends my evening of reflection.

It's too bad. I had hoped Emmett would make my decision easier. Or make it for me.

Chapter Twenty

Neely

"I DON'T WANT TO close down the vlog."

Once again on Wednesday, I meet with Shae and Dawson to decide the fate of ExpiryDate. While it's only been a few days since Shae's world turned upside down, we've always posted regularly, and our viewers will be expecting something soon. Whether we announce another trip or post a collage of pictures, we need to have new content online quickly.

"I don't think we have to," I soothe, flipping through my emails until one catches my eye. "Pearly White Travel Toothpaste," I read. "New sponsor."

"We need to travel with their toothpaste then," Shae says.

"I don't think back and forth to Ashbury is what they're looking at." Dawson's grin fades when Shae drops her head. "You didn't fix things with Emmett, did you?"

"How am I supposed to do that?" Shae says bitterly. "From what Neely told me, he's finished with me because I lied."

"Technically, it wasn't a lie. You withheld the truth," Dawson points out.

"I doubt Emmett is thinking about technicalities." Shae's face falls at my words. She did lie to him, just like she lied to every other man who cared about her, so why does it bother me that she's sad about it?

Unless Shae faces the consequences of her actions, she's never going to learn.

But like a new mother, too soft to deal with enforcing those consequences, I cave. "Grayson thinks there's still hope," I say reluctantly. "Emmett might need a little time to process. It's confusing being told you should be happy about something that you knew nothing about."

"I know, I know. It's all my fault," Shae moans.

"I didn't say that," I say quickly. Years of appeasing the dying girl is going to be hard to break.

"Your face did."

"I can't control my face."

"If you can't control it, then who can?" Dawson wants to know.

"Are you on her side?" I snap. "She did lie to him."

"You said it wasn't my fault!" Shae protests.

"Well, it was," I concede. "And Dawson thinks so too."

He raises his hands. "Keep me out of it. I am neutral. I am Switzerland."

"We've never been to Switzerland," Shae muses. "Don't fight."

"I'm not fighting. I'm pointing out what you did is wrong, so you won't do it again."

"But I'm not dying now."

"You're missing the point, Shae!" Is this how parents feel?

Shae crawls over to where I'm sitting on the floor and throws her arms around me. "You're annoyed with me. Please don't. I'll grovel if you like, but I can't bear it when you're mad."

"You're like a puppy," I groan. "Such a pain at times."

"But lovable," she adds, laying her head on my shoulder. Dawson watches us with a smile I don't recognize.

"Yes, you're lovable." I pat her head. "I think we need to put out something about how we won't be doing the trips for a while."

"But I thought we were going to Switzerland?" Shae demands.

Dawson laughs. "No one said anything about Switzerland!"

"You just did."

Sometimes I wonder how we get anything settled. Oh, I know—I decide everything. But my heart isn't in it today. I haven't been able to think of anything but Grayson. Or rather, the way Grayson kissed me and what that will mean.

I still haven't told Shae. I don't think it's fair to share my confusion when she doesn't know what's going on with Emmett. Talking to him would be a start, but she's really dragging her feet.

"I need to make a statement," she said earlier. "A grand gesture."

"Tell him how you feel," I suggested. "It's a start and at least you won't be in limbo trying to come up with your grand gesture."

Will Grayson give up the show for me? Is that his grand gesture?

I don't know how I feel about that. On one hand, no one has ever done anything like that for me. He would be telling the world that I come first. It's a scary thought, because of the pressure that comes with it.

What if it doesn't work out? What if I can't get over Dawson?

What if Grayson isn't the relationship type after all and I give up everything for him?

I close my mind to the questions of what exactly I'd be giving up because I don't have the mental energy to think about that now.

Shae rolls onto her back and checks her phone, something she's done at least ten times since I've been here.

"Anything from Emmett?" I ask, even though there's been no telltale Pink song from her phone that signals an incoming text. She shakes her head. "Talk to him. I feel like a broken record."

"Do you know Rufus has never played a real record or seen a record player?" Shae asks. "Isn't that sad?"

"Fix things with Emmett and you can buy him one," Dawson suggests.

"You talk to his eleven-year-old nephew, but not Emmett?" I shake my head with disbelief. "Something's not right there."

"I'm scared," she admits, looking much younger than her twenty-seven years. "I don't know how people do this relationship stuff."

"You're looking at me like I should know what you're talking about. Ask Dawson, since he's got the string of broken hearts to remind us what a ladykiller he is."

"I'm not a ladykiller," he says in a quiet voice.

"Really? Who are you with this week?"

I can't read the expression in Dawson's eyes. It's almost...hurt? And something else I've never seen before. But before I ask him, Shae clears her throat.

"Uh...Neely....?" Shae waves her phone before my face. "Is Grayson a sure thing for *The Suitor*?"

"He hasn't signed the contract yet, so it's not official."

"That's not what Instagram says."

I grab her wrist to stop her waving the phone and squint at the picture of Grayson. "What does it say?"

"That he's the next Suitor." Shae pulls her hand back to read the rest of the post. "Oh no."

"What?"

"This isn't from the show." She looks straight at Dawson. "Natasha posted this. Natasha just told the world that Grayson is the next Suitor."

Grayson

I GET THE CALL from Ria and Raoul on Wednesday afternoon.

"Grayson, who did you tell about *The Suitor*?" Ria demands as soon as I pick up the call.

"It's all over Instagram, with Twitter picking it up," Raoul adds. They must have me on speaker.

"No one," I say immediately, even though I remember the discussion at Fred's diner with crystal clarity. "Who...who posted it?"

"There's a picture of you with the rose from Chrissa's season," Ria says in a disappointed voice. "Along with a comment about how you will be the next Suitor; about a hundred people have already jumped on it."

As Ria is talking, I've put them on speaker to open Instagram. It's not hard to find the photo in question—I find a steady stream of tags as well DMs from about everyone I know on Insta and a lot I don't.

"This was not to be released to the public until next week," Raoul says, his voice nasally with annoyance.

"Who posted it?" *It can't be Neely*. She wouldn't. She couldn't. But it was only her and her friends that knew, and I doubt Shae would do something like this without telling her.

Dawson, on the other hand...

"It's from @natashanotromanoff," Ria supplies. I don't bother to hide my groan. "Do you know her?"

"If it's who I think it is, I met her once, but I have no idea why she'd say that. Or even how she'd know...It had to be a shot in the dark." Or was it? Natasha would know if Dawson told her. Neither Shae nor Neely would post something like that, so it has to be Dawson.

"Whatever the reason, we need to either confirm or deny, Grayson. And the studio won't do either until we have a signed contract, so those couple of days you needed are over. If you want to be the next Suitor, get in here and sign this."

I stop at Pepper's bakery before I head to the production office. It's the closest and quickest way I have to getting hold of Dawson, without physically getting close to Dawson, which might result in my grabbing him by the front of the shirt and putting a fist in his face.

I can't believe he told Natasha. It feels like a betrayal. It is a betrayal.

"Thanks, dude," I mutter as I push open the door, the mouth-watering aroma of freshly baked bread hitting me in the face. "Now I'm going to steal your girl."

Because now I'm forced to make a decision that I should have had a week more to make. I'm going to have to say yes to the reality show, or yes to Neely. And I'm going to have to do that right now.

"Who are you talking to?" Pepper stands at the cash register with a frown on her face. It's a different place with the empty tables and lack of lineup.

"Your boyfriend," I growl.

The spots of colour on Pepper's cheeks fade quickly to leave her pasty white. "How did you—?" she sputters just as the swinging door to the tiny kitchen opens. A bearded man appears, apron-clad and holding a tray full of apple pie tarts. I stare with no recognition until he opens his mouth.

"Hullo, brother," he says in a thick Scottish accent.

"What are—Reuben, right?" I turn to Pepper with surprise. "From Pain au Chocolate?"

"*Aye.* How're ye?" he asks. The big man looks comfortable behind the counter and I stare dumbfounded as he starts to fill the glass display case.

What's going on here? But I push the question away; there'll be time enough to figure it out later. "Where's Dawson?" I demand.

"Why would I know where Dawson is?" She gives Reuben a nervous sideways glance.

"I thought you were seeing him?"

"Even if I was, it doesn't mean I'm his keeper," she says in a too-loud voice. "Why, what's the problem?"

I heave a sigh of disgust. "That girl Natasha from the wedding posted something about me being the Suitor. The only way she'd even know is if Dawson told her."

"Oh no! What did the producers say?" She gives Reuben another glance as he disappears into the kitchen with his empty tray.

"Not happy and they're making me sign the contract right now. I don't appreciate—" "Dawson would have never told Natasha," Pepper interrupts.

"And how could you possibly know that? Thought you weren't his keeper?"

"He wouldn't do that. He'd never do that to someone. Natasha probably guessed after all the fuss you got at the wedding. Did she say anything to you about it, or a *Wouldn't it be cool if...* comment? C'mon, fans have wanted you to take over the spot since you were first on. It's not a big stretch."

Things settle into place, lessening some of my anger. "Maybe...I guess..."

"You guessed wrong if you think it's Dawson. Give him the benefit of the doubt," she urges.

"Why, because you're dating him? When were you going to tell me about that?"

"We're not dating," she hisses with another glance at the kitchen. "Just shut up about that."

"What's up with you?" But then the kitchen door opens and Reuben brings another tray out, and it all becomes clear. "Really?"

If an expression could tell me to shut up, with a few curse words thrown in, Pepper's got it nailed. "Not yet," she says through gritted teeth.

"Whoa." I can't help the smile breaking across my face, Pepper's furious expression making it even sweeter. "Okay, then, I'm out of here. Got a meeting with a couple of angry producers."

Some of the fury fades from Pepper's face. "What are you going to do?"

I run my hand through my hair as I study my sister for a long minute. "You're sure Dawson wouldn't have said anything?" I ask finally.

"Dawson's a stand-up guy," Reuben says before Pepper can open her mouth. "One of the best I've met, and I've known him for a while."

"Thanks," I say in a curt voice and give Pepper a wave as I duck back through the door.

"Good luck," Pepper calls after me.

I'm going to need it.

Chapter Twenty-One

♥

Neely

"HOW COULD YOU?" I demand. We stand around Shae's phone, staring at the screen. Natasha's post has been liked so many times and got so many comments, it's now the first thing on my Instagram feed.

"I told you, I didn't do anything," Dawson says patiently. "I haven't spoken to Natasha since the wedding. I'm sure it was just a good guess. She's a huge fan of *The Suitor*, so of course that's where her mind would go." His shoulders slump miserably.

From guilt?

"How could she know?" I persist, shaking my phone at him.

"Like I said, a good guess. C'mon, Neely, really?" His quick glance at Shae has her shaking her head, so I know she's stepping out of this fight. "Pepper asks us not to say anything, so of course I wouldn't. Why do you even have to ask?"

"So you'd keep your mouth shut for Pepper but not for the rest of us?"

"What does that even mean? You know I'd do anything for the two of you and your friends. Where's this coming from? Are things that bad with you and Grayson?"

"There is no me and Grayson thanks to this." My voice is shrill and heightens the tension in the room like the blare of an alarm.

"What's that supposed to mean? I thought—I don't know what I thought," Shae says quickly, her gaze moving from me to Dawson and back to me. Right away I regret saying anything about a fake relationship to Shae because Dawson is looking at both of us and Shae can't keep anything a secret other than herself.

"What's going on?" Dawson asks. "Neely? Talk to me. There's more to this, isn't there?"

I don't want to do this anymore. I can't lie to him about Grayson. I can't find the words or the energy or the need.

My heart has had enough of Dawson. I can't take his friendship anymore.

"I can't," I groan, collapsing into the chair.

"You can tell me anything." His voice sounds confused and concerned. "C'mon. You're my best friend."

"I don't want to be your friend!" I burst out. Dawson rears back, eyes wide. "I can't watch you and Pepper. I can't do it anymore. There's always someone new, and it takes a bit for me to get my head around it, but Natasha was gone and there was Pepper and I can't do it anymore. I won't."

The kitchen is silent, save for the drip of the coffee maker and Shae's soft sigh.

"Why won't—?"

"I'm in love with you." My words crash through the quiet room with all the tact of a Bingo-playing grandmother at a baby shower.

I want to take them all back, gobble them back into my mouth like Shae eats a cupcake. But I can't. They're out there, like the first breath of a drowning man pulled from the waves, his chest pushed and pummelled from CPR. It's an instinctive breath physically forced to come out.

It's the regret that comes the second after saying something that hurts another.

It's the relief like the glass of water after sleeping with your mouth open.

I had to tell him.

Dawson swallows, his gaze flicking between me and Shae. She looks as shocked as I feel—dark eyes wide and staring, hand clasped over her mouth. How could I have let that slip? All those years, all those girlfriends I had to watch him with. How can I keep feeling this way? I let my head fall into my hands, wanting nothing more than to curl up in a ball and wish Dawson away.

I can't look at him.

"Just go," I groan.

"Neely..."

"I'm going if you won't." Jumping to my feet, I find Dawson right there, forcing me to look at him. I can't—but I want to. I want to stare into those dark green eyes with the brown flecks, at the shock of black hair that won't stop from flopping into his eyes, at the scar on his chin, because I know exactly what he was doing when he got that scar.

He was with me.

He's mine, has always been mine, and it hurts so much that he can't see it.

"Neely." His voice is soft, and I can only stare at him, in mute anguish for what I've ruined.

And then I hear the chime of an incoming text. Because his phone is in his hand, it's instinct for him to glance down. What isn't natural is the astonished expression on his face.

"I've got to go," he says before he rushes out the door.

Grayson

T HERE'S MORE REGRET THAN I imagined as I put pen to paper.

Seated in the office of Selina Sams, the executive producer of *The Suitor*, I scratch my name on the contract binding me to the next season of the show and everything it entails.

Photo shoots. Promotions. Giving up my privacy, giving them access to my life. Making this my life for the next six weeks leading up to the show, and then twelve weeks after that. And after that...

"This could mean really big things for you," Selina says with a big smile.

I set the pen down. It's done. The end of Grayson Grant, former professional baseball player and my life in limbo. It's the beginning to Grayson Grant, reality show star.

It's the end of Neely but could be the beginning of something even better. I force my mind to focus on the positives. I have no idea what the future will hold and have to hope it's going to be good.

"Glad to have you aboard, Grayson." Selina reaches for my hand and pumps it vigorously. "I think this will be a great season."

"The most dramatic one ever?" I mimic the oft-used *Bachelor* tagline, but Selina looks at me blankly.

"Drama is all and good, but we hope we can help you find love," she says, surprising me by how earnest she sounds. "Now we've organized a photo shoot for later today, so we'll need you in wardrobe right away. "And there's an interview tomorrow..."

I tune out Selina, thinking about how I promised Neely the first shot of an interview with me. I wonder if she'll still want to talk to me.

Chapter Twenty-Two

♥

Neely

I SINK ONTO THE floor in Shae's kitchen.

Shae stares open-mouthed after Dawson, sinking onto the floor beside me after the door slams behind him. "You said it." The awe and pride in her voice cuts away at my overwhelming regret like a bread knife attacking an ice-covered car.

It's not very effective.

"What did I do?" Covering my face, I double over until the back of my hands touch the cool linoleum floor.

"You told him you love him!" Shae cheers. "I told you to do it years ago!"

I sit up at the glee in her voice. "And what good has it done for me? He's gone, Shae. Dawson is...gone. I ruined everything." I return to my position of anguish.

"You didn't ruin anything."

"Dawson is gone," I remind her.

"He'll be back," Shae says with a confidence I can't imagine ever feeling.

"Maybe for you. He'll never want to see me again."

"Neely Scalzo, you look at me," she orders. When I don't move, she takes a hank of hair and pulls me upright. "Look. At. Me."

"You're pulling out my hair!"

"Got your attention, didn't I? Now, you know Dawson as well as I do—do you honestly think he's going to abandon us? He's not going to throw away thirteen years of friendship over this."

I want to believe her, I really do. Over the years, Shae has been able to convince me to put my life on hold, facing fears of heights and speed and eating things that crawl in the dirt. Maybe if I listen hard enough, she can convince me Dawson will come back. But what if he does? "How can we get past this? I told him I *love* him. You can't move past that." I bury my face in my hands again, hating how dramatic I'm being. It's not me to moan and wail and not immediately try to fix it.

I don't know how to fix this so maybe a little moaning and wailing are in order.

"Who says he can't get over it?" Shae demands. "We make the rules. We can do anything."

"That's when you thought you were dying and the universe owed you one." I hear the resentment in my voice and don't like it. I don't like this one bit.

This isn't me. Maybe being in love with Dawson is me, but fake relationships and lying to my best friends isn't me. Shae's faced the changes and mistakes in her life with more grace than this.

Crying on the floor about a man isn't me at all. At least it shouldn't be.

I heave a ragged breath and sit up.

That's enough. It's done, I can't undo it. There's no sense in pretending this won't change anything but I have to accept it. It had to be done.

"No one owes you anything anymore now that you'll be an old lady alongside of me," I say with resignation.

"We're going to be old ladies together," Shae says with a happy sigh. "You can dye my hair purple because all the cool old ladies have purple hair, and I'll remind you to take your heart medicine."

"You're going to remind me to take my pills?"

"Hey, after listening to you for years, I think it's my turn."

I turn to Shae, not realizing my face is damp with tears until I bury it in the crook of her neck. "I understand if you pick him," I say in a soft voice.

"Stop it!" Shae exclaims, pulling away. Her face is serious for once, dark eyes full of concern and strength as she grabs my shoulders and hauls me off the floor. "You sit and listen," she says, pushing me into a chair. "There's no picking. You're mine and will always be my best friend."

She's being strong for me. This time *Shae* is trying to fix things for me because that's what friends do. She's trying to take care of *me* now.

The realization makes me melt; sagging into more happiness and gratitude than any man has ever given me. I may not want to be Dawson's friend, but Shae isn't going anywhere. Nor do I want her to.

"I'm not picking either of you because neither of you are going anywhere," she continues, sitting across from me. "That little, horrible period of time when I thought I was really going to die was the worst in my entire life because I was going to lose the two of you. I know you want me to say I'd pick you over him, and maybe I would, but I need you *both*. So there." And she slaps her hand on the table for emphasis, loud enough to make me jump. "I need Dawson to go along with all my crazy ideas, but it's you who gives me the strength to come up with them," she says, her voice softening after her outburst. "You're the leader in our little trio. I need you."

"Me?" I stare wonderingly at her. "I thought I was your side-kick."

"No, Dawson is clearly the sidekick," Shae says quickly. "You're—you're the Hermione out of us. She rules those boys. You're...you're not even a hobbit—you're Aragorn, leading the Fellowship, keeping the hobbits safe. You're Captain America, Neely, not a sidekick."

I swipe my hand across my cheek. "Do you think it's Captain America or Iron Man who's really in charge of things?" I ask, my heart lifting just enough.

Shae laughs. "Only a twelve-year-old boy would debate that for you. You need to go talk to Rufus."

"You need to talk to Emmett," I point out, leaning forward to grab the paper towel roll on the counter. I feel sick to my stomach, but my shoulders do feel a tiny bit lighter now that everything is out in the open. Maybe it's Shae's optimism, or wishful thinking, but things might be okay.

Things will be different now, but maybe that's okay too.

"I think I do," she says ruefully. "I'll figure something out. But first—you. And Dawson. I'm sure it was some family emer-gency—"

"Do you think everything's all right?" I demand, and Shae groans.

"You amaze me. And I know you amaze him. He'll come around and see you for the amazing woman you are. And if he doesn't, I'll kick his nice bum and you'll use his temporary absence to get over him and then we'll go on our merry way." She throws her arms around me, trapping my hand that is trying to clean myself up.

"I don't think it's going to be that simple. I'm going home." Detangling myself from Shae's embrace, I smile tightly. "Begin the getting-over process."

"Wait to talk to him first," she begs.

"Unless there is a family emergency, I think his running out of here said enough."

Once home, I maneuver around Mama like an obstacle course before I can make it to my room. As I flop onto my bed, resisting the urge to crawl under the covers, I catch sight of my stars, nearly invisible in the sunlight flooding my room.

Maybe I'm destined to be like my father—in love with a person that I can never fully have.

I wonder what it's like for him?

I spend the next, forever-long forty-five minutes imagining the worst—my life without Dawson in it.

They are not pretty thoughts.

To make it worse, when I finally pick up my phone, pictures of Grayson have flooded social media, announcing him as the next Suitor. It's official.

I'm glad he didn't give it up for me. It wouldn't have been worth it. My love for Dawson will burn in my heart forever, like the coals of a campfire that need to go out before you can fall asleep in your tent.

A knock on the door has me sitting up in horror. "Just a minute," I call, frantically wiping my face. But Mama opens the door anyway.

"Neely, there's—what is the matter?"

"Nothing." I pick up the stuffed zebra I'm holding and hunch over it. "I'm fine."

Out of the corner of my eye I see her frown, like she wants to get to the bottom of this, and I steel myself for the Inquisition. I'm not about to confess the mess I've made of my life. She wouldn't understand.

"Neely, Dawson is here," Mama says instead. "He says—"

"What? No!"

"I have to talk to you." Suddenly Dawson is there, and Mama, horror of all horrors, is stepping out of the way. She's never once let me have a man in my room and now she's practically pushing him in.

"I'm fine," I babble. "Everything is fine."

"It's not but it can be." Without looking up I can tell he's in the room, standing at the end of my bed, smelling of coffee and sweet things and—"I brought you a cupcake."

I stare up at him in disbelief. "You left to buy a cupcake?"

"I went to talk to Grayson."

Through all this, Mama is still at the door, her head swiveling between us like she's watching a Grand Slam match. Dawson turns, and smiling apologetically, begins to close the door. "Thanks, Mama S., but do you mind?"

"Keep both feet on the floor," she cries as she's cut off from the drama.

The door shuts, leaving Dawson alone with me, and my room has never felt smaller.

"Twenty-seven years old and she still thinks I need a chaperone," I grumble, staring at the zebra in my lap, now faded and tattered from years of being under the covers with me. "Where's my cupcake?"

"Downstairs. Mama S. wouldn't let me bring food up here." Gingerly he lowers himself to the bed.

"Of course she wouldn't." I toss the stuffed toy on the floor. Why am I doing that? Making conversation, small talk that will relax Dawson. I don't want him relaxed, I want him gone so I can begin to get over him. I don't want to hear what he has to say because I'm sure it won't be good. It won't—

"Grayson says you've only been pretending to date him."

My eyes roll with suppressed frustration. Can today get any worse? "So?"

"I'm glad."

"That you're humiliating me right now?"

He laughs. "I'm not trying to. I'm trying to tell you that I love you too."

My heart stops. It literally stops beating, only to give a great skip and resume double time. Slowly, ever so slowly, I meet his eyes. "Why?" I whisper.

"Have you seen yourself?"

"You mean as a friend...right?" My voice becomes as flat as if he's told me he's dating someone new. There's no point in getting excited by what can never happen. If it hasn't already, it never will.

I convinced myself of that fact years ago.

"Do you know how frustrating you are?" Dawson asks instead, his lips curving upward into the smile I know better than my own.

"I'm frustrating?" I push away from him. "You run out with your tail between your legs just after I tell you something utterly, horribly embarrassing, leaving me—"

My words are cut off by Dawson. His mouth. On mine.

Kissing me.

His lips are soft and mold to mine like they are meant to be there: more than a peck, less than a full-on lock. But it's enough to muddle my thoughts and send tingles racing out of the caverns they've been hiding in. And then he stops.

"What...?" My eyes flutter open to see Dawson grinning, looking smugly satisfied. "Why?"

"Ready to listen now?" he asks quietly.

Mutely, I nod.

"Just to be clear—you really love me?" His eyes look uneasy.

"You're not getting me to say anything unless you explain why you kissed me," I snap.

"Grayson texted me about three times today."

That isn't what I expected or even hoped to hear. "Why?"

"The one that came in just after you said what you said was literally a 9-1-1 call," Dawson continues as if I hadn't spoken. "It even said 9-1-1, in shouty caps, so I read it. He wanted to see me—needed to see me. So I ran over to Pain au Chocolate to talk to him." He pauses and I impatiently motion for him to continue. "He said he knew there isn't anything between me and Pepper."

"He texted you about Pepper?" My heart, which had given a leap when I saw Dawson at the door, sinks a little at her name.

"Because everyone thought we were getting together. Or he thought it, and therefore, you, too. Did you?"

"I've stopped thinking of you with anyone," I whisper. "At least I try not to." I'm afraid to look at him in case he sees the hurt. Dawson has *hurt* me.

He tips a finger under my chin, lifts it so I'm forced to look at him. "I didn't know how you felt. I hoped...but I never knew."

"You...hoped?"

"Of course I hoped. It's everything I've ever wanted." He smiles sheepishly. "At least for the past week it has been."

I shake my head, mind whirling at a dizzying pace. This isn't fair, none of this is fair. I can't do this; Dawson sitting here, looking like he is, smiling at me like he cares more than he should. "Dawson..."

"Grayson needed to know how I felt about *you*."

"Me?"

"Yes, you." Dawson mouths the words, in the most perfect Jake Ryan impression, from the movie we've watched together countless times. A flood of something that I can only describe as elation, mixed with anticipation, erupts in me. Maybe this...maybe it's going to be—

"It's always been you," he says in a halting voice, "only I never realized it. I mean, deep down I knew it but I didn't know you knew it."

"You're not making sense." None of this makes any sense but I can't push too hard against it because what if it goes away? What if this is one of my daydreams that seems so real and it goes away? What if he's not really here, sitting on my bed?

I reach out and poke at Dawson's knee, feeling the soft denim of his jeans. The baggy ones that Shae always tells him not to wear because it makes Dawson look like he has no bum, but Dawson loves how comfortable they are—

"I'm real." Dawson smiles, his eyes more green than brown today and crinkling in the corners.

"Why?"

"Jeez. For a smart girl, you are absolutely clueless."

"I'm not, I'm just confused."

"I know. I love knowing something you don't. But now—can I kiss you now, and explain everything later?" His warm hand cups my face. "We should have been doing this for years."

Happiness bubbles over like a glass of champagne. "Oh."

"That's all you have to say?"

Suddenly, I don't want to say anything more. For once, I don't need to know everything, not now. This can wait, because if I'm hearing right, if I understand this, we have time. Dawson and I have time.

The only thing I want to know right now is if he's gotten any better at kissing. Because if he has... "Take your feet off the floor," I whisper.

And then we're kissing, and yes, he has improved so that kissing him is better than anything, even finding out that Dawson's in love with me, and I didn't have any idea about it.

It takes a while before we stop kissing and I find that out.

Grayson

I GET THE TEXT from Neely as I walk to my car, after officially signing away the next four months of my life to the producers of *The Suitor*.

NEELY: Thank you xox

Sometimes it's tough being the nice guy.

Grayson is a good guy, which is why he'll get another chance at his HEA in Falling for the Suitor!

But first, find out what happens with Neely and Dawson, as well as Pepper and Reuben in Don't Stop Me Now.

If you enjoyed Neely and Grayson, I'd love it if you joined my mailing list and find out more about my books and me!

When you sign up for my mailing list, you'll get a copy of the short story, **Cupcake Connections**!

In Pain au Chocolate patisserie, the cupcakes are becoming more popular than the pastries. Reuben, the big, burly Scotsman, is an expert on sugar and sweets, but his love life has fallen flat.

And when one of the customers catches Reuben's eye, Adam decides to help him win her over. While planning a makeover for Reuben, Adam digs into Reuben's past and discovers that Reuben is doing just fine on his own.

Packed full of character cameos from Beautifully Baked, Unexpectingly Happily Ever After and The Hidden Past of Pippa McGovern, Cupcake Connections is a sweet story about finding your own way.

Sign up now!

About Author

Holly Kerr is the author of over twenty-five chick-lit, romantic comedy, and women's fiction novels. She grew up a farm girl but now calls Toronto home, where she lives with her three very tall children, following their sports exploits like any dutiful mother.

She's a lover of Marvel movies, Star Wars movies...really, any movies, and has a surprising amount of worthless pop culture info stored in her head. She likes oceans over mountains, tea over coffee, and can mix a darn fine dirty martini, with extra olives, of course.

Visit her at www.facebook.com/HollyKerrAuthor and www.hollykerr.ca to sign up for her newsletter.

Acknowledgments

Another book written during the pandemic and another book that ignores how much has changed in the world. Once again, I've made the decision to bypass Covid-19, and I do hope you'll forgive me for that. It's difficult enough living through it; I don't want to bring it into my writing, or in that matter, my reading.

I need to thank my family for this one—we've become very close during the past ten months and being home so much, they've finally realized what I do all day! Butt in chair, fingers on keyboard! Thanks to Kaitie, Sam, Sarah and Jeff for understanding that I have voices continually talking in my head; I love to hear what you need to tell me, just as soon as I write down what's going on in my imaginary world.

Thanks to Regina, Paula and Terry; thanks always to Nita for teaching me so much.

Thanks to my readers, especially my ARC readers who are so awesome in every way!

And again, thanks to my mom for all our talks and for wanting to understand my process, and to E who listens and supports.

LOTS OF LAUGHS.
LOTS OF LOVE.

Suitor Science

Hating the Chemistry Teacher
Falling for The Suitor
Fraternizing with the Ex
Marrying the Billionaire Best Friend
Loving the Wrong Guy
Finding the One

Love & Alliteration

Perfectly Played
Beautifully Baked
Pleasantly Popped

Don't

Don't Tell Me You Love Me
Don't Want to Be Friends
Don't Stop Me Now
Don't They Know It's Christmas

Sisters in a Small Town

Coming Home
Hanging On
Stepping Up

Charlotte Dodd

The Secret Life of Charlotte Dodd
The Missing Files of Charlotte Dodd
The Best Worst First Date Ever
The Hidden Past of Pippa McGovern
The Last Stand of Charlotte Dodd

Unexpecting
Unexpectingly Happily Ever After

Absinthe Doesn't Make the Heart Grow Fonder

Oceanic Dreams – I Saw Him Standing There

Kid Lit

The Dragon Under the Mountain
The Dragon Under the Dome

www.ingramcontent.com/pod-product-compliance
Lightning Source LLC
Chambersburg PA
CBHW051329020726
47501CB00007B/1992